Visit www.jamesbhendryx.com for more information on
forthcoming installments in the Halfaday Creek
uniform matching series.

STRANGE DOINGS ON HALFADAY CREEK

STRANGE DOINGS ON HALFADAY CREEK

JAMES B. HENDRYX

ILLUSTRATIONS BY
PETE KUHLHOFF

ALTUS PRESS • 2016

EDITED AND DESIGNED BY
Matthew Moring

SERIES EXECUTIVE CONSULTANT
Richard Hall

PUBLISHING HISTORY
"All the Evidence" originally appeared in the May 25, 1938 issue of *Short Stories* magazine (vol. 162, no. 6). Reprinted by arrangement with the Estate of James B. Hendryx.
"Bear Paws" originally appeared in the December 10, 1938 issue of *Short Stories* magazine (vol. 165, no. 5). Reprinted by arrangement with the Estate of James B. Hendryx.
"Black John Assists at a Wedding" originally appeared in the October 25, 1937 issue of *Short Stories* magazine (vol. 161, no. 2). Reprinted by arrangement with the Estate of James B. Hendryx.
"Black John Files a Claim" originally appeared in the July 25, 1937 issue of *Short Stories* magazine (vol. 160, no. 2). Reprinted by arrangement with the Estate of James B. Hendryx.
"Father John" originally appeared in the March 10, 1941 issue of *Short Stories* magazine (vol. 174, no. 5). Reprinted by arrangement with the Estate of James B. Hendryx.
"Mail Order to Halfaday" originally appeared in the March 10, 1942 issue of *Short Stories* magazine (vol. 178, no. 5). Reprinted by arrangement with the Estate of James B. Hendryx.

THANKS TO
Everard P. Digges LaTouche, Robert Loomis, Richard Moore, Rick Ollerman, Cynthia Whyte, & the Leelanau Historical Society

TABLE OF CONTENTS

ALL THE EVIDENCE

JOE WEST LEANED on his paddle and looked down into the upturned eyes of the girl seated on a stone at his feet, her hands clasping her knees.

"I wish you wouldn't go," she was saying. "I—I'll miss you. I don't know what I'll do without you."

"You don't have to do without me," replied the young man quickly. "That's what I'm tellin' you, Elsie. You go with me. We'll get married as soon as we hit Dawson."

The girl shook her head wearily. "No, Joe, I can't go. It wouldn't be right—"

"It is, too, right!" he contradicted vehemently. "It ain't right for old Tom to stand in the way of our gettin' married. You love me, don't you?"

The girl's eyes dropped before his burning gaze to scrutinize the sand at her feet. She nodded. "You know I love you, Joe."

"Sure, I know—an' I love you. Why, Elsie—I never knew what it was to love a woman till I come here to Goose Crick an' got acquainted with you. An' old Tom ain't got no right to keep us from gettin' married."

"He's my father," the girl replied.

"Yes, an' you're goin' on twenty, an' you've kep' his cabin, an' done his cookin', an' cranked his windlass fer him ever since you was big enough to, an' it's time you was thinkin' about yer own life. You got a right to a home of yer own, an' a man of yer own."

"But, Joe, what would he do without me?"

"Jest like all the others does—batch it, er marry some woman."

"Why don't you stay on the crick? Maybe next year he'd—"

"No, he wouldn't. Not next year, nor the year after—an' you know it. An' as fer me stayin' on the crick—what would I do here? I finished my clean-up today—seventy-six ounces, twelve hundred dollars fer a whole winter's hard work. I could have got four time that much workin' fer wages upriver. Old Tom's got the only decent claim on Goose Crick. Everyone else quit an' went upriver last year. I stayed on account of—of you. I was hopin' I'd locate a good pocket, like old Tom, but there ain't no more pockets—she's been prospected from one end to the other."

"There's one other man on the crick," said the girl. "He's up to the cabin, now. He and dad are playing the phonograph."

Joe West gave a contemptuous snort. "Huh—Charlie Gamble, eh? He's too damn lazy to locate a claim an' sink a shaft. Too lazy even to work fer wages. He fools along snipin' the bars, an' hen-scratchin' the flats fer a bare livin'. All he wants to do is tootle-te-toot on that flute of his, an' play his phonograph, an' listen to himself sing. I come to this country to make a stake. An' with my claim what it is—there ain't nothin' on Goose Crick fer me."

"I'm on Goose Crick," reminded the girl, without raising her eyes.

"Yeah—an' what good does that do me? Come on, Elsie—look at it reasonable. Marry me, an' we'll go somewheres an' hunt us up a location. Them seventy-six ounces I took out will give us a grubstake. We'll make good—the two of us together—we couldn't help it."

THE SHADOW had crept higher and higher on the opposite rock wall, till only the rim rocks caught the early evening sunlight. The deep blue eyes of the girl lifted to the gilded

2

pinnacles. "I love you, Joe. You know that. And I'd marry you this very minute, if it wasn't for him."

From the direction of the cabin, a short distance back from the creek, came the scratchy cadence of Charlie Gamble's phonograph:

"When you and I were y-o-u-n-g, Maggie—"

Joe West stooped, drew his canoe a bit higher onto the sandbar, tossed his paddle into it, and turned abruptly onto the foot-trail that led to the cabin.

The girl rose hastily from the stone. "Wait, Joe! Joe—where you going?"

The man paused on the brink of the short, sharp pitch. "I'm goin' to tell old Tom—"

"No, no! It won't do any good! He told you once you can't marry me. He won't change his mind."

"It's time someone changed it for him, then," retorted the man bitterly, "That other time I *asked* him; I'm *tellin'* him this time!"

"No, no, Joe! Please! He'll be angry, He—he might—" She paused, as though wondering, herself, what he might do. And again the doleful, wailing cadence of the phonograph broke upon their ears:

"But now were growing o-o-o-o-l-l-d, Maggie—"

"Listen to that!" The girl detected a grim note in Joe West's voice. "It's like us. Bye an' bye we'll be growin' old, an' it'll be too late!" He turned, and was gone.

She called, "Joe, Joe!" But there was no answer, and she sank back onto her stone and buried her face in her hands.

II

CHARLIE GAMBLE WAS slipping the cylindrical wax record into its pasteboard case. Tom Nolan looked up at the sound of footsteps, and frowned as he recognized young Joe West. He

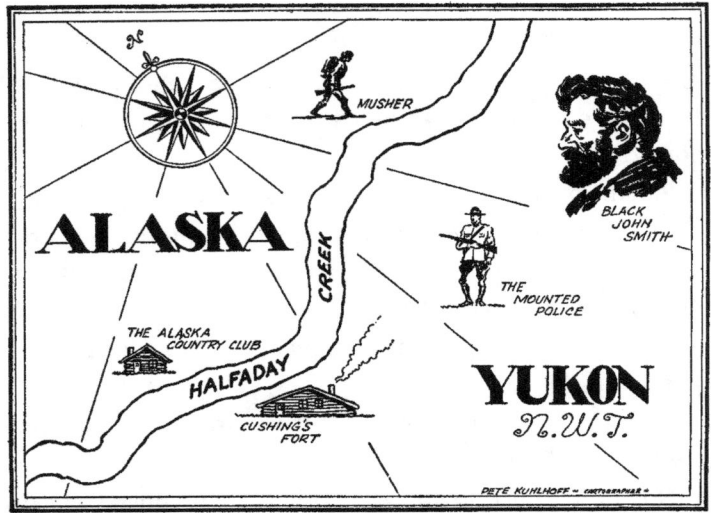

and Gamble were seated, one on either side of a smudge before the door of the pole and mud cabin, a partially emptied black bottle between them. As the younger man came to a halt before the smudge, Nolan lifted the bottle from the ground and proffered it, without rising. "Have a snort?" he asked, but with no cordiality in his tone.

"No," West declined shortly. "I come to tell you that me an' Elsie is goin' to get married."

Tom Nolan leaped to his feet, jaw thrust forward, eyes blazing. "Yer goin' to what?" he roared, swaying a bit unsteadily on his feet.

"You heard it," replied the younger man curtly.

"Yeah, an' you heard me when I told you, a month back, that she couldn't marry you!"

"Listen, Tom, you're a little drunk, an' there ain't no use gettin' excited about this. But the fact is I finished cleanin' up my dump today, an' I ain't made wages—nor nowheres near wages. I'm through with Goose Crick. I'm pullin' out in a day or so—an' Elsie's goin' with me."

"Like hell she is! Who's goin' to crank my windlass? Tell me that—an' who's goin' to do my cookin' if she goes off?"

"Do yer own cookin'—or get married again."

"Married! Me—goin' on sixty, an' git married agin! Look at me! Where's any woman to marry? An' who'n hell'd have me, if there was? Some klooch, mebbe, er some skirt that would try to grab off my dust!" Stooping, the man recovered the bottle and took a deep pull at it.

Across the smudge Charlie Gamble picked up a rude case fashioned from a length of hollow balsam, opened it, and removed the filthy cloth covering from a dilapidated flute. Picking up the bottle which Nolan returned to the ground, he took a drink, wet his lips with his tongue, fitted the mouthpiece of the flute to them and blew a few notes, apparently entirely oblivious of the heated words that were passing back and forth between the other two, as his fingers fumbled uncertainly at the keys.

None of the three noticed the girl who hastened up the trail, from the creek and slipped silently behind a scrub spruce at the edge of the tiny clearing.

"That's what they'd be after—my dust—any woman that'd marry me," Nolan continued, belligerently. "But they don't git my dust—not a damn ounce of it! They can't no woman make a fool out of me! Twelve hundred an' twenty-seven ounces in my cache—an' three, four ounces more goin' in every day."

"An' by all good rights, the half of it belongs to Elsie—the way she's stuck here on Goose Crick, workin' like hell every day. She's never havin' no fun like other girls."

Nolan leered drunkenly. "So that's it, eh? That's why yer so hell-bent on marryin' Elsie—figgerin' to git the half of my dust along with her!"

"You lie!" cried West, his voice trembling with anger. "I wouldn't touch an ounce of yer damn dust! I've got enough fer the two of us—an' some day I'll have more dust than you ever seen! An' if you wasn't half drunk I'd make you eat them words, along with yer front teeth!"

The older man lurched toward him, fists clenched. "Git off this claim, an' don't you never set foot on it agin!" he roared. "Ye'll never marry her while I'm alive!"

"The sooner yer dead the better then! Come on—start somethin'! But if you do, by God, I'll finish it!"

The older man hesitated, and at that instant, the girl slipped swiftly from behind the tree and, stepping between the two, faced West with flashing eyes.

"Go away from here!" she cried hysterically. "I won't marry you—ever. You—you tried to make him fight so you could—could kill him!"

Joe West stared aghast into the outraged eyes of the girl. "Elsie!" he cried. "You know that ain't so, Elsie. You know—"

"I know what I've seen, and heard!" retorted the girl. "Get off this claim and don't ever come back. I hate you!"

For long moments the two stood facing each other. When Joe West spoke his voice sounded toneless and flat.

"I guess there ain't nothin' more to say, then." Turning upon his heel, he disappeared in the direction of the creek. With a low, choking sob, the girl dashed into the cabin and threw herself face downward upon her bunk, while from outside came the discordant notes of Charlie Gamble's flute. After what seemed an interminable time, she heard the man depart, and a few moments later her father entered the cabin and groped his way to his own bunk beyond the curtain partition.

III

AT BREAKFAST NEXT morning neither referred to the events of the night before. When the meal was over Nolan took five sticks of giant from the case stored in the winter dog kennel, tied them into a bundle, and crimped a cap to a six-foot length of fuse. In the doorway he paused.

"Goin' to shoot down a lip of rock that sticks out into the shaft," he said. "It's in the way."

The girl nodded indifferently as she gathered the dirty dishes into the dishpan. "Let me know when you're ready," she said, "and I'll come down and crank you out."

"No need. I got some cleanin' up to do in the shaft first. It ain't only twelve foot down, anyhow. I kin shin up the rope."

"Some day the rope's goin' to break or something and drop you back into the shaft."

Nolan scowled. "You tellin' me how to fire a shot" he asked grouchily. "Hell—I was shootin' down rock before you was born. What if it did drop me back? I could jerk out the fuse, couldn't I?"

The girl shrugged and went on about her dishes as the man left the cabin.

Along toward the middle of the forenoon she heard the dull boom of the shot, and giving no heed to it went on with her work about the cabin. It was with a heavy heart that, an hour later, she laid aside her sewing and kindled the fire for the preparation of the noonday meal. As she waited for the kettle to boil she stood leaning against the door jamb, her eyes on the distant peaks.

"I oughtn't to have been so cross to him," she murmured, as she remembered the dull, hopeless tone of Joe West's voice as he turned away. "He wouldn't really have hurt dad. And—oh—I do love him! I'll go up to his claim this afternoon and tell him I'm sorry. I—I can't let him go away, like that—away from Goose Crick—away from me. If I could only marry him!" she added as, hastily brushing a tear from her eye, she turned back into the room. "But dad wouldn't ever cook himself the right kind of meals, or he'd get drunk and break his neck, or something.

I guess life is like that—and when Joe's gone, it's going to be—hell."

AT NOON she placed the meal on the table, and when her father failed to appear after a few minutes of waiting, she stepped to the door and called loudly. But there was no answer from the direction of the shaft situated a hundred yards or more from the cabin and screened from it by a thicket of spruce and scrub birches. Her father was rarely late to his meals, and—why didn't he answer? Hastening down the short trail, her growing feeling of apprehension was dispelled, as she broke through the copse, at sight of the heavy galvanized bucket hanging from the windlass, where it had been drawn tight against the roller. The windlass evidently had been chocked to prevent its running back down.

"Pulled up his bucket," she muttered. "He must have gone some place." Throwing back her head she called loudly, and receiving no answer, walked idly to the shaft and glanced down. The next instant she recoiled with a low moan of horror and, scarcely conscious of what she was doing, turned and dashed for the canoe that was always kept overturned on the shingle at a bend of the creek. She must get help; must find Joe—Joe would know what to do! Reaching the creek, her eyes widened in sudden terror. There was the canoe—smashed into a useless tangle of ribs and planking and canvas! Wildly she glanced about her. Who had done this? Who had pulled up the bucket and left her father to be blown to bits in the bottom of the shaft? And who had smashed the canoe? Then, fearful lest the fiendish marauder should seek to still her own lips, the girl plunged across the shallows of the creek, and disappeared into the thick bush of the opposite side.

Nearly two hours later she burst into the little clearing that surrounded Joe West's cabin four miles up the creek, her face, hands and feet bruised and the clothing half torn from her body by her frenzied haste through the trailless bush. Joe West was not at home. His cabin was empty, and she received no answer to her repeated calls. Yet the girl realized he had not gone for good—had not left Goose Creek as he had threatened to do. His canoe was there on the bank, and all his effects were in the cabin. Only his rifle was missing.

Without hesitation, the girl shoved the canoe into the water and headed back down the creek, paddling with frantic haste.

At her father's claim, she beached the craft, and dashing for the cabin, snatched the rifle from the wall, jacked a shell into the barrel, and stepping to the doorway, allowed her eyes to travel slowly about the clearing, scrutinizing each tree or shrub that could conceal a lurking assassin.

Satisfied that she was in no immediate danger, she hastily changed her torn clothing, bolted some food from the table, threw some more into a pack sack and, catching up pack and rifle, hastened back to the canoe. When she had nearly reached the creek, she paused, turned at a right angle, and hurried toward the rock wall.

"I'll need some dust when I get to Dawson," she panted, and then halting abruptly before a cavity in the rock face, stared in dumb panic. The rock fragment that fitted into the entrance to the crevice that was Tom Nolan's cache had been pulled aside. It needed but a glance to tell the girl what the misplaced fragment had already told her—that the cache was empty!

With tight-pressed lips, she dashed for the creek, and a few moments later, was paddling frenziedly downstream. Night forced her to camp with still some eight or ten miles to go to the big river. She dared not build a fire, for fear the light might bring her father's murderer to finish his grisly work.

It was mid-morning when her canoe finally shot out onto the broad waters of the mighty Yukon, and she headed upstream for Dawson.

IV

OLD CUSH, PROPRIETOR of Cushing's Fort, the combined trading post and saloon that served the little community of outlawed men that had sprung up on Halfaday Creek, close against the Yukon-Alaska border, wagged his head somberly as he mopped perfunctorily at the bar with a rag.

"First we're fightin' them Spanish, down there in Cuby, an' then the next thing we know, we're tanglin' up with a lot of niggers halfways around the world. What I claim, this here fightin' mightn't never stop—one thing leadin' to another that-a-way."

"There's a hell of a lot of powder bein' made," opined Black John Smith, picking up the leather dice box and rolling the little cubes onto the bar, "an' it's got to be used up some way. Beat them three sixes in one."

Cush lowered the square, steel-rimmed spectacles from forehead to nose, verified the three sixes, gathered the dice into the box, and cast them. "There's four fives—an' a horse on you. An' here's three fours right back at you—beat 'em in one, if you kin. What I mean, if the U.S. keeps right on fightin' one country an' then another, it ain't only a question of time till all the men will git killed off except a lot of old ones, an' women, an' kids— an' then some other country could step in an' knock hell out of us."

Black John shook the dice, frowning at the three deuces that showed. "The drinks is on me," he admitted, as Cush set out bottle and glasses. "But you don't need to worry about all the men gittin' killed off. Accordin' to the Malthusian theory—"

"Listen," Cush interrupted, filling his glass, "if yer figgerin' on startin' in on a string of big words, you might's well button yer lip. I don't know what they mean; an' if I did I wouldn't give a damn about no theories old Methuselum might have, when anyone would know he must of been in his second childhood eight, nine hundred years before he died."

Black John grinned. "Well, switchin' to Methuselah, then—do you really believe he lived that long?"

"Shore I do! Hell—it's right there in the Good Book! Nine hundred an' sixty-nine years old when he died. Must of been somethin' he et kep' hid goin'. Too bad he couldn't of lived thirty-one years more to make it an even thousan'. Cripes—that would be a record to shoot at! But I s'pose 'long to'ards the last, the old gentleman's health kinda went back on him—er mebby it was a stroke."

"I guess," grinned Black John, "his record's safe fer some time to come, as it stands. Here comes someone."

BOTH EYED the newcomer, who paused for a moment in the doorway, then advanced to the bar.

"Is this here Cushing's Fort on Halfaday Crick?" he asked, lowering a pack sack to the floor.

"This is the place," answered Cush, sliding a glass toward him. "Fill up. The house is buyin' one."

"The police don't dast to show up here, eh?"

Black John frowned. "Corporal Downey comes whenever he feels like it," he replied, noting that the pack sack seemed very heavy for its size.

"Huh. Thought you was all outlaws. But yer right up agin the line, where you kin duck acrost when he does come, ain't you?"

"Some of the boys occasionally take advantage of the fact that we're close to the line."

"It's up that gulch yonder," supplied Cush, " 'bout a mile. Kinda uphill—but it's been run in thirteen minutes."

"Yer Old Cush, ain't you?" He turned to the other. "An' I figger yer Black John Smith. That there's my name, too—John Smith—same as yourn."

"Yer a little late," observed Black John.

"Late! What you mean—late? How'd you know I was comin'?"

"We didn't know. In fact, we wouldn't hardly of believed it, if we'd been told. I was referrin' to yer choice of names. No more Smiths on Halfaday. We got too many as it is."

The stranger's wide lips stretched into a grin, disclosing uneven ill-spaced teeth. "I git you!"

Black John pointed to the tin molasses can that stood at the end of the bar. "The name-can, there, has proved a great boon to mentalities like yourn, furnishin' em a sort of synthetic name, without subjectin' 'em to the agonies of deep thought."

"Cripes sake! You musta been a preacher, er a lawyer, er somethin'! I don't even know what yer talkin' about."

Black John grinned. "Don't let that worry you none. Neither does Cush—more'n half the time."

Old Cush sniffed audibly, and shoved his spectacles from nose to forehead. "What I claim—if a man can't talk words which someone would know if they was even words er not—he might's well shet up in the first place."

"I've got another name figgered out a'ready," said the new-comer proudly. "John Brown. How's that?"

"Clever!" exclaimed Black John. "An' it didn't take you hardly no time at all! Accordin' to the way the song goes, John Brown's body lies a-smolderin' in the grave, an' I wouldn't be a damn bit surprised an' what hist'ry would be repeatin' itself before long."

"Hell—don't you never talk without you've got to make a speech? What in hell you drivin' at?"

"I was wonderin'," replied Black John gravely, "what particular malfeasance precipitated you into our midst."

"What?"

"What John's drivin' at," explained Cush, mopping a few drops of liquor from the bar, "is how come you to come here? What was it you done, back where you come from, that put you on the run?"

"Who—me? Hell, I never done nothin'. I ain't on the run. You got me wrong. I jest heard tell about this place, an' I come here. Hell—I ain't no outlaw! I'm a prospector."

"Prospector eh? Do any good fer yerself?"

"Yer damn right I done good. I ain't broke, by a damn sight. Fetched plenty dust right along with me."

"Had a claim on Bonanza er some of them good cricks, I s'pose."

"Hell, no! I don't fool with no claim—don't like to be tied down."

"There is times when a man don't."

"I git mine snipin' the bars along the different cricks. Fill 'em up agin'," he added, tossing a well stuffed, pouch onto the bar.

"Was you figgerin' on snipin' the bars along Halfaday?" asked Black John.

"Oh shore. I don't believe in a man workin' himself to death in the bottom of a shaft. They's easier ways to git dust than that. You gents like music?"

"Well, I ain't no more'n what you'd call medium fond of it," replied the big man. "Cush there, he's got an accordian; an' there was a fella come along one time with a fiddle—but we hung him."

"Hung him! What fer?"

"He got a little off key, one night. Seems like he flatted his *A* in the upper register—er mebbe it was his *B*. I rec'lect I wasn't whole-heartedly in favor of the hangin' at the time, bein' as the fella was a little drunk—but it didn't seem worth while augerin' about, so we went ahead with it. You a fiddler?"

"No, I—I play the flute."

"Flute, eh? Keep on the key, kin you?"

"Well—I try to. 'Course I ain't what you'd call no fancy player, ner nothin' like that. But I wouldn't like to git hung fer gittin' off key."

"Better stay on it, then," advised Black John. "The boys is mighty tetchy about their music. Would you care to give us a tune?"

"Mebbe you'd ruther hear the phonygrapht," suggested the man. "I got some good pieces—some of them war songs is new, like 'Dolly Gray,' an' 'Jest as the Sun Went Down.' I got other ones, too. Then I got some I made myself."

"Made yerself?"

"Shore. I rigged up a dingus that fastens on where the needle goes that trims down a record into a blank. When I git holt of a piece I don't like, er if I git tired of one, er it gits kinda blurry, I slip this dingus on an trim off the old piece—jest like in a lathe. Then I put on the blank, put in a needle, an' start her goin' an' sing er play my flute, an' it makes a new record. Like to hear some of 'em?"

"If it's jest the same to you, I believe I'd rather take a chanct on some of the store records—like them new war songs. They might sound pretty good."

DIGGING INTO his pack, the man produced a phonograph and several cylindrical records, and for a half hour, or more, the three listened to the scratchy wailing of the instrument.

"That's all the store ones I've got," he announced. "But here's one I made. It's one of them new songs. 'Jerooshelum' is the name of it. It's a hell of a good song. Want to hear it?"

"On key?" asked Black John, suggestively.

"Well, I made it back on a crick, an' I ain't got no way to check up. It might be a little off. Hell—you couldn't hang no one if a phonygrapht played off key!"

"Yer in error," opined Black John. "The offence would come under vicarious skullduggery, an' as sech, would be hangable on Halfaday."

"Mebbe I better not play it till I git a chanct to do it over," suggested the man. "Could I set up my tent in the clearin'?"

Cush was about to reply, when Black John forestalled him. "You might—but I wouldn't advise it. If you got to playin' yer flute, er singin', an' made some slight mistake that would offend our ear, we might call a miners' meetin' an' hang you willy-nilly, as a poet would say. If yer aimin' to locate, why don't you throw yer stuff into One Eyed John's cabin. He ain't had no use fer it sence the time we hung him a while back."

"Another one you hung? What'd you hang him fer?"

"Oh, prob'ly somethin' he done. The offence was too trivial to remember, so it don't make no difference, one way er another. As I was sayin', this here cabin of One Eyed's is in good shape, an' yer welcome to use it. It ain't only a little ways from the fort here—an' yet it's far enough so any annoyin' sounds incident to off-key singin' er playin' wouldn't disturb the peace an' dignity of the crick none."

"Yeah—but s'pose someone was goin' by an' heard it?"

"That," assured Black John, "wouldn't cut no figger. We aim to be fair an' reasonable, on Halfaday, an' what a man does in the sanctity of his own home, ain't no one else's business."

"Yer shore hard-boiled up here," grumbled the man. "Where's this cabin at?"

"Go down the crick about a quarter of a mile, an' you'll come to a cut bank. The cabin sets back off the trail about a hundred foot er so. You can't miss it. An' by the way—we figger One Eyed must of had sixty, eighty ounces of dust cached away that time we hung him, but we couldn't never locate his cache. If you happen to find it, remember that dust belongs to us."

"Oh, shore," the man replied, as he swung his pack to his shoulders. "I don't want nothin' except what belongs to me."

When the man had left, Old Cush eyed Black John. "Looks like he's got a consid'ble heft of dust in his pack," he observed. "But I bet he never got it snipin' no bars. What do you think?"

"If yer askin' fer my candid opinion," replied the big man, "he's prob'ly the most onprepossessin', onmittigated, an' oncon-vincin' prevaricator I ever heard prevaricate."

"Yeah, an' on top of all that, he's a damn liar besides. His eyes sets too clost together. An' they don't wink no more'n a snake's."

"It's what he lacks between the ears that's goin' to git him in trouble," said Black John.

"Them big words you said about him—is any of 'em hangable?" Cush asked hopefully. "I don't like to have no sech party on the crick. He ain't no one you could trust."

BLACK JOHN'S grin broadened as he filled his glass from the bottle on the bar. "Not *per se*—"

"He claimed his name was John Brown—not Percy," corrected Cush.

"That's so," agreed the big man. "But in either event, I don't believe we could rightfully hang him, as yet. At that, I don't anticipate that his sojourn amongst us will be onduly protracted."

"Which?" asked Cush, scowling across the bar. "Ain't they a damn thing kin happen that you kin say it in little words?"

"I mean," chuckled Black John, "that it's my guess that pack of his has got seventy, eighty pounds of dust in it—which is too damn much dust fer a man of his mentality to git away with without causin' a ripple amongst the authorities. In other words, I'm lookin' fer someone to come up an' take him off our hands."

"D'you reckon he'll find One Eyed's cache—that there section of log that pulls out?"

"Oh shore. I keep that trap baited, so in case we want to gain access to the occupant's cache, we kin do it without huntin' all over hell. I left a short end of cord stickin' out right where he'll hang his coat, an' when he pulls it, the section of log'll come loose. The hole behind it has got a poke in it—stuffed with gilt iron filin's."

"Yeah," said Cush dubiously, "an' he ain't a-goin' to turn in that poke. He's goin' to blow that dust—an' I'll have to set out good licker fer iron filin's!"

16

"That's what we want him to do."

"But where in hell would my profit go!"

"He'll figger that if we couldn't find that cache it's a good place to stick his own dust in," explained Black John. "Your share of the dust in his pack ought to show profit enough on any licker you'll be settin' out fer them iron filin's. An' the fact that he's tenderin' iron filin's in payment fer licker is a palpable fraud in itself, an' as sech, is hangable under our skullduggery law. An' he can't wiggle out by claimin' he found the poke— because, bein' as we warned him to turn it in, he'd be guilty of conversion."

"Yeah—an' it would be stealin', besides. We could hang him fer that," opined Cush.

"Jest so. An' if Downey was to come an' take him off our hands, we kin divide the contents of his cache, the same as if we'd hung him."

"That's right," Cush agreed, "'cause he wouldn't never tell Downey about that dust. That phonygraft would be kinda nice to have, too. I like that piece about 'When I an' you was young, Maggie.' My third wife use' to sing that before she run out on me."

V

IT WAS EVIDENT from the start that the man who called himself Brown was living in mortal terror of pursuit, and equally evident that he was endeavoring in every way possible to incur the good will of the men of Halfaday Creek.

He spent his days in aimless and desultory sniping the sandbars, or playing his flute or his phonograph in One Eyed John's cabin. In the evenings he would carry the phonograph to the saloon and exhaust its repertoire of "store records" even essaying one or two of his own attempts, both instrumental and vocal, under solemn promise of immunity from blame if they were not exactly on key.

"I'm practicin' up on a minin' song I heard back in Californy, an' when I git it so it goes purty good, I'll shave down one of them flute pieces an' make a record. It's a song name of 'Clementine.' They's a lot of verses to it, an' it sounds good if it's sang right."

When the man had been on the creek a week, One Armed John burst into the saloon one day just as Black John and Old Cush were about to hoist a drink.

"Hey!" he cried, his eyes round with excitement, "John Brown—he's deader'n hell!"

"H-u-u-m," said Black John, pausing with his glass halfway to his lips. "What did he do—swaller his flute?"

"He's shot! I come by his door, which it was open, an' I seen him layin' there on the floor, an' he's got his rifle in one hand, an' blood had run out where someone plugged him right in the middle, an' it hain't been so long ago, neither, 'cause the blood hain't only partly dry."

"Mostly," opined Old Cush, as he reached to the back bar for a glass which he slid toward the speaker, "you come in here with bad news. It shore is nice to have you fetch in a pleasant item now an' then. Have one on the house."

"How d'you mean—pleasant?"

"Well," Cush replied, "much as you git up an' down the crick, fishin' an' whatnot, you mostly wait till a corpse has laid around till there ain't no comfort in holdin' the inquest, before you find it, er else it's to hell an' gone up er down the crick, er it's when the mosquitoes an' flies is bad, er the ground is froze, er somethin'. But this time the corpse is new, an' it ain't only a little ways off, an' there ain't no mosquitoes to speak of, an' it's easy diggin'—an' besides of all that, I sort of like the idee of Brown bein' a corpse. On top of his damn flute playin', he's been spendin' iron-filin's fer licker."

"Oh, I don't know," One Armed John replied, returning the empty glass to the bar and drawing the back of his hand across his lips. "That there piece about Dolly Gray he had on his phonygraphy was kinda sad. I shore liked to hear it."

"Well, hell—he didn't take his phonygrapht with him," replied Cush. "After we git the inquest over, an' him planted, there ain't no reason we can't fetch the phonygrapht over here to the saloon an' use it till sech heirs as he might have comes an' claims it."

"The p'int," agreed Black John, refilling his glass from the bottle, "seems well taken. The matter of paramount importance, at present, however is the callin' of an inquest to inquire into how the deceased came to his demise."

"How he done what?" asked Cush, wrinkling his brow.

"How he died."

"Well—hell, didn't One Armed jest git through tellin' us he was shot? Oh—you mean, mebbe it was a murder, eh?"

"Well, some sech thought entered my mind—provided the knockin' off of a flute-player could be so designated."

"Cripes—we might have a hangin', too, eh?" exclaimed One Armed John hopefully.

OLD CUSH shook his head. "I don't believe whoever done it could be very guilty," he opined. "I'd hate like hell to hang any of the boys fer a little thing like that."

"We'll hold the inquest first, an' then if necessary, call a miners' meetin'," decided Black John. "We can't neither permit nor condone a murder on Halfaday. It might fetch in the police, an' that would make it mean fer all of us." He turned to One Armed John. "Cush, he's the coroner, an' he app'ints me an' you an' Pot Gutted John fer a jury."

"They ought to be six, by rights," interpolated Cush.

"'Tain't necessary only fer the report," explained Black John. "A six man jury is all right—if you've got one—but we want to git this over with, an' bein' as Pot Gut lives right clost, One Armed kin slip down to his shack an' fetch him over to One Eyed's cabin right now. We kin hold the inquest, an' you kin fill in three other names in yer report, later. We got to be careful an' keep things like that legal. Git along, One Armed, an' fetch Pot Gut, an' me an' Cush'll go on down."

A few minutes later the four men stood in the small cabin and regarded the body that lay sprawled on its face, a rifle still clutched in one hand. Black John glanced at Cush. "As coroner, what in your opinion is this man's status?"

"His what?"

"Is he alive; er dead?"

"Dead—" Cush grunted, "any damn fool would know that."

"Having established the fact of death," announced Black John, "we will now proceed to investigate the cause of his death." Stooping, he removed the rifle from the man's hand, and working the lever, ejected an empty shell. Holding the shell to his nose, he sniffed at it, and passed it to the others who did likewise. "It's plain to see the deceased fired a shot from this rifle, an' plain to smell that he done it this mornin'. Ain't that right?"

THE OTHERS agreed. Stopping, the big man rolled the body onto its back and drawing aside the blood-soaked shirt, pointed to a wound in the chest, just a trifle to the left. "An' it is evident that a bullet entered this man's body at this point, undoubtedly penetrating his heart, and equally evident, from the condition of the blood, that the wound was received this mornin'. Therefore, in the absence of any evidence that any other gun was fired in this room this mornin', the coroner finds that this man, to wit, alias John Brown, came to his death by reason of a gun-shot wound inflicted by his own hand. The verdict bein' suicide. Is that right, Cush?"

"Shore."

"Hold on," interrupted Pot Gutted John. "Damn if I believe a fella could shoot himself through the heart with a rifle an' not leave no powder marks on his shirt, er his hide."

Black John frowned at the speaker. "That there's immaterial an' irreverent—bein' a mere matter of opinion."

"Well," insisted the other, "how in hell could he? You show me."

"Listen," thundered the big man, "it's a well known fact that the deceased could play tunes on a flute, ain't it?"

"Shore."

"All right—I don't believe it. How in hell could he? You show me!"

"But Cripes, John—I can't play no flute!"

"An' I can't shoot myself through the heart with a rifle jest to show you how it's done, neither. An' yer fined a round of drinks fer contempt of an inquest. An' on top of that, you an' One Armed is ordered by the coroner to take this here corpse up to the graveyard an' bury it. Ain't that so, Cush?"

"Yeah. We can't leave corpses layin' around."

When the two had gone with the body, Black John stepped to the wall, and removing sixteen small moosehide sacks laid them on the table beside the phonograph. "They'll run about eighty ounces to the sack—better'n twelve hundred ounces. There's eight of 'em apiece. Here is yours."

"How about them iron-filin's I took in fer licker? Don't I git paid back fer them?"

"Paid back for 'em!" exclaimed Black John. "Hell, you've got 'em, ain't you? What d'you mean—paid back? An' we might's well divide up his other stuff, too. Here, you kin have the flute, an' I'll take the phonograph an' what records he's got."

"But Cripes—I don't want no flute!"

"Me neither," replied Black John. "I don't know how to play one. An' a flute ain't no good to a man onless he kin play it."

"I can't play none, neither."

"You kin come a damn sight closter'n I kin. Hell, you kin play the accordian, an' it hadn't ought to be so hard to ketch onto the flute. If a man's musical, that way, it's only a matter of practice."

"But I don't want to play no damn flute," objected Cush.

"Well, you can't be blamed fer that. Take it along, anyway—it's liable to come in handy, some time."

"How could a flute come in handy?" grumbled Cush, picking the instrument up gingerly.

"How the hell would I know? I never run a saloon." As Black John talked, he wound up the phonograph and placed the needle on the record. The instrument whirred for a moment, and suddenly the voice of the dead man blared forth in a popular song.

THEN, THERE was a sudden break in the melody, and there came words in a tense voice—a voice of sudden terror. "Joe West! What—"

"Yes, Gamble—it's me. Where's Elsie?"

"Elsie—how the hell do I know."

"You know, all right—you murdered her."

"You lie!"

"An' you murdered old Tom Nolan, too—blew him up in his shaft. An' you robbed his cache."

"Sure—blow'd Tom up! What's that to you? He hated you! But I never touched the girl!"

"Where is she?"

"I don't know! My God, put up that gun! Don't shoot! Don't—" there was an indistinct sound—then the sudden sound of a shot—and another—other indistinct sounds, and the needle ran off the end of the cylinder, with a dry scraping noise.

In the cabin, both men looked at each other in strained silence. Black John was the first to speak. "So his name's Gamble, eh—an' he murdered Tom Nolan. I know'd Tom—a long time ago—on Fortymile—his girl, too—she was jest a kid then. Maybe he murdered her, too. If he didn't, she'll be needin' this dust, Cush—"

"Shore," agreed Old Cush heartily, and tossed his eight little sacks back onto the table. "We'll pack the dust over to the saloon an' lock it in the safe,"

"Yeah, so we kin turn it over to Downey—in case the girl ain't dead."

"Downey?"

"Shore—if a guy that ain't got no more brains than this Gamble commits a murder, Downey'll be on his tail—don't worry."

"He'll come too late," opined Cush, "an' I'm glad of it, 'cause the damn skunk already got what's comin' to him."

"Yeah," grinned Black John, "now none of them obstructions to justice that the law brings in can do him any good. But—who in hell is Joe West?"

Old Cush wangled the corner from a plug of tobacco and spat into the wood box. "Oh—him? Well, he might be the young fella that come along yesterday whilst you was off huntin'. Seems like he did claim his name was West."

"Funny you didn't say nothin' about it."

"Kinda slipped my mind, I guess."

"Where is he, now?"

"He's prob'ly up the crick. Claimed he might locate on Halfaday, an' I told him about Whiskey Bill's old cabin above here."

"What did he have to say? Ask any questions about anyone?"

"Well—not many. Wanted to know if anyone name of Charlie Gamble had showed up here lately. Claimed this here Gamble done a couple of murders down on Goose Crick. Claimed Gamble packed a phonygrapht an' a flute along with him."

Black John slanted the other a keen glance. "An' what did you tell him?"

"Well," Old Cush replied, pausing to mouth his quid, "I don't never give out no information—you know that, John. This here West, he's a hell of a nice lookin' young fella, an' he claimed how one of the parties that Gamble murdered was a girl—West's girl. The other one was her pa—an' he claimed Gamble had robbed their cache besides. Now you know damn well, John, that ain't no way fer a man to carry on—murderin' folks an' robbin' caches—an' you rec'lect how narrow this here damn cuss was between the eyes, an' all—an' how he lied like hell about gittin' that dust snipin' the bars."

"Yeah—but even at that, you hadn't ought to tip West off. We don't want no murders on Halfaday."

"Tipped him off! Who in hell tipped him off? I told him right out that there wasn't no one named Gamble on the crick— an' the only one on the crick that had a phonygrapht er a flute, either one, was a damn liar name of John Brown that had moved into One Eyed John's cabin. But the way it turned out seems like this here Brown an' Gamble might be the same fella."

"Yeah," agreed Black John dryly, "it does kind of look that way, from here. Guess I'll go hunt up this West, an' have a talk with him."

"He claimed he'd come back today fer some supplies."

"He come back, all right. Mebbe he's got guts enough to be waitin' fer you to open up. Let's git up to the fort. I'm takin' this phonograph along. Better fetch the flute—it's your share of the deceased's estate."

Cush picked up the instrument gingerly. "I wouldn't give a damn fer no flute, even if I could whistle a tune on it," he said sourly. "Come on—let's go."

VI

BLACK JOHN STERNLY eyed the young man that stood waiting while Cush unlocked the door. Then he glanced mean- ingly toward the little graveyard at the farther end of the clear- ing, where two men were digging a grave, an ominous, blanket- covered figure laying on the ground beside them.

"A man was shot in a cabin down the crick a piece this mornin'," he said. "We hang murderers, on Halfaday."

The other nodded, his clear blue eyes meeting Black John's glance squarely. "I shot him," he announced, in a matter of fact tone. "My name's Joe West. It wasn't a murder. He had it comin'."

"I know that he murdered a couple of people on Goose Crick, down below Dawson."

The door swung open and the two followed Old Cush into the saloon where, after depositing the phonograph beside the flute on the huge iron safe, Black John joined the younger man at the bar. "Accordin' to your way of thinkin', it ain't murder to murder a murderer—is that right?"

"He had it comin'," reiterated the other. "I'll be damned if I was goin' to let him get away with it."

"The law," Black John reminded him, "has got men paid to see that no one gits away with murder."

West nodded, "An' most times they do a damn good job. But this time they're makin' a mistake—they're huntin' me. They think I murdered Tom Nolan an' Elsie. The damn fools! Why—I—me an' Elsie was goin' to get married—but old Tom wouldn't let us."

"So, you knocked him off, eh?"

"No!" flared the younger man angrily. "I'm no damn murderer! Tom an' I quarreled, an' Charlie Gamble heard it. The next day he murdered the Nolans an' robbed their cache, an' stole my canoe to get away in. He either tipped the police off that old Tom an' I had quarreled, or else he left my canoe where they could find it, because when I got to Dawson, figurin' to report the murders to the police, a fella I know there told me that the police were already huntin' me for the murder. I wasn't goin' to get arrested an' let Gamble go free, an' I couldn't stay around Dawson—too many people there know me. I'd heard of Halfaday Crick, so I came here, an' then, on the White River, I met a couple of fellas comin' down, that told me they'd camped, a couple of nights before, along side of a man headed upriver that had a phonograph an' a flute with him—so I knew that Gamble was headin' for here, too.

"When I got here I asked Mr. Cushing about him, and he told me that there was no one named Gamble on the crick, an' that the only man here who owned a phonograph an' a flute was a John Brown, who had moved into One Eyed John's cabin only a few days before.

"I was afraid the police might trail me here, an' arrest me for the Goose Crick murders, an' that Gamble would get away with 'em—an' old Tom's dust, besides. So this mornin' I went down to see him. He admitted killin' Nolan, but denied killin' Elsie. I pulled a gun on him an' demanded to know what he had done with the girl. He grabbed up his rifle an' fired, an' I fired, too. He fell—"West paused abruptly and stared, wide-eyed, toward the doorway where a young woman darted swiftly past an officer in the uniform of the Northwest Mounted Police. She came rapidly toward him with a glad cry that held in it also a note of fear.

"Oh—Joe! They—they think that you killed dad!"

Rapidly crossing the floor, the officer reached the young man's side almost as soon as did the girl. "Joe West," he said, "I arrest you for the murder of Tom Nolan—an' it's my duty to warn you that anything you say may be used against you."

"Oh Joe—tell him you didn't do it," cried the girl. "Tell him about Charlie Gamble!"

The formality of arrest over, Black John's glance strayed from the girl to the face of the officer. "Hello, Downey—it looks like you'd introduce a fella to yer friend."

"This is Miss Nolan, John. Her father was murdered down on Goose Crick. I'm up here after the murderer."

"H-u-u-m-m—well, it looks like you wouldn't have much trouble locatin' him."

"I've located him already."

"Kind of looks like you an' Miss Nolan has got different idees on the subject."

"She's either tryin' to cover up for him, or she really believes he's innocent—I don't know which. I ain't exactly blamin' her, either way—she's in love with him."

"How come you to fetch her along?"

"I didn't. Some friend of Joe West's tipped her off in Dawson that he'd hit for Halfaday, an' she followed. When I couldn't locate West in Dawson, I figured he'd hit for here, so I took the trail, and this mornin' I overtook her on the crick."

"H-u-u-m—you must have worked up considerable in the way of evidence agin him, to be so shore it was him done it."

"I've got plenty to convict him on. It's a plain case. I went up to Goose Crick an' made the investigation, myself. In the first place, there was Tom Nolan's body—what was left of it—in the bottom of his shaft. He'd been blown up with a shot of giant. The girl told me when she reported the murder, that Nolan had rigged the shot with a six foot length of fuse that would allow him three minutes to git out of the shaft after touchin' it off. I found, on the dump beside the shaft, a length of fuse that measured jest five foot an' nine inches. I also found the bucket drawn tight up against the roller of the windlass, an' the windlass chocked. Apparently what happened was this: not wantin' to take the capped dynamite into the shaft with him, Nolan lays his shot on the ground beside the shaft an' slides down the rope to do some cleanin' out, figurin' to come back up an' get it when he's ready to shoot. The murderer comes along, cranks up the bucket so Nolan can't get out of the shaft, cuts off all but three inches of the fuse, which allows only five seconds fer the fire to reach the cap, lights it an' tosses it into the shaft. Nolan ain't got time to snatch the fuse out—an' the giant lets go."

"Sounds reasonable, so far," agreed Black John. "But that ain't sayin' that the man that done it was West."

"Next I found that the murderer had smashed up the Nolan canoe with an ax, evidently to prevent the girl's followin' him.

Also, I confirmed the girl's statement that Tom Nolan's cache had been robbed."

"But you didn't find out who stole my canoe!" interrupted West.

Corporal Downey smiled, as the girl exclaimed, "Why, I took your canoe, Joe! Ours was smashed all to pieces, and when I found out what had happened, I rushed to the crick and found the canoe all broken up, so I made my way to your claim as fast as I could. I wanted to get you to help me. I knew you'd know what to do—but you weren't there, and your rifle was gone. I took your canoe, and went to notify the police."

"I was huntin'," said West. "I was figurin' on pullin' out in a few days, an' I wanted to smoke me some meat. When I got home an' found the canoe gone, I went down to your place an' found—what you found in the shaft. I struck out afoot fer the big river—figgerin' you'd been killed, too."

Black John glanced at the officer. "An' that sounds reasonable, too," he said.

Corporal Downey nodded. "It does."

"You ain't said nothin' yet that would link West up with this murder."

"I'm comin' to that. When Miss Nolan reported the murder to me she admitted that her father had quarreled with West the night before Nolan was killed. West told him he was goin' to marry her, an' Nolan told him he never would so long as he was alive. Then West told him that the sooner he was dead the better, whereupon Nolan ordered him off the claim—an' West went away. There you've got a motive—an' what amounts to a threat.

"But the thing that really links West with the murder is fingerprints. A few years ago Sir Francis Galton wrote a couple of books on fingerprints—an' I got hold of 'em an' studied 'em. A man's fingerprints never change from birth to old age—an' there ain't no two of 'em alike. I examined the bucket that hung on the windlass. There was blood stickin' to it that had been blown up out of the shaft. An' there was plenty of good plain fingerprints where someone had handled the bucket after Tom Nolan was killed, an' before the blood had dried. I took the bucket with me to West's cabin, an' found plenty of fingerprints there—on a tin drinkin' cup an' some tin plates, an' other places. I got some fine ashes out of the stove an' blew 'em on the prints to bring 'em out—an' then I compared 'em with the prints on the bucket. They were identical to the man who handled West's dishes. An' when we take West's fingerprints we'll know it was him that made 'em all."

"Sure, I handled that bucket!" exclaimed West. "When I got to Nolan's, that afternoon, I looked all around to see if I could find out anything that would help the police when I reported the murder. I reached over and took the bucket, and there was blood on it that had clotted, but hadn't quite dried yet. I didn't find anything about the bucket that would help, so I put it back jest as I found it."

"Jest when," asked Downey sarcastically, "did you figure on reportin' the murder?"

West flushed. "I'd have reported it as soon as I hit Dawson, except that I met a friend of mine while I was headin' for the detachment, an' he told me the police were huntin' me for the murder of Tom Nolan. It seemed like a joke, at first—me murderin' old Tom. Then I happened to think that him an' I had quarreled the night before, an' Charlie Gamble had heard it an' he'd prob'ly beat me to Dawson after killin' Nolan an' reported that I done it. It looked as if, what with him fer a witness an' all, I was in a mighty tight spot. I got kind of panicky, I guess—an' instead of goin' on to the detachment, I skipped out an' came up here."

Downey glanced at Black John with a smile. "An' I s'pose that sounds reasonable, too?"

"Well—tolerable. Off hand, Downey, it looks like you'd worked up a pretty good case agin West, what with them fingerprints an' all—"

"Oh—but he's not guilty!" cried the girl.

"Yeah—an' that's the hell of it," observed the big man. "That's where I claim the law's all wrong—dependin' on evidence, like it does. Evidence is all right—if you've got it all. The trouble is, the police never know if they've got all the evidence. They git all they kin an' go to trial with it—but that might not be all of it by a damn sight. Take this here case, Downey—both Miss Nolan an' Joe West mentioned this here Charlie Gamble, an' you ain't said a damn word about him. How do you git around Charlie Gamble?"

Downey's smile broadened. "I don't have to get around him. In the first place, Miss Nolan told me there was no one but West on the crick when he and Nolan quarreled. When she saw I suspected West, she invented this Charlie Gamble—a most improbable person. An' more improbable that she would forget to mention him at first. I guess we can ignore Gamble as a—a figure of the imagination."

"Yeah, I guess he can be ignored, all right. He was sort of improbable, at that; what with his phonograph, an' flute—"

"What!" exclaimed Downey, his eyes suddenly widening as his glance followed Black John's toward the big iron safe. Suddenly he pointed to the instruments. "Where the devil did those things come from?" he demanded, in a hard, tense voice.

"Them? Oh, them's Charlie Gamble's estate—part of it."

"Charlie Gamble! You mean, there is a Charlie Gamble? That he's here on Halfaday? Do you know anything about him?"

"Well, I can't say as I know much about him. Fact is, Downey, Charlie met up with a little tough luck. He ain't here no more."

"Ain't here! Where is he?"

"Your guess would be as good as mine—that's up to the theologians."

"You mean, he's dead?"

"That's what Cush claims—an' he's the coroner."

"How did he die?"

"Fairly sudden, from the looks of things. We figger it was his heart."

"His heart?"

"Yeah—we found where a bullet had tore through it,"

"You mean, he was murdered?"

"Well—from what evidence we had at the time we held the inquest, we figgered it was suicide. We turned in a verdict to that effect—an' Pot Gut an' One Armed John is right now engaged in buryin' him as sech. But from some evidence that turned up later, me an' Cush feels constrained to believe that the verdict is open to question. Like I was tellin' you, Downey; we thought we had all the evidence, but we didn't."

"You mean," exclaimed Downey, "that West killed him? That he knocked off the only witness to his quarrel with Nolan except the girl—to keep him from testifyin'?"

"I shot him," said West in a hard, dry voice, "but not to keep him from testifyin'. I knew he'd murdered old Tom—he was the only one who could have done it—an' I was afraid he'd murdered Elsie, too. I accused him of it, an' he admitted blowin' Tom up—but denied touchin' the girl. I pulled a gun on him to make him tell what he'd done with her. Then he grabbed up his rifle an' fired—an' I fired—an' he dropped."

"Self defence, eh? Can you prove it? An' can you prove he admitted blowin' Nolan up?"

"No—I can't prove it. There was no one in the cabin but Gamble an' me. But it's the truth, just the same."

AT A sign from Black John, Old Cush opened the safe and tossed the sixteen little sacks they had taken from Gamble's cache onto the bar.

"Dad's dust!" cried the girl, her eyes lighting with excitement. "I made those sacks myself—I'd know them anywhere."

"An' them sacks," observed Black John, "constitutes the balance of Charlie Gamble's estate. Me an' Cush found 'em in his cabin after the inquest."

"It's possible," said Downey, "that Joe West planted 'em there, to throw suspicion on Gamble after he shot him."

"Nope," denied Black John. "West never seen them sacks. Gamble had a heft of dust in his pack when he come here. An' besides, West couldn't of found the cache."

"And everyone that knew Charlie Gamble can swear he never had two ounces of dust to his name at one time!" exclaimed the girl.

Corporal Downey cleared his throat "I'll admit," he said, "that I'm not nearly so sure of my case as I was when I came here. This Gamble business throws a new angle on it." He turned and regarded young West searchingly. "It may be that you're tellin' the truth. I'd hate like the devil to make a mistake—especially in a murder case. It's as much a policeman's duty to protect the innocent, as it is to convict the guilty. If your story is true, I sure hope you can make the jury believe it. But unsupported by actual evidence—"

"Oh, they'll prob'ly believe it, all right, when all the evidence is in," said Black John casually. "That is—if the case ever goes to a jury."

"What do you mean?" Downey asked.

"You know, this here Gamble—he was a sort of a queer cuss in his way," Black John said irrelevantly. "He rigged him up a dingus that would shave one of them phonograph records down to a blank, an' then he'd start the machine up with a needle on it, an' sing songs in front of it, an' the songs would go on the record so you could play 'em. Look—I'll show you."

As he lifted the phonograph from the safe to the bar, Corporal Downey frowned. "I ain't got time to be standin' around playin' records," he said. "I want to take a look at Gamble, before they bury him, an' the cabin where he was shot. It's possible I can dig up some evidence that'll support West's story."

"That's the trouble with you police—always worryin' about evidence," grinned Black John. "Hold on a minute, an' listen to this." He wound up the machine, and carefully placed the needle. There was a moment of meaningless grinding, and then a man's voice—singing. Then as before the words of the song broke suddenly, and there came the voice fraught with mingled surprise and terror. "Joe West! What—"

"Yes, Gamble—it's me. Where's Elsie?"

"Elsie—how the hell do I know?"

"You know, all right—you murdered her—"

"You lie!"

"An' you murdered Old Tom Nolan, too—blew him up in his shaft. An' you robbed his cache."

"Sure—I blow'd Tom up, all right. But what's that to you? He hated you! But I never touched the girl!"

"Where is she?"

"I don't know I My God—put up that gun! Don't shoot! Don't—" The words broke off abruptly, there was an indistinct sound—then the sudden roar of a shot—and another, followed by indefinable scraping sounds and then a loud scratching noise as the needle ran off the record.

In the saloon the three stood before the instrument in stunned silence, while Black John stopped the machine, and Old Cush wiped at an imaginary spot on the bar with his rag.

The girl was the first to find her voice. "It's the proof!" she cried hysterically, throwing her arms about West's neck. "It proves Joe told the truth! The jury will have to believe it!"

Corporal Downey smiled. "It's the proof, all right," he said. "But no jury will ever hear it. There ain't goin' to be no arrest." He turned gravely to Black John. "This case is closed," he said.

The big man nodded. "Yeah," he agreed, "you've got in all the evidence."

Behind the bar Old Cush set out bottle and glasses. "Fill 'em up," he invited. "This un's on the house."

BEAR PAWS

THE STRANGER PAUSED in the doorway for a long and searching scrutiny of the room before advancing to the bar and ranging himself beside Black John Smith who stood, dice box in hand.

"This here's Cushing's Fort, ain't it—on Halfaday Crick?" he demanded, a note of truculence in his voice.

"Yeah," admitted Cush, the somber faced proprietor, as he slid a glass across the bar, "this is the place. Have one on the house."

The man filled the glass and returned the bottle to the bar without offering it to either of the others whose glasses stood empty. Reaching for it, Black John filled his own glass and shoved the bottle toward Cush as the newcomer downed his liquor at a gulp without waiting for the others.

"There's certain amenities," observed Black John in a mild tone of voice, "that obtains even in a saloon."

"What?" asked the stranger, reaching again for the bottle.

"I was jest remarkin' that there's a few rules of barroom etiquette that you seem to have overlooked."

"Oh, you mean manners, eh? Well, tellin' you about me, I ain't got no use fer manners. I go ahead an' mind my own business an' let other folks mind theirn. If I feel like takin' a drink I take one. An' if I feel like eatin' I eat—an' to hell with what anyone else is doin'—er how they like it."

"It's prob'ly a good policy—if you kin make it work," the big man admitted. "Takin' it by an' large, though, I'd hesitate, to predict any outstandin' success fer the system."

The man scowled. "What the hell be you—a preacher, er a lawyer, er somethin'?"

"The question is framed wide enough to admit an' affirmative answer."

"Wise guy,'eh? Well listen, bo—you might talk like a preach-er an' act like one, but you ain't foolin' me none. I know all about this here Halfaday Crick. I know you ain't nothin' but a bunch of outlaws up here that lives clost agin the line so you kin dodge acrost into Alasky if the police should show up—which they don't dast to. An' I know that anythin' goes up here, an' it ain't no one's business—the police's least of all."

"Yer knowledge seems to be damn near as comprehensive as it is erroneous," observed Black John.

"Yeah? Well where's this Black John Smith they tell, about? I want to see him."

"I'm the character that's know'd more er less locally as Black John Smith."

"You!"

"Yeah—me."

"Well—I'll be damned!"

"Too obvious to brag about, I'd say."

"What?"

"Jest a random observation. What was it you wanted to see me about?"

"Listen—if yer tryin' to put somethin' over on me—fergit it. I ain't no one to fool with. Hell—there's more police huntin' me back in the States than you've got in the Yukon!"

"Bad man, eh?"

"I'll say I'm bad."

THE BIG man smiled. "Is that what you come up here to tell me?"

"If yer Black John Smith—okay; but if yer some guy that's tryin' to string me you better begin pickin' 'em up an' layin' 'em down before I find it out. I ain't got no more use fer preachers than preachers has got fer me. If yer Black John I want to j'ine up with yer gang."

"What gang?"

"What gang! Why yer gang of outlaws up here, of course!"

"There ain't no gang—an' never was. Fact is you seem to have absorbed more misinformation than a head that size could be expected to hold. It's a fact that some of the boys on Halfaday is outlawed, fer one reason er another here er there—but we ain't a gang. We're a community of simple law abidin' prospectors, an' the reason the police don't bother us is because we don't give 'em no reason to."

The saturnine face twisted into a knowing grin and the man winked a comprehending eye. "Oh shore—I git you. I guess we talk the same language, bo—barrin' you usin' a few bigger words than me. But le's git down to cases. I want to j'ine up like I says. My line was hick banks an' post offices an' grain elevators around harvest time when their boxes had plenty of the needful in 'em. I ain't afraid to use a gat er a blackjack. An' I kin handle soup like nobody's business."

The big man regarded him gravely. "If you'll promise to confine yer criminal activity to banks an' post offices an' grain elevators I guess there won't be no objection to yer operatin' on Halfaday. But about the soup—I'm goin' to request you not to swoozle it in public."

"What?"

"I say you've got my permission to rob any bank er post office er grain elevator on Halfaday, with the onderstandin' that yer criminal tendencies is curbed then an' there. Oversteppin' the bounds of this verbal license will earn a prompt an' thoroughgoin' hangin' fer yerself."

"But there ain't none on Halfaday!"

"The lack of sech institutions ain't our fault, an' up to now we ain't felt the need of none. If you feel that yer sphere of usefulness will be curtailed here, I suggest that you either move on, er go to work."

"Go to work! You mean crawl down some hole an' muck around in the mud with a shovel?"

"The shovel is optional."

"You tryin' to make me believe you ain't got no outlaw gang up here?"

"That's the idea I was endeavorin' to convey. An' I might add the information that any misconduct on the part of a resident of Halfaday sech as murder, larceny in any form, claim jumpin', an' general skullduggery is promptly an' effectively dealt with by miners' meetin'. A casual stroll through our graveyard out back will ondoubtless disabuse yer mind of any lingerin' doubt of the sincerity of our determination to keep the crick free from the taint of crime. The check letters on the slabs is indicative of the mode of departure used by their owners—*M* standin' fer Murdered, *H* fer Hung, an' *D* fer Died natural without human aid er abettal. The preponderance of *Hs* over *Ms* is owin' to our habit of hangin' folks fer much more trivial offenses than murder."

THE MAN was plainly disappointed. "That's a hell of a note!" he exclaimed at length. "But I gotta stay here fer a spell, anyhow. The name is John Smith—same as yourn."

"Not on Halfaday it ain't," corrected Black John. "The name has become hackneyed hereabouts. When we run out of descriptive adjectives like black, red, pot-gutted, long-nosed, an' so forth. Me an' Cush devised the expedient of the name-can. It's that molasses can there on the end of the bar. We copied down the names out of a hist'ry book that One Eyed John left behind him when we hung him one time, an' juggled 'em around a little

an' wrote the results on slips of paper. Jest reach in an' pick out a name which will become yer property ontil sech time as a rope er some other circumstance removes you from our midst, as a newspaper would say."

Reaching into the can the man drew out a slip of paper from which he read the name: "Benedict Hale."

"It's a name," opined Black John, "that is fraught with possibilities."

"What?"

"Jest a couple of big words that John seen the chanct to work in," observed Cush sourly. "An' speakin' of drinks, them last three you've took is on yerself."

"Oh yeah—I did have three more, didn't I? Take 'em out of that," the man said, tossing a sack onto the bar. "An' here's another thing I heard—that a man kin bank his dust in yer safe. I ain't got no hell of a lot, couple hundred ounces mebbe. But I wouldn't like fer it to git stole out of no cache."

"Yer welcome to bank it here," Cush replied. "I'll weigh it in an' give you a receipt."

The man tendered a second pouch and, after taking payment for the drinks, Cush weighed the contents of the two and handed him a receipt for a hundred and eighty-four ounces.

"Looks like you done fairly well, Ben, on some crick er other," observed Black John, his eyes on the two small pouches.

"Oh, jest tol'able. It was down on Fortymile. I prospected around there a couple of months. I don't like prospectin'. Too damn much work. That's why I come up here—heard there was a gang. There's a damn sight easier ways of gittin' money than workin' fer it."

"Not on Halfaday there ain't," reminded Black John. "I s'pose you'll be locatin' a claim?"

"No, I won't bother. I've got a hunch I ain't goin' to stop here long."

"Our hunches runs sim'lar."

"I throw'd my stuff in an empty cabin about four, five mile down the crick on the right hand side comin' up. Guess there won't be no one care if I hole up there temporary, will they?"

"Temporary is the best anyone's be'n able to reside in that cabin to date," said Black John. "Some of the tenancies could best be described by the word 'fleetin'."

"That's Olson's old shack," Cush volunteered. "It's onlucky."

"How do you mean—unlucky?"

"Well," Black John explained; "it's so considered from the fact that murders, hangin's, an' arrests has took a toll that runs right around a hundred percent of its former occupants."

"Hell—that ain't the cabin's fault!"

"No, thinkin' back over the list, I'd say it was its virtue."

"Ain't the claim no good?"

"No one ever worked it long enough to find out."

"Well I ain't goin' to work it neither. I'll jest lay up there a spell an' hunt an' fish an' take it easy. I'll be goin' back now. I want a couple of bottles of booze, an' some flour, an' some pork fer grease, an' some sugar, an' tea. You kin charge it up agin my dust."

AS THE man left the room with his pack Cush returned to the bar and shoved the bottle toward Black John. "Seems like," he observed with a sigh, "The run of folks that shows up on Halfaday gits ornier an' ornier as time goes on."

"Well, you got to remember, Cush, that proximity to a boundary line ain't no inducement to the average citizen. An' besides, big camps like Dawson has got a lot to recommend 'em that we ain't. Personally, I sort of like the peace an' quiet of our little community. Its humdrum existence pleases me. I s'pose we could organize a Chamber of Commerce an' institute an exploitation drive that would—"

"Listen!" Cush interrupted with a frown. "All I says was that the folks that come here was gittin' ornier. An' there ain't no call fer you to begin onloadin' all the big words you know onto me, which I wouldn't know what they mean even if I would listen to 'em. Take this cuss that was jest in here—I bet he never panned er sluiced out a damn ounce of that dust he's got."

"Let's take a look at it."

Cush produced one of the little sacks from the safe and opening it, Black John poured a portion of dust into his palm.

"Not on Fortymile, he didn't," agreed the big man. "This is upriver gold. No chechako could take out better'n three ounces a day on Fortymile anyhow. Ben has proved himself a liar."

"Humph—I could of told you that by jest lookin' at him!" snorted Cush. "He stole that dust off'n some one—that's what he done."

"The amount is too trivial to contemplate."

"I'll bet that there Koogler that come to the crick four, five days ago fetched in more'n that. He didn't bank none in the safe—but I'll bet he's got plenty cached somewheres."

"Much the same thought occurred to me," admitted Black John. "But so far, sech observation as I've be'n able to carry on has failed to disclose the location of any cache."

"Be'n watchin' him, eh?"

"Well, suspectin' as I do that the man is possessed of important wealth, I deemed it prudent to ascertain, if possible, the whereabouts of his cache, jest in case hangin', murder, er sudden death should remove him. It would be a damn shame fer him to leave any considerable amount of dust buried in some cache where it wouldn't never do anyone any good."

"He ain't no damn chechako," opined Cush. "You kin say that much for him. He would know how to cache the stuff where it would be hard to find. Plays a damn good game of stud, too."

"Yeah," agreed Black John, "an' that's the reason I ain't be'n able to locate his cache. Bein' way ahead of the game, he ain't be'n drove by the vicissitudes of fortune to replenish his exchequer from his reserve supply."

"If them words means his luck's runnin' good, yer right," replied Cush sourly. "It's prob'ly owin' to that there luck-piece he packs around in his pocket. It's about a four-ounce nugget in the shape of a bear. An' when he sets in a game he pulls it out an' lays it amongst his chips."

BLACK JOHN nodded thoughtfully. "Barrin' his adherence to the pardonable superstition that attaches to a luck-piece, the man seems to be smarter'n most of the riff-raff that drifts in on us. He's resourceful enough to hit on the name 'Koogler' instead of the usual 'John Smith'. He's close mouthed. He filed a claim, an' spends his days workin' it."

"Yeah, an' every night he's in here playin' stud."

"That's right," agreed Black John. "If the weather'd change I might be able to locate his cache."

"What's the weather got to do with findin' someone's cache?"

"It would be a contributin' factor in a sequence of circumstances."

"Does that mean his luck might change if it rained?" growled Cush.

"Exactly," Black John grinned. "Your education is progressin'."

"It ain't no sech a damn thing. If a man has got to guess what you mean every time you open yer head he would be bound to git it right onct in a while. But how could rain change a man's luck?"

"Only by analogy."

"Oh shore," replied Cush, with elaborate sarcasm, "funny I didn't think of that!"

Black John's grin widened. "I mean if it should rain some day so Koogler couldn't work on his claim, he might drift up here. An' if we could git him in a three-handed stud game an' run them markers in on him we could relieve him of what dust he carried an' thus drive him to his cache to git more."

Cush frowned. "You know damn well, John, I don't favor runnin' in no markers when we don't have to—like if we know'd someone was cheatin' er somethin'. It somehow don't seem honest."

"I'll admit that the use of markers does raise a question of ethics," replied the big man. "An' under ordinary circumstances I'm every bit as punctilious as you. I would scorn to ring in markers on a man if winnin' his money were the sole object. But, in the present case, the winnin' of his dust is only a secondary an' incidental consideration. The main one bein' to force him to visit his cache. So under the circumstances, I deem it a just an' a proper subterfuge. Distasteful as it may be it is sometimes necessary to employ questionable means to accomplish a laudable end."

"Humph!" snorted Cush. "A man can't auger with you no more'n what he kin with a preacher er a lawyer. They go ahead an' do as they damn please; an' then say big words enough to make it sound all right."

"There is much truth in what you say," laughed Black John. "But as the signs seem to indicate a continued spell of good weather, I guess I'll slip out in the hills for a couple of days an' try to kill us some meat. What's left of that hindquarter is beginnin' to smell a mite high. Guess I'll swing around by Solomon Albert's place. He generally knows where a man kin pick up a nice young moose."

II

PROCURING HIS BLANKETS and rifle, and stowing a few days' provisions into his pack sack, Black John stepped into his canoe and paddled swiftly down Halfaday. At Olson's old shack he landed to pass the time of day with the saturnine Benedict Hale.

"What the hell a man's going to do all by hisself in a damn dump like this is more'n I know," grumbled the man. "Here I come to Halfaday lookin' fer action—an' this is what I git!"

"You might try workin' the claim here. Some of the claims on the crick is payin' out pretty good. If you struck somethin' worth while you could file on it."

"Listen—there's a lot of ways of makin' money, an' work ain't one of 'em, as fer as I'm concerned. What does a man do nights around here? Ain't there no card game er nothin'? Er be you all so damn sanctimonious you hold prayer meetin's every night?"

"We have services in the saloon when some preacher happens along. The boys rather enjoys it fer a change. Other nights a man kin generally find what he's lookin' fer in the way of poker er stud."

"That's more like it. I know damn well I ain't goin' to break my back on no shovel."

"Without seemin' to cast no hints nor aspersions," said Black John, as he stepped into his canoe, "it ain't no more'n right to warn you that cheatin' at cards comes under skullduggery on Halfaday—an' as sech is hangable. So long. I'm slippin' down the crick to hunt me some meat."

Dropping down Halfaday to its confluence with the White, Black John headed up the larger river and late in the evening shoved a short distance up a feeder to the cabin of Solomon Albert, a Belgian by birth, who had been a resident of the Yukon since the days before even such sourdoughs as Old Bettles and Skiff Mitchell first saw the big river. The old recluse was a dour person who preferred the solitudes to the companionship of men and his camps were always located far from the seats of activity.

IT WAS in one of these lone shacks that Bettles and Tagish Jim had come upon him, years before, suffering from an advanced stage of gangrene that had followed the freezing of his feet. Acting promptly the two sourdoughs had succeeded with the aid of a butcher knife in amputating all ten of the man's toes—an operation that undoubtedly saved his life, but left him seriously hampered in the matter of locomotion until, quite by accident, he discovered that by skinning out a bear's paws and using them for moccasins he could navigate with little or no inconvenience—the paws furnishing the toe hold necessary for taking steps.

The old man welcomed Black John, who was one of the few men he tolerated, and readily agreed to pilot him to a creek where a young moose might be procured without much trouble.

The moose was shot the following day, the meat cut up and packed to the canoe where it was stowed for the trip to Cushing's Fort.

"I'll be goin' back with ye," the old man said that evening as the two sat in the cabin. "I'm needin' some grub, an' I be'n figgerin' on hittin' across to Cush's. This way I'll git me a ride there."

"Cripes!" exclaimed Black John, "I'd think you'd take a canoe every time! All you've got to do is drop down the White an' paddle up Halfaday to Cush's."

"I got the rheumatiz in my shoulders an' clean down one arm an' it hurts more to paddle a canoe. What with them portages around the rapids an' the stidy paddlin' an' polin' agin the current, it's easier to hit out acrost country. With two in a canoe it's easier work. A man kin rest up a few minutes when the pain ketches him bad without driftin' back downstream further'n he's shoved up."

"But it's a rough country between here an' Cush's. I should think a pack would hurt yer shoulders."

"It ain't only about twenty mile acrost, the way Halfaday bends around. I kin make it easy in a day, when the days is long, like now. I won't be packin' no more'n fifty er sixty pound. Onct I git the pack on it don't hurt much—not like paddlin' where I got to be movin' my arms all the time."

"But crippled like you be, I'd call twenty miles a long trip."

"I ain't crippled no more'n you be. Them bear paws is all right. Hell—I wouldn't go back to toes fer nothin'. It's better this way."

THE TWO started at daybreak the following morning and arrived at Cushing's Fort shortly after dark. With a nod toward the players of stud among whom Black John recognized Benedict Hale and Koogler, he led the way to the bar where Cush had already set out bottle and glasses.

"Got some meat?" asked the somber one.

"Oh, shore. Solomon, here, he had a nice yearlin' all fattened up fer me. I'll fetch you a chunk in the mornin'."

"You'd ought to be'n here night before last," said Cush, as they refilled the glasses. "Koogler's luck went back on him an' they cleaned him out of what dust he had on him—so he went an' got more. He didn't do so bad with the second batch—played a little ahead fer the rest of the evenin'. I guess he got his bear to workin' agin."

"What d'ye mean—his bear?" asked Solomon Albert, who was sensitive to any mention of bears.

"Jest a luck piece he's got. It's a layin' there amongst his chips—a nugget shaped like a bear. He claims it fetches him luck."

"Who was it got the heft of his losin's?" asked Black John casually.

"It was Ben Hale, that chechako with the mean lookin' eyes."

"H-u-m-m, was he perchance, forcin' his luck—I mean in a manner incompatible with the honest run of the cards?"

"If you mean was he cheatin' I would't know. Not settin' in the game myself, I couldn't say. I was busy back of the bar."

"How long was Koogler gone to git his reinforcement of dust?"

"Jest long enough to go to his claim an' back. You know where it's at—about a mile down the crick, mebbe a mile an' a half."

"An' durin' his absence did Ben Hale continue to set in the game?"

"Well, he set in fer a few minutes, then he cashed in, claimin' he had to step out back. He came after a while an' was settin' in the game agin when Koogler got back with his dust."

The glasses were filled, emptied, and refilled as the three talked of this, and of that. Old Solomon Albert, filling his to the brim each time, soon began to show evidence of the potency of the liquor. His loud talk attracted the attention of Koogler who noticing the man's incongruous footgear laughed aloud:

"First time I ever seen a bear standin' up to a bar drinkin' out of a glass!" he said, in a tone loud enough for Solomon Albert to hear.

Despite his years, Albert had the reputation of being plenty tough. He scowled at the words and Black John spoke to him in an undertone.

"Don't mind Koogler, Solomon. He was only kiddin'."

Ignoring the words, the old man picked up his glass and strode across to the table, the long nails of the bear toes scratching and clicking upon the floor. Pausing beside the man he glared into his face.

"Koogler, eh?" he snarled. "I've saw yer face before; somewheres—an' the name wasn't Koogler, neither! Drink that—if you think a bear ain't got no right to stand up to a bar!" With the words, he dashed the contents of his whiskey glass full into the man's face.

LEAPING TO his feet with a roar of rage, Koogler struck straight from the shoulder. His fist, catching Albert squarely upon the jaw, sent him sprawling on his back. The old man was on his feet in a second, his face livid with anger. Drawing a keen-bladed knife from his belt, he lunged toward Koogler just as Black John caught his wrist in a grip of iron.

"Hold on there, Old Timer," he soothed. "Jest take it easy. We don't want no one should git carved up in here. It's agin the law of the crick, an' besides it would mess Cush's floor all up."

"By God, they can't no one knock me down without I stick a knife in 'em!" yelled the oldster, his stubby gray beard fairly quivering with rage.

"But you got to remember you was the aggressor in this fracus. You can't hardly blame a man fer knockin' you down if you intimate he's livin' under some name he wasn't born with, an' slosh a glass of raw licker in his face to boot."

"But the polecat called me a bear!" shrilled Albert, struggling to free his arm. "Leggo! I'll, cut his guts out!"

"Not here an' now you won't," grinned Black John, giving the man's wrist a sudden twist that sent the knife clattering to the floor. "Come on back to the bar an' git on with yer drinkin' an' let them stud players alone." Stooping, he picked up the knife and handed it to Cush who laid it on the back bar out of its owner's reach.

As Black John released his wrist the old man took a step toward the table and fixed Koogler with a baleful glare. "Damn you!" he cried. "I'll kill you jest as shore as I'd kill a rattlesnake if I'd see one! You ain't never goin' to have no luck no more! That luck-piece of yourn is an onluck-piece from now on! Us bears sticks together!"

"You ain't got no call to git so hostyle," said Cush, as he shoved a bottle and glass toward the oldster a few moments later. "He prob'ly didn't mean nothin'. An' anyways it wasn't no killin' matter."

"An' besides which," added Black John, "if you'd kill him on Halfaday we'd hang you shore as hell."

"Hang an' be damned!" retorted the tough old sourdough. "I'll kill him all right—an' don't you fergit it!"

III

EARLY THE FOLLOWING morning Solomon Albert, his drunken rage of the night before considerably cooled, crowded his supplies into his pack sack and took his departure. A short time later Black John stepped into the saloon, stood his rifle in a corner, and deposited a quarter of moose meat on the bar.

"What's yer idee in parkin' yer rifle?" asked Cush, as he set out the bottle and glasses. " 'Fraid this moose ain't dead yet an' would try an' git away on you?"

"No, jest figgered on takin' a siyou down the crick a piece to see if there's any game stirrin' around."

"But cripes, we got meat enough now to last us quite a spell! Take it in weather like this it's hard to keep. It's damn pore policy killin' off game you don't need."

"As an abstract proposition yer thesis is onassailable. But there's times when a man's soul longs to commune with nature in her vastest solitudes—"

"Dry up on them big words an' ketch holt of the other side of this rinse tub," interrupted Cush. "They's drownded mice in it, and the glasses look kinda cloudy. We'll empty it an' fetch a fresh tub up from the crick. The klooch is busy worshin'—an' I like fer to be neat around the saloon."

"Yeah," agreed Black John, as he downed his liquor with a grin and passed around behind the bar to lay hold of the tub, "but I'm afraid yer gittin' plumb fastidious."

"Guess the curse old Solomon put on Koogler's luck-piece worked," said Cush, after the tub of fresh water was in place and the glasses refilled from the bottle. "Koogler went home 'long about three this mornin' skun out again an' talkin' to hisself."

"Dependence upon an insentiate an' inanimate talisman is obviously—"

"Good God!" exclaimed Cush in disgust. "If all the big words you kin say was wrote down end to end they'd reach from here to Dawson! Can't you never say nothin' that someone would know what it means when you git it said?"

BLACK JOHN picked up his rifle and left the room chuckling. He returned early in the afternoon, having left the rifle in his cabin.

"Well," queried Cush, eying him with disapproval, "what did you kill?"

"Nothin'," replied the big man. "But I'm dryer'n a post hole. Shove that dice box out here an' I'll beat you out of a drink." The cubes clicked and rattled as he shook the leather box and cast them out onto the bar. "Three fives," he announced. "I feel lucky. I'll leave 'em in one."

Dropping the square steel framed spectacles from forehead to nose Cush inspected the dice and gathering them into the box rolled them out. "Four fours," he declared, "an' mebbe that'll learn you not to send a boy to do a man's chore." Returning the cubes to the box he cast them again, saved a pair of aces, added another on the second shake, and threw a trey and a four on his third.

Black John collected four treys in two throws. "That's a horse apiece," he said, "an' here goes fer the drinks." He shook the box and cast out the dice with a flourish. "Five aces in one—count 'em!" he grinned. "I told you I felt lucky."

Cush scowlingly verified the cast and picking up the dice examined them closely. "Prob'ly be'n out in the hills practicin' some new trick," he grumbled as he returned them to the box. "Any five ties," he stated as he shook the box slowly back and forth.

"Not by a damn sight! That's a question that has be'n mooted in here a dozen times. Last time we decided it took five higher ones. There ain't nothin' higher'n aces so the best you kin do is tie—an' if you'd care to make a sportin' event out of it, one ounce'll git you five hundred if you kin tie 'em in one throw."

"This is fer drinks; not ounces," Cush replied. "An' what's more, it don't make no difference what we decided last time. This is this time, an' bein' as this is my saloon, an' my licker, an' my dice, an' I says first that any five ties; any five does. An' if I roll out five of anythin' you don't git no drink till you pay fer two of 'em—an' you've got it all in little words that means somethin'."

"Oh, all right! Roll 'em out—onless yer waitin' to git a little more age on that licker. I'd trust you with a million in dust, Cush—but there ain't no subterfuge you wouldn't stoop to to beat a man out of the drinks."

Cush cast the dice, gathered up three deuces, returned the box to the back bar, and set out the bottle and glasses. "So you didn't see nothin' to shoot at, eh?" he asked, shoving the spectacles to his forehead.

"Seen a bear."

"Take a shot at it?"

"Nope. It was one of them big old he ones. I didn't deem it advisable to shoot."

"Some of them lone ones gits ornier'n hell. You'd ought to shot him to git shet of him. They ain't safe to be let live. He's liable to git on the prod an' attack someone."

"I didn't give him no provocation to attack me. He never even seen me." Black John swallowed his liquor and turned toward the door. "Guess I'll slip over to the shack an' ketch me some sleep," he said. "There'll prob'ly be a stud game tonight, an' what with one thing an' another, it's be'n quite a while sence I've set in."

"If you'd of set in t'other night instead of bein' off on that moose hunt you could mebbe of follered Koogler to his cache an' wouldn't have to wait fer a rainy day an' spring them markers on him."

"Possibly," admitted Black John, "but we'd still be eatin' tainted meat. An' besides, from certain observations I made in the hills today I am now of the opinion that it will be onnecessary to await an' atmospheric disturbance—"

"Does them words mean you located Koogler's cache?"

"Oh, no. I was much farther down the crick than Koogler's. From a high hillside in the vicinity of Olson's old shack I heard the sound of a shot closely followed by three others. Making my way to the rim of a deep dry wash I peered in an' beheld a sight that may well portend dire an' ominous events in the lives of a couple of our esteemed citizens—an' may casually have some effect upon the fortunes of others."

"What the hell you gassin' about?"

"I was merely stating that I peered over the rim of this drywash an' seen Ben Hale skinnin' a bear he's jest shot."

"Well—what's so damn funny about that?"

"Funny? I saw no humor in it. I merely state it as a fact. Later I followed Ben to Olson's an' watched him cache somethin' in that hole in the rock wall near the shack—you know the one. Everyone that's ever lived in that shack has used that hole fer a cache. It's a natural—'specially as I always see to it that there's a slab lyin' there handy that fits over the hole so clost you can't see it. It don't hurt a man none to know where them caches is—in case anythin' should happen to their owners."

"Yeah," deprecated Cush, "but I don't believe that damn Ben Hale cached nothin' in there worth havin'—chunk of bear meat, mebbe, an' prob'ly so damn tough a man would break a tooth on the gravy. I don't figger he's got no other dust than them hundred an' eighty-four ounces he banked in here. An' he's shore as hell too lazy to dig any."

"Yer right," agreed Black John. "An' I happen to know the cache was empty earlier in the day because I swung around that way an' found Ben missin'."

"Then what was all them big words—like what you seen would be effectin' lives an' fortunes—an' all that rot?"

"Merely a prognostication, Cush—merely a prognostication."

"Yeah, an' if I'd have to carry around words as big as that in my head I'd need some sleep, too."

IV

THE STUD GAME that evening lasted far into the night and it was nearly noon the following day when Black John strolled into the saloon just as Cush was finishing his bar chores.

"Guess that curse old Solomon Albert put on Koogler's luck-piece didn't last very long," observed Cush, as he set out bottle and glasses. "I see Koogler win agin last night."

"Yeah, he done pretty well fer himself," agreed the big man, pouring his drink. "But I noticed he didn't depend on his luck-piece. He didn't flash it all evenin'."

"That's prob'ly why he won then," opined Cush. "D'you believe, John, that a man could put a curse on a luck-piece that would be worth a damn?"

"Oh, shore he could! He could absolutely an' completely nullify its potency."

"I doubt if Solomon Albert could do that. Chances is he don't even know what them words means. All he claimed was that the little gold bear would be an onluck-piece from then on. An' it must of worked, 'cause sence then Koogler lost when he had it amongst his chips; an' won when he didn't."

"A luck-piece is worthless once a man loses faith in it."

"Mebbe Koogler would sell it then. I wouldn't mind havin' it. I'd give him twict its weight fer it. That ought to be a good dicker if it ain't no more good to him."

A shadow darkened the doorway as One Armed John Smith catapulted into the room. "Koogler's dead!" he panted. "I was fishin' down the crick an' I come around that bend an' there he laid right by his spring! A bear done it! He's messed up somethin' fierce an' there's bear tracks in the mud!"

Old Cush frowned as he slid a glass along the bar toward the man. "If they's any corpses along a crick you always find 'em," he said. "This un ain't so bad though, bein' only a mile er so away, an' the weather bein' good, an' the flies an' mosquitoes about gone. An' bein' as he was in here last night he's bound to be fresh.

"Mostly when you find one it's snowin' er rainin' like hell, er the ground's froze too hard fer diggin', er it's hot an' he's laid there so long it ain't no pleasure to hold the inquest."

"Well, Cripes, Cush," defended One Armed John, "if a corpse is along a crick you've got to find him where he's at! It ain't my fault if it's snowin', er the bugs is bad, er he's laid there till he's sp'ilt."

"Well, Cush, you're the coroner," said Black John. "We better go down an' hold the inquest." He turned to One Armed John. "Throw that drink into you an' then git busy an' notify Pot Gutted John, Long Nosed John, Short John, Red John, an' Benedick Hale—them bein' the ones Cush app'ints fer a jury. I'll make the sixth member. Tell 'em to be at Koogler's claim at four this afternoon—that'll give 'em all time to git there."

"This here Benedick Hale, now—he might not want to come," objected One Armed John. "Him not bein' on the crick long,

JAMES B. HENDRYX

an' a chechako to boot, he might not know our ways—like if a man's app'inted on a coroner's jury he's got to serve."

"Any objections he might have will ondoubtless vanish when you put it accost to him that shirkin' a civic duty, like servin' on a jury, is deemed to be skullduggery on Halfaday, an' as sech is hangable. Jest tell him if he ain't at Koogler's at four, he'll shore be here at Cush's at five, an' in hell by six sharp. I noticed him out back the other day contemplatin' them slabs in the graveyard. You might drop a hint that we ain't had no unsuccessful hangin's to date, an' p'int out that we've still got considerable room left fer more of them *H* slabs. Of course, if he'd like to make a test case of it, that's up to him—but I doubt if he'd win."

"You mean he kin either serve, er git hung—an' you don't give a damn which?"

BLACK JOHN nodded. "That seems to be a comprehensive an' onprejudiced presentation of the proposition. A bit abrupt, perhaps, but succinct an' onequivocal, an' easily onderstandable even to a mediocre intellect."

"Which?"

"Git goin'!" growled Cush. "That's jest John's way of sayin' O.K."

At three o'clock Cush locked the saloon and accompanied by Black John proceeded down the creek. "It's jest like I said," he opined as they approached Koogler's claim. "If you'd shot that bear you seen yesterday, this wouldn't of happened. Them old lone ones is mean."

"That one wasn't," grinned Black John. "When I seen him Ben Hale had already shot him. But at that, Koogler can't be deemed no hell of a loss."

"He's a damn sight more of a loss than he would of be'n if you could of located his cache," grumbled Cush. "A man can't never tell when somethin' like this is goin' to happen. I've got a hunch he had plenty of dust cached somewheres. We prob'ly won't never find it now. Chances is a man like him wouldn't have no heirs that could be located, an' we could of divided that dust between us. The way it is now we don't hardly git paid fer our trouble. You kin take his last night's winnin's fer your share. An' we'll divide his other stuff amongst the boys fer jury pay. I'll take his luck-piece fer my fee."

"Considerin' the luck he's had yer welcome," grinned Black John.

"Solomon Albert ain't got nothin' agin me," Cush replied. "I'll bet if I was to offer him a couple of ounces, an' throw'd in a few drinks on the deal, he'd oncurse that luck-piece fer me."

"He might," admitted the big man. "I see the boys is all here. I hope they ain't tromped around in that mud till we can't see them bear tracks."

The two halted beside a flowing spring from which water found its way in tiny burbling cascades to the nearby creek. The body of a man lay sprawled on its back close beside the spring, and huge bear tracks were visible in the nearby mud.

"We ain't touched him," explained Pot Gutted John who, with the four other jurors and One Armed John, were awaiting the arrival of the two. "An' we ain't messed up them tracks none."

"That's good," replied Black John, and turned to Cush. "Go ahead an' swear in yer jury, Coroner. You're runnin' this inquest. I ain't got nothin' to say."

THE JURY being duly sworn Cush stooped and examined the body. He pointed to the dead man's head. "You kin all see how he was hit a hell of a crack which stove in the side of his head like a bear's paw might. An' you kin see how his face is all clawed to hell. Nothin' but a bear's toenails could make scratches like them. An' them tracks in the mud bein' hind tracks shows where the bear r'ared up on his hind legs like bears does an' fetched Koogler a clout side of the head when he come to the spring, an' then he clawed him." He paused and two or three of the jurors nodded agreement.

Black John met Cush's eye. "Then it's the verdick of this jury that deceased come to his death at the hands, er the paws rather, of a bear whose identity an' present whereabouts are onknown. Is that right?"

Cush wangled the corner from a plug of tobacco and spat into the mud. "It's all right with me—if the boys votes that way."

Black John's glance traveled over the faces of the others. "How about it—do you so vote?"

Pot Gutted John frowned. "I be'n in the country quite a spell an' I never know'd a bear to attackt a man before. 'Course, if Koogler come onto him sudden here at the spring the bear might of r'ared up an' smacked him like Cush said. But it ain't no ways reasonable a man could git that clost to a bear without neither one of 'em knowin' the other was there. If the bear heard er seen Koogler he'd of run off. An' vicy vercy, so would Koogler. It don't look reasonable."

"That's right," agreed Benedict Hale, "an' there's a couple of other things too. Take them tracks there—if a half-ton bear had made them tracks they'd be sunk a damn sight deeper in the mud than what they be. An' them scratches on Koogler's face. They was made by bear claws all right, accordin' to their looks—but I don't believe no bear ever clawed him. If one had he'd of ripped his hull face off, an' not jest left scratches that don't go more'n half an inch under his hide."

Other members of the jury were nodding agreement. Black John turned to the speaker. "You seem to be quite an authority on bears," he observed.

"Who—me? Hell, no—never killed one in my life! Ain't got no rifle I'd tackle one with. I was jest sayin' how things looked to me—jest common sense."

"He's right," seconded Long Nosed John. "A bear heavy enough to make tracks that size would shore have sunk 'em in the mud deeper'n what them is."

The others nodded agreement and thus encouraged, Hale continued. "So it looks like a man done this job instead of a bear. We was all in the saloon t'other night an' heard that old Solomon, er Albert, er whatever his name is, threaten to kill Koogler fer knockin' him down."

"By God, that's right!" exclaimed Red John.

"Shore he did, I heard him myself!" agreed Long Nosed John.

"An' old Solomon Albert always wears bear's paws fer moccasins!" said Pot Gutted John. "An' he leaved the toes on, nails an' all!"

"Yeah," agreed Short John, "an' you rec'lect that there luck-piece of Koogler's—shaped like a bear—an' when old Solomon seen it he says, 'Yer luck-piece is an' onluck-piece now,' he says. An' he says, 'You ain't goin' to have no luck from now on—us bears stick together.' Them was his very words."

BLACK JOHN nodded agreement, "Yer right. I heard him myself. In fact, old Albert would have carved Koogler up right there in Cush's if I hadn't stopped him. But if Solomon did kill him he must have used a club of some kind. It's a cinch he never stove in Koogler's head with his fist."

"That's right," agreed Pot Gutted John. "Le's hunt around in the bresh an' see if we can't find where he throw'd it."

The club was presently found by Benedict Hale in a clump of willows where the murderer had tossed it. It was a piece of heavy green spruce, clinging to the rough bark of which close scrutiny disclosed dry blood and a few hairs.

When all had again gathered at the spring Black John cleared his throat. "Owin' to further discovered evidence it's Cush's opinion that the verdick of this jury be amended to state that the deceased, alias Koogler, come to his death at the hands of a person onknown but suspected of bein' Solomon Albert, an' recommends that the said Solomon Albert be apprehended an' arrested wheresoever he may be found an' fetched into Cush's Fort fer trial by miners' meetin' at four o'clock day after tomorrow afternoon, if an' providin' the aforementioned suspect is duly delivered thither by then. Gentlemen of the jury do you so vote?"

The verdict being unanimous Black John proceeded. "An' by virtue of his authority as coroner of Halfaday Crick, Yukon Territory, as duly made an' provided, Cush app'ints Red John, Short John an' Benedick Hale to go an' fetch the said Solomon Albert to the Fort, an' instructs 'em to have him then an' there, dead er alive, by four o'clock day after tomorrow afternoon. An' he adds that he better be alive an' in good condition because maltreatin' a prisoner er killin' him is both hangable offenses, *pro tem,* on Halfaday—an' no questions asked."

"But hell, I don't want to go chasin' off to hunt this fella up an' help fetch him in," objected Hale. "It looks like two ought to be enough to git him. I've got work to do."

BLACK JOHN regarded him with a frown of disapproval. "By the time you've abode amongst us longer, if ever, you'll learn, Ben, that on Halfaday industry is never allowed to clog the wheels of justice. You kin either go along now with Red John an' Short John to Solomon's place; er you kin remain here an' git hung after supper, jest as you prefer. An' in either case yer fined a round of drinks fer contempt of a coroner, which will be charged again yer poke an' drunk when we git back to the saloon. This merely nominal fine bein' assessed to remind you that on Halfaday we're a serious minded folk. Further back talk will be rewarded by further fines. An' you'll leave yer rifle here. We'll pack it up to Cush's. With three of you to fetch old Solomon in, there ain't no call to do no shootin'."

When the three had departed the big man turned to One Armed John. "You hustle up an' down the crick an' notify the boys about the miners' meetin', an' tell 'em I say they better be here—er else. You kin add that there'll ondoubtless be a hangin', follerin' which drinks will be had to the full extent of the hangee's available assets."

Black John turned to the spring. "We'll want these bear tracks fer evidence at the miners' meetin', so—"

"How the hell you goin' to pack some bear tracks made in soft mud clean up to Cush's?" interrupted Long Nosed John.

"Easy enough. You an' Pot Gut slip up to the Fort an' fetch down ten, fifteen pounds of cement out of that sack in the shed, an' while yer at it you kin lug the *corpus delicti* up there. Jest h'ist him up on the meat cache to keep him out of the way of the dogs, an' hurry back. In the meantime, me an' Cush'll be huntin' up whatever we kin find in the way of additional evidence."

Loading the body into Koogler's canoe the two shoved upstream.

When they had disappeared Cush allowed his eyes to rove unhopefully over the landscape.

"I don't s'pose," he opined lugubriously, "we'll ever locate his cache."

"I located it already," replied Black John. "It was in the mud at the bottom of the spring. Smart trick—cachein' yer dust in the spring. Only a sourdough would think of it. If anyone was snoopin' around spyin' on a man he wouldn't think nothin' of his goin' to the spring fer a pail of water."

"When did you find it? I didn't see you pokin' around in the spring."

"I didn't have to. Whilst we was huntin' fer the murder weapon I found this." Stepping to a clump of bushes nearby Black John retreived a sodden, muddy flour sack which he held up for inspection. "Here's what he kep' his dust in. Prob'ly had it in moosehide sacks an' the sack's in here to keep 'em from gittin' separated an' sunk in the mud."

"You mean his cache is empty!" Cush exclaimed.

"It don't look very full," grinned the big man.

"Then that damn Ben Hale was right! It wasn't no bear killed Koogler! A bear wouldn't give a damn about a man's gold cache.

We'll hang old Solomon Albert—but you kin bet he'll never tell where he cached Koogler's dust!"

"That's right," agreed Black John. "Solomon'll never tell."

"Hell's fire!" exclaimed Cush, suddenly, fixing Black John with an accusing stare. "What did you let Pot Gut an' Long Nose git away with that corpse fer before we'd searched him? Them two's middlin' honest, as folks goes—but they shore as hell ain't goin' to overlook no bet like goin' through his pockets. I'll bet anythin' you want that when we search him we won't find a damn thing on him! An' he must of had that luck-piece, an' his last night's winnin's in his pockets—onlest old Solomon got them too."

BLACK JOHN grinned, and produced a pouch from his pocket. "I deemed it prudent to remove temptation from the path of them two characters whose morals ondoubtless hangs by a slender thread at best. So whilst the boys was busy huntin' fer the club I took occasion to give some onobtrusive attention to his honor the corpse. Three of his pockets assayed nothin' but a hole apiece. From the fourth I extracted this poke which contains, I'd say, right around forty-five er fifty ounces, which sum, constitutin' his last night's winnin's, will be divided equally between us in lieu of any claim we may have fer services rendered. The luck-piece was not upon his person. Either the murderer got it er we'll find it amongst whatever he's got in the way of personal effects in his tent. I suggest we go look the stuff over before Pot Gut an' Long Nose gits back with that cement."

Search of the tent failed to unearth Koogler's luck-piece. Cush picked up Koogler's gun. "This ain't sech a bad rifle," he said. "I wouldn't mind havin' it."

Black John frowned. "It don't never pay to be avaricious, Cush. We'll be dividin' the contents of this poke which should net us right around four hundred dollars apiece. The rest of this junk—tent, rifle, blankets an' all won't appraise more'n a couple of hundred. We better let the boys divide it amongst 'em. We don't want to appear niggardly in the matter of jury fees. We've got to be public-spirited."

"I wouldn't see nothin' niggerly in a man's gittin' him a good rifle if he got the chanct," grumbled Cush, laying the gun aside. "But like you say, I s'pose we got to be public-spirited."

When the two men returned with the cement Black John mixed a thin batter in a pail and poured it into the bear tracks, and leaving Cush and Long Nosed John to collect Koogler's effects and convey him to the Fort in the canoe, he ordered Pot Gutted John to accompany him and struck off down the creek.

In a deep dry wash not far from Olson's old shack the big man grinned as Pot Gutted John, who at the moment was in the lead, halted abruptly and pointed. "Looky there, John! Someone kilt a bear an' never skun out nothin' but his hind legs!"

"Yeah," replied Black John, "an' them hind legs is what we come down here after."

"But what the hell—?" He paused abruptly as a great light seemed to dawn on him. "By God, I'll bet them was the paws that made them tracks by Koogler's spring! By the size of this bear they'd jest about fit!"

"Exactly," agreed Black John. "Git busy an' cut them legs off an' put 'em in yer pack sack. We'll be wantin' 'em fer evidence. An' while yer about it dig out a couple of bullets from the carcass an' save 'em. I'm goin' to hunt fer an empty shell er two, if I kin locate where he stood when he shot the bear."

"But Solomon Albert had bear's feet! He can't git around without 'em!"

"Yeah, but Benedick Hale didn't have none—not till he shot this bear he didn't."

"You mean it was Benedick Hale knocked Koogler off?"

"I believe the evidence will support sech assumption."

"Why, the damn dirty, low-lived skunk! An' him tryin' to put it off on old Solomon Albert! Cripes, John, don't it beat hell what some folks would stoop to! It would be bad enough to knock a man off fer his dust without tryin' to git someone else hung fer it! 'Course, if he know'd Koogler had quite a heft of dust cached somewheres, an' ondertook to git it peaceable, without killin' him, a man couldn't hardly blame him none."

"Couldn't blame him!" exclaimed Black John, fixing the fat one with a disapproving frown. "I'll have you to remember that cache-robbin' on Halfaday is hangable, murder er no murder!"

"Oh, shore—I wouldn't claim it was plumb honest. An' if a man was to git ketched at it, it ain't no more'n right he should git hung. But at that, it wouldn't show no moral trepitood."

BLACK JOHN grinned. "What do you know about moral turpitude?"

"Well, not a hell of a lot—only what a jedge said when he practically throw'd the book at a pal of mine. Handed him a ten-to-twenty fer an express job we tried to pull off back in Ioway one time. We was in on this job together an' it was a cinch—but when Duffy started to slug this messenger with a half a brick in a sock, I sailed into him an' knocked him cuckoo. That's how come we got pinched. But hell—I couldn't stand there an' see him lam this pore guy on the dome with half a brick! It didn't look right. I only draw'd a one-to-three on account of the jedge claimin' Duffy had this here moral trepitood that I showed a lack of. Anyways, I would do a one-to-three any time before I would stand there an' see a guy git his conk stove in with a half a brick because he wouldn't fork over the company's dough."

"Yer attitude," commented Black John, "is a worthy one an' shows an innate sense of rectitude that would entirely escape the eye of the casual observer."

"I got paroled in eighteen months—if that's what you mean."

"That's near enough, Git to work on that bear now—an' when you git done pack them legs an' the bullets up to Cush's an' put 'em in the storeroom where they'll be handy fer the miners' meetin'. I'll nose around a bit an' see if I kin dig up any more incriminatin' evidence ag'in Ben Hale."

A short time later, after pocketing two empty rifle shells, Black John proceeded to Olson's old shack where he went directly to the cache and removed a pair of freshly skinned bear paws with a foot of hide attached. He noted that mud clung to the hair and was packed between the toes, and laying them aside, removed twenty damp and muddy moosehide sacks of gold. "They'll run right around eighty ounces apiece," he muttered as he slipped them into his pack sack, returned the bear paws to the cache, and replaced the stone. "That would figger better'n twenty-five thousan' dollars—an' I wouldn't be surprised if every damn ounce of it was the emolument of some crime."

Proceeding directly to his own cabin he cached the dust and strolled over to the saloon.

V

SHORTLY AFTER NOON on the day set for the miners' meeting the three who had been appointed to bring in the suspect appeared at the Fort with old Solomon Albert who angrily and defiantly denied that he knew anything about the killing of Koogler.

Reaching into his pocket Benedict Hale withdrew an object which he handed to Black John. "This here don't look like he didn't have nothin' to do with the killin'," he said. "Both Red John an' Short John kin swear we found this little gold bear in his pocket when we searched him. It's Koogler's luck-piece—an' there's plenty on the crick that's set in stud games with him kin swear to it."

"That's right," agreed Black John, slipping the object into his pocket, "I've seen it myself."

"It looks like he won't have a chanct in the world to wiggle out of it, what with havin' the luck-piece an' all," continued Hale eagerly. "I never be'n to a miners' meetin' before. I'd shore enjoy to be in on a hangin'."

"Well," replied the big man dryly, "it looks like yer goin' to be in on one this time—an' yer shore as hell welcome to all the enjoyment you kin git out of it."

Promptly at four o'clock, with the saloon crowded to the doors, Black John thumped the bar for order. "Miners' meetin' called fer the purpose of tryin' the prisoner, to wit, Solomon Albert, fer feloniously murderin' one, alias Koogler, again the peace an' dignity of Halfaday Crick, an' the statutes made an' provided. I'll app'int myself chairman of the meetin' an' we'll go ahead with the evidence. Meanwhile, Pot Gut kin cut a len'th of rope an' be tyin' a proper knot." He turned to the prisoner who stood before him in an open semicircle in front of the bar, accompanied by his three guards and surrounded by the crowd. "Solomon, you've be'n in the country long enough to know all about miners' meetin's so we'll go ahead with the evidence agin you, an' when it's all in you'll be given a chance to think up whatever you kin in the way of a defense.

"In the first place there was a dozen er more of us in here the night Koogler knocked you down fer throwin' a glass of licker in his face. We seen you throw the licker an' we seen him knock you down an' we seen you jump up an' go after him with yer belt knife with intent to do him great bodily harm. An' they all seen me take yer knife away, an' we heard you threaten to kill him, an' heard you put a curse on his luck-piece. This evidence shows a motive fer murder. So many of us seen an' heard these facts that it's a matter of common knowledge, an' I'll therefore waive swearin' in each an' every one, as it would be a waste of time.

"Regardin' the evidence that goes to show you did, in fact, carry out yer threat we'll be more explicit. Fer the first witness I'll call Lyme Cushing, Coroner of Halfaday Crick." He turned to the somber-faced proprietor who stood behind the bar upon which rested his elbows.

"D'you swear to tell the hull truth er any part of it s'elp'e God?"

"Oh, shore."

"Did we, er did we not hold an inquest over the corpse of alias Koogler down to his spring day before yesterday?"

"Yeah, that's what we done."

"An' after due consideration of what facts an' evidence was available, wasn't it the unanimous verdick of the jury that the said corpse had be'n murdered an' that suspicion p'inted agin this prisoner, to wit, Solomon Albert?"

"Yeah—that's what you claimed; an' that's the way they voted."

"That's all. I'll now call Benedick Hale. Speak up, Ben, so them in the back kin hear. D'you swear to tell the hull truth er any part of it s'elp'e God?"

"I do."

"What's yer name?"

The man hesitated a moment before replying. "You mean—?"

"Yeah—the name-can one will do. This ain't a probe into yer past."

"Benedick Hale."

"Where do you live?"

"Down the crick in Olson's old shack."

"You was on the aforementioned coroner's jury?"

"I was."

"Did you ever kill a bear?"

"No."

"Wasn't it you that first p'inted out that it couldn't have be'n a bear that killed Koogler on account of them tracks in the mud not bein' sunk in as deep as a bear would have sunk 'em?"

"It was."

"An' didn't you first p'int out that them claw scratches on the *corpus delicti's* face couldn't have be'n made by a bear because if

66

a bear had swiped him one with his paw his nails would have ripped Koogler's face off?"

"I did."

"An' wasn't you furthermore the one that found the murder weapon, to wit, a green spruce club with blood an' hairs stickin' to it in a bunch of willers where the murderer had throw'd it?"

"I was."

"An' didn't you hand me Koogler's luck-piece today when you fetched the prisoner in?"

"I did."

"Will you now state where you got holt of this luck-piece?"

THE MAN glanced about, smiled, and cleared his throat importantly, apparently well pleased with himself at being the center of attention. "Me an' Red John an' Short John went to Albert's shack an' found him settin' on a box mendin' a net. We surrounded him an' grabbed him an' throw'd him down an' tied his hands. I searched him an' found the luck-piece in his pants pocket."

"Which pants pocket?"

"Why—the ones he had on."

"I mean which pocket?"

"The right hand one, lookin' at him from behind. He claimed Koogler give it to him, which is prob'ly a damn lie—"

"A witness," interrupted Black John, "is s'posed to stick to facts an' not voice no opinions. However, as you seem to have done most of the figgerin' on this case, I'll ask you to state under oath yer honest opinion to the best of yer knowledge an' belief. Is Solomon guilty of this murder; or ain't he?"

"He is. There ain't no doubt but what he done it, figgerin' we'd think it was a bear."

"That's all. I'll now submit the exhibits, to wit, cement casts of bear tracks that was left in the mud at the scene of the murder. He motioned to Cush who lifted the several casts to the bar.

"Next is the club which Cush will lay on the bar so you kin all see it—an' them that cares to will be given the chance to examine it an' verify the fact that there's dry blood an' hairs stickin' to the bark. An' here's the luck-piece Ben swore to findin' in Albert's pocket. You all know this nugget in the shape of a bear was Koogler's luck-piece—most of you havin' played stud with him. An' finally there's the *corpus delicti* himself, to wit, alias Koogler. Anyone that's in doubt about his status bein' that of a corpse kin verify the fact by climbin' up on the meat cache an' lookin' him over.

"That concludes the case agin Solomon Albert, who will now be give the chance to say whatever he kin think up in his own defense an' produce any witness he might have to prove he never committed this murder. Speak up, Solomon—are you guilty, er not guilty? We won't bother to swear you in because we all know a man would lie like hell to save himself a hangin', whether he was swore er not."

"I didn't kill him," said the oldster and relapsed into silence.

"H-u-u-m-m, that's a plain statement, but it ain't no elaborate defense. Can't you think up no reason why you didn't kill him? You don't deny tryin' to carve him up in here that night, do you?"

"I was mad that night he knocked me dawn, an' partly drunk. I would of killed him then mebby."

"Didn't you threaten to kill him after I took yer knife away?"

"Yes, I guess mebby I did."

"You heard what the witness, to wit, alias Ben Hale, said about findin' the late Koogler's luck-piece in yer pocket. Is that the truth?"

"Yes, I had it in my pocket. Koogler give it to me. It was the next day when I was hittin' back fer home. When I passed his tent he hollered at me. I told him the night before that his luck-piece would be an onluck-piece from then on an' he wouldn't have no more luck. So when he begun to lose in the stud game he figgered I'd put some kind of a curse er hoodoo on the luck-piece, an' I guess it kinda scairt him when I told him us bears stuck together. So he wanted to know how much I'd charge him to take back the curse. I was sober by then an' I'd kinda cooled down an' fergot all about wantin' to kill him. So jest fer a joke I told him the only way he could change his luck was to give me his luck-piece. He didn't want to do it, but when I told him there wasn't no other way to git out from inunder that curse he handed it over an' I stuck it in my pocket an' went on home."

"An' you ain't seen him sence?"

"No."

"Is that all you've got in the way of a defense?"

"That's all. That's jest like it happened."

CALLS OF disbelief and derision issued from the crowd. "He's lyin' like hell!"

"Shore he is!"

"He done it all right!"

"He's the only one had a grudge agin Koogler!"

"Let's string him up! Koogler would never give that luck-piece away!"

Black John thumped the bar with a huge fist and when the clamor subsided he scowled as his eyes swept the faces of the crowd. "There ain't no doubt how the verdick of this meetin' would go if it was put to a vote. You've all heard the evidence—an' you'd all vote fer conviction. Ain't that right?" A chorus of affirmation greeted the question and the big man continued. "I don't s'pose there'd be even one vote again it, would there?" No one ventured a reply and Black John's scowl deepened. "I was hopin' there'd be someone amongst you that had sense enough to see from the evidence right here before you that Solomon Albert couldn't of made them tracks beside Koogler's spring, an' therefore that he couldn't have had no more to do with killin' him than I had! But it seems sech hope ain't got no foundation in fact." Pausing he lifted the cement forms from the bar, placed them beside Solomon Albert's feet, and pointed to his bear paw moccasins. "What paws is them he's wearin'—hind, er fore?"

There was a great crowding and craning of necks as those in the rear strove to see.

"They're front feet!" exclaimed someone.

"Damn if they ain't!" agreed another.

"Shore they be!" echoed a third.

"An' now," thundered the big man, "look at them casts of the tracks at the spring! Anyone that ever seen a bear track would know at a glance that they're hind tracks—in' half agin as big as Solomon's moccasins, to boot!"

"Fore feet!" exclaimed a man who by dint of much shoving and worming between close-backed bodies finally succeeded in gaining the edge of the open semicircle where he scrutinized the prisoner's footgear, then raised accusing eyes to his face.

"So you're the damn cuss that made me quit drinkin'!" he cried angrily.

"Quit drinkin'! What's Solomon got to do with that?" asked Black John. "You told me a while back you quit 'cause you was afraid you was gittin' the jim-jams."

"Shore I thought that! An' he was the cause of it! I was huntin' that day an' I run onto some bear tracks on a crick over by the White, an' I figgered the bear had r'ared up an' was walkin' like a man—so I follered along, hopin' fer a shot at him. Seemed like it was a hell of a ways fer a bear to be walkin' on his hind legs, an' I looked at the tracks closter—an' then I throw'd away my bottle an' hit back here as fast as God would let me. They wasn't hind tracks! An' damn if I was goin' to run onto no bear walkin' around on his front feet! I ain't took a drink sense—an' it's all his fault!"

Black John grinned. "That's tough luck. However, yer average is still 'way ahead of most folks. Whatever grievance you've got agin Albert, like damages er anythin', would be a matter fer the civil courts, an' not a miners' meetin'—so shet up, an' we'll be gittin' on with the case."

"But," cried a man in the crowd, "if a bear kilt Koogler, then how about that club? That's evidence, too!"

"No one is claimin' a bear killed Koogler," replied Black John.

"Who done it, then?" someone demanded, and a bedlam of demands broke loose. When comparative quiet was regained Black John turned to Pot Gutted John who, having completed his hangman's noose, had laid the rope on the bar and been an interested listener. "Go to the storeroom an' git that pack you fetched up here day before yesterday," he ordered.

When the fat one returned with the pack, Black John dumped its contents onto the floor beside the cement casts. "The one that done it," he said, "is the man that skun out this pair of hind paws!" He paused as the crowd surged forward to stare at the two bear legs. When the commotion had somewhat subsided Black John noticed that Benedict Hale was no longer standing beside the prisoner. A slight disturbance toward the rear of the crowd showed that someone was swiftly but unobtrusively worming his way toward the door.

"Stop that man!" he roared. "Stop Benedick Hale an' fetch him back here! He claimed he'd hate to miss out on a hangin'— an' we'd hate like hell to disapp'int him!"

The man was seized and shoved squirming and cursing from one to another until he once again stood within the semicircle facing Black John. His look of prideful importance had given place to one of pasty-faced terror as he stared in horror at the bear legs on the floor.

Thumping the bar for order, Black John bellowed, "As chairman of this meetin' I don't care to say nothin', one way er another, that might influence yer vote. But it's the unanimous verdick of them present that the prisoner, to wit, Solomon Albert, is hereby acquitted of the murder of the late alias Koogler. All them in favor of sech verdick signify by hollerin' 'Aye.'"

A thunder of "Ayes" shook the room.

"Contrary—'No'," said the big man, who followed the ensuing silence by announcing "The Ayes have it. Miners' meetin' adjourned an' another one called to try alias Benedick Hale fer the same offense, to wit, the murder of alias Koogler.

"I'll swear myself in as the first witness, an' swear to tell the hull truth er any part of it s'elp me God so here goes. I was huntin' a few days ago when I heard some shots in a dry wash near Olson's old shack. I looked over the rim an' seen Ben Hale workin' on a bear he'd jest shot, contrary to his sworn statement that he'd never killed one.

"I watched him skin out the hind legs an' leave the rest of the carcass lay there, an' next day One Armed John found Koogler's corpse layin' by his spring, an' we held an inquest. Seein' the tracks, the boys was about to conclude a bear done it when Pot Gut claimed he didn't believe a bear would attack a man that way, whereupon Ben Hale become mighty interested in provin' it couldn't have be'n a bear on account of neither the tracks in the mud nor the scratches on Koogler's face bein' deep enough fer a bear to have made 'em. He further p'inted out that Solomon Albert wore bear's feet fer moccasins, an' reminded us that he'd threatened to kill Koogler here in the saloon. We rendered a verdick agin Albert an' Cush sent Red John, an' Short John, an' Ben Hale to git him.

"When they was gone I made them casts of the tracks, an' then me an' Pot Gut went down to the dry wash an' fetched these hind legs up here. Whilst Pot Gut was diggin' the bullets out of the bear I found the empty shells they was shot from." Pausing, he drew the shells and battered bullets from his pocket, placed them on the bar, and turned to Cush. "Hand me Hale's rifle," he ordered, and throwing a cartridge from the chamber, he laid it beside the bullets and shells.

"All them on the coroner's jury kin swear to this bein' Hale's rifle, Cush havin' ordered him to leave it when he went fer Albert, knowin' damn well he'd shoot the old man, hopin' with the evidence we had agin' him the case would be closed. You kin all see that the empty shells I found where the bear was shot is the same as this cat'ridge from Hale's rifle. Anyone inquisitive enough to give a damn kin verify the fact by examinin' the dents in the caps, an' Hale's firin' pin with a magnifyin' glass. Furthermore, while we ain't got the actual hind paws fer comparison, the prisoner ondoubtless havin' cached 'em, anyone kin see at a glance that the paws from a bear that size would match up with them casts.

"YOU ALL heard Ben lie about not killin' a bear, an' you kin see the evidence that links him up with the crime. Further evidence would be merely corroborative, an' a waste of time.

"As chairman I ain't in no position to say anything that might influence yer vote, but I might add that any damn skunk that would murder a man to rob him an' then try to put it off on an innocent old man—the quicker he's hung the better fer the community. Jest remember you heard him state under oath that it was his honest opinion that old Solomon murdered Koogler, when he know'd damn well he done it himself. This closes the case again the prisoner who will now be give the chance to try an' lie out of it—a feat that ondoubtless won't be attended with much luck." He turned to the trembling prisoner. "What you got to say, Ben?"

"It—it's a lie! I never done it!"

"You mean," thundered Black John, glowering at him, "that I lied about you killin' that bear an' skinnin' out them feet?"

"No! No—I—that is—I done that. But it was jest fer—fer to git me some warm moccasins—fer winter."

Derisive laughter, and loud angry demands to hang him forthwith caused the prisoner's face to go a shade whiter. He rolled his eyes wildly about, and catching no friendly glance, realized his case was lost. A sudden gleam of hope lighted his eyes. "I done it!" he cried. "I follered him to Halfaday to rob him. I know'd he'd robbed the Detroit-Yukon outfit of better'n twenty-five thousan' in dust—an' I aimed to git it. I did git it, too. It's cached where no one in God's world kin ever find it. I'll deal with you men. There's right around a hundred pound of dust—sixteen hundred ounces. I'll tell you where my cache is with the dust an' them bear paws in it if you'll turn me loose an' let me slip over into Alasky!"

Black John's face darkened like a thunder cloud. "Bribery!" he roared, allowing his eyes to travel slowly over the crowd in a glance of outraged horror. "Ain't there no limit to the depths the human soul kin sink to? This here self-confessed thief an' murderer has actually had the temerity—the guts to you men— to impugn the honor of every man on Halfaday! He has brazenly compounded a felony to our very face. There's fifty er sixty men in this room—how fer would sixteen hundred ounces go betwixt us? I call fer a vote—guilty; er not guilty?"

The verdict was unanimous. And Black John turned to the prisoner. "There you've got the answer of men who hold honor above gold! The answer of the onbribable citizens of Halfaday! As quick as Pot Gut kin git the noose adjusted you'll be strung up to the nearest rafter in accordance with the verdick—an' you kin take the secret of yer cache with you. If that twice pilfered dust won't do us no good—it shore as hell won't do you none, neither!"

VI

THE VERDICT OF the meeting was promptly carried out and a few minutes after a sudden and violent commotion broke loose in the saloon. Nearly half the occupants of the room—those who had reason to fear the Yukon law—jammed the rear exit in a frantic endeavor to all leave at once. Black John glanced toward the front doorway in which stood framed an officer of the Northwest Mounted Police. Raising his voice, he called loudly:

"Hello, Downey! Come on in! We're jest about to h'ist one!"

"What does this mean?" asked the officer sternly, pointing to the late prisoner.

"That's what's left of a self-confessed murderer, one Benedick Hale, accordin' to the name-can—duly convicted an' executed by verdick of a miner's meetin'."

"He committed a murder, you say?" asked Downey, advancing into the room.

"Murder, an' robbery, an' perjury, compounded after the verdict with attempted bribery. He murdered a man known to us as alias Koogler, robbin' him accordin' to his own admission of a matter of sixteen hundred ounces, which accordin' to alias Hale, the said alias Koogler had feloniously obtained from the Detroit-Yukon dredge outfit down along the river. Hale claimed to have stole this dust from Koogler an' cached it, havin' the gall to go so fer as to offer to turn it over to us if we'd let him slip acrost into Alasky."

"Where is this cache of his?"

Black John pointed to the late and alias Hale. "His secret died with him," he said somberly.

Stepping to the dead man Downey stared into his face. "He's a murderer, all right—an' a damn mean one, too. Bashed in the head of a prospector on Dominion Crick an' robbed him of what little dust he had—less than three thousan' dollars' worth, accordin' to the man's wife, but all they had in the world. This Hale's right name is Mike McQueen. Constable Brink got a hot tip that he'd hit out downriver. He's huntin' him now."

"What brings you amongst us if you wasn't huntin' him?" asked Black John. "Jest takin' a stroll? Er is there perchance some other malefactor loose in the land?"

"I'm huntin' a fellow named Joe Parker who robbed the Detroit-Yukon outfit of right around twenty-five thousan' in dust. I guess the trail ends here. He's the man McQueen murdered. Have you buried him? If so we'll have to dig him up for identification."

"Nope, yer in luck. We couldn't bury our *corpus delicti*. We kep' him fer evidence. You'll find him on the meat cache. We'll bury 'em both in the mornin'."

After viewing the body Corporal Downey returned to the bar and Cush set out bottle and glasses. "It's Parker all right," the officer said. "But I don't s'pose there'll be a chance in the world of locatin' that dust."

"Off hand, I'd say no—but we kin try," replied Black John. "Caches is mighty hard to find. Anyhow, Downey, yer playin' in luck, at that."

"What do you mean—luck?"

"Like you said, the chances is so slim as to be practically nil of findin' where McQueen cached Parker's dust. But you'll be able to return the dust he stole off that prospector. You claimed his wife was left with practically nothin', didn't you?"

"That's right. A fine woman, too. She shore took it on the chin. But she's keepin' that chin up. She's takin' in washin' in Dawson. But how'm I goin' to get that dust, if I don't get the other? He prob'ly, cached both lots together."

"Yer in error. When McQueen first come he banked his dust with Cush. A hundred an' eighty-four ounces which he claimed he got on Forty Mile—but I seen at a glance it was upriver gold."

DOWNEY FIGURED for a moment with a pencil. "That makes twenty-six hundred an' twenty-four dollars," he announced. "Jest about what he got off her husband."

"There's sixty-two dollars fer supplies, an' seventeen fer a round of drinks charged agin that dust," said Cush.

"Oh shore," Black John agreed, "but we ain't so pickyune as to make this pore widow pay it. Jest turn over the whole hundred an' eighty-four ounces to Corporal Downey."

"How do you mean—we?" grumbled Cush, as he reached into the safe for the two sacks.

"Oh I jest used the plural form off hand as you might say," grinned Black John. "Of course the donation is yours. However, bein' as this widow is a woman an' has met up with more er less hard luck, I'll jest trouble you to weigh out another hundred an' eighty-four ounces fer this widow an' charge it to me. That'll fix it, mebbe, so she kin quit takin' in washin'."

"You mean—yer donyatin' another hundred an' eighty-four ounces out of yer own pocket?" asked Cush.

"Shore. You rec'lect what it says in the Good Book about castin' yer bread upon the waters?"

"A woman kin git anythin' out of you she wants," growled Cush, as he weighed out the dust. "But I'm jest as big a damn fool as you be. I'll match yer pile. I guess she kin use it, at that—what with losin' her man, an' all."

The following morning Black John accompanied Downey down the creek where the two spent hours searching around Koogler's claim in a futile search for a cache. At Olson's old shack, after another long search, they discovered the hole in the rock wall and removed the slab. Reaching in Black John withdrew two bear paws—hind paws, with skin flaps attached for lacing onto the feet of a man.

"There!" he exclaimed, holding them up for inspection, "I shore wish I'd of found this cache before the trial! It would have clinched our case to compare these paws with them casts. I know'd he was guilty, but if he hadn't confessed, some of the boys might not have voted to hang him."

Satisfying himself that the cache contained no dust, Corporal Downey regarded the big man searchingly. "Take it first an' last, John," he said, "you've turned back a lot of dust that had be'n stolen an' taken to Halfaday by crooks. But in every instance this dust you turned in had been stolen from individuals who couldn't afford to lose it. An' it has all been returned either to them or to their heirs. Never once have I succeeded in recovering any dust from Halfaday that had been stolen from a big outfit."

"H-u-u-m-m, is that right, Downey? Well now, that's a coincidence, ain't it? But I can't seem to work up no grief about it. Them big outfits is ruinin' the country fer the pore man. Somehow I don't seem to take no more'n what you might say, a casual interest in their losses."

Later in the day, after Downey had departed for Dawson, Black John returned to the Fort to find Cush alone in the barroom. Stepping to his cabin, he returned with twenty heavy little sacks which he placed upon the bar. "Weigh 'em in, Cush," he said, "an' credit 'em to you an' me, equal."

"But where in hell did you git 'em?" asked Cush.

"Don't ask no questions," grinned the big man. "This here's our bread come back—that we cast upon the waters."

BLACK JOHN ASSISTS
AT A WEDDING

OLD CUSH, PROPRIETOR of Cushing's Fort, the combined trading post and saloon that served the little community of outlawed men that had sprung up on Halfaday Creek, close against the Yukon-Alaska border, carefully folded the voluminous Sunday newspaper he had been reading, shoved the square steel-rimmed spectacles from nose to forehead, and set out a bottle, two glasses, and a leather dice box, as Black John Smith entered the saloon and approached the bar.

"What I claim," he began, as he shoved the box toward the other, "is why in hell can't a newspaper print news that's somewheres up to date?"

"Well," replied the huge, bearded man, as he picked up the box and rattled the dice, "you got to remember, Cush, we're quite a ways from where them papers is printed. It takes time to git 'em to Dawson, an' a damn sight longer fer 'em to git up here where we ain't got no reg'lar mail. There's three sixes to beat in one. What's the date on that paper?"

Cush gathered up the dice and cast them. "That's a horse on me," he admitted somberly. "The date is Sunday, March the third. An' there's four deuces right back at you."

"An' there's four fives to beat 'em," announced Black John, returning the box to the bar with a flourish, and reaching for the bottle. "March the third, eh? Well, it's only the middle of June. What the hell do you want—an' extry, er somethin'?"

"It ain't that," explained Cush, filling his glass, "I wouldn't kick on three months, er even six. But when news gits three, four thousan' years old, it looks like it was kind of stale to be printin' in a newspaper."

"They prob'ly wanted to make shore they wasn't foistin' no canard on the public," grinned Black John. "But holdin' off that long—it looks like they stood in danger of gittin' scooped, at that."

"I don't know what yer talkin' about," replied Cush, "but I don't s'pose it makes no difference, most of what you say bein' onintelligent, anyway. I was referrin' to a piece I was readin' in the paper about these here old Egyptian mummies. They was some pitchers of some it claimed had been dead fer three, four thousan' years—an' damn if they don't look it."

Black John nodded. "Yeah, them old Egyptians was artists at that sort of thing."

"Artists! Huh—if them pitchers in the paper was anythin' like them mummies look, they shore ain't no job no artist would turn out. They look like some old piece of leather that had turned black an' shrank—but mebbe these here Egyptians was niggers to start out with."

"They wasn't exactly what you'd call niggers, but they was prob'ly sort of dark—livin' down there in Egypt."

"What was the idee of embalmin' 'em?"

"Why, to preserve 'em fer posterity, I s'pose—so future generations could tell how they looked."

"Cripes," snorted Cush, "if I looked like that, damn if I'd want anyone to know it. Not even a future generation—prosperity, er no prosperity. I don't blame old Moses an' all them Jews fer wantin' to git to hell out of there, if them's the kind of people they had to live amongst."

"They didn't look like that, you damn fool. They was prob'ly pretty good lookin' folks. Mark Antony an' Julius Caesar seemed to think Cleopatra was, anyway."

"If they was, then these here embalmers done a damn pore job. Them old kings an' queens would of kep' better if they'd pickled 'em—er mebbe corned 'em."

"Anyhow, Cush, you've got to admit that what with the paintin's, an' the jewelery, an' writin's, an' other things they put in them old tombs, folks nowadays has got a pretty good idea of how them old Egyptians lived."

"Who would give a damn how they lived? What do I care if, three er four thousan' years ago, an Egyptian lived one way er some other. An' as far as them paintin's goes—bulls an' horses with wings an 'em like a bird, an' folks with different animals' heads on 'em—it's like a bunch of kids done it. An' them carvin's looks like them totem poles the Siwashes makes, down on the coast. An' as fer the writin'—there was a sample of it in the paper, an' no one but a Chinee could read it. If a newspaper has got to print pitchers, why don't they do like the Police Gazette an' print good lookin' women that folks likes to look at—an' not no mummies—which their face looks like a apple that had hung on the tree an' dried?"

"Look at 'er comin'!" exclaimed Black John, his eyes on the doorway beyond which a level space stretched to the brink of the steep descent to the landing. "A woman! An', by God—she looks like she'd stepped right out of one of a page of the Police Gazette, at that? Cush—I've got a premonition of evil!"

II

THE WOMAN, A buxom, deep bosomed creature, apparently in her late twenties, entered without hesitation, advanced to the bar and, ignoring the two men completely, studied the names on the row of bottles that ornamented the back bar.

"Shake me up a dry martini," she ordered.

"Any cocktail you git in here, mom," replied Cush, without making any move to comply, "will be so dry you can't even taste it."

The woman frowned. "Come on—make it snappy. I need a drink. You've got the ingredients there. Don't you know how to mix a martini—or do I have to step around there and show you?"

Black John grinned and lifted his hat. "If you kin show Cush how to mix a martini out of what he's got in them bottles yer shore welcome on Halfaday. There ain't nothin' but whiskey in any of 'em. They're all filled out of the same barrel."

"Them names on the bottles don't cut no figger," supplemented Cush. "I use' to run a saloon back in Seattle, an' when the gold rush come I boxed all my bottles up an' fetched 'em along. What was in 'em them days has be'n drank up long ago. There ain't no call fer fancy drinks here on Halfaday. I don't sell nothin' but whiskey."

The woman sniffed. "A hell of a saloon—and a hell of a country! Give me some whiskey, then." Cush set a glass on the bar and shoved the bottle in front of her. "Don't I get a chaser?" she asked, eyeing the single glass.

"You mean like—some water, mom?"

"Water'll do, I suppose, if you ain't got somethin' better."

"Oh, shore. You'll have to wait till I fetch some from the crick, though. Yer the third one, since I be'n rennin' this saloon, to want water with their licker. I don't keep none, except fer my rinse tub. But the way folks is clamorin' fer it nowadays, I s'pose I'll have to keep a bucket handy. What with the flies an' the mice like they be, though, I'd think they'd rather drink their licker straight. There ain't hardly a mornin' but what I find anywheres from one to a dozen mice drownded in the rinse tub."

As Cush disappeared through the doorway, Black John turned to the woman: "Was you figgerin' on locatin' on the crick, mam?" he asked.

"What if I am? Who wants to know?"

"Well, I guess all the boys'll be more or less interested. There ain't no other woman on the crick."

"Their interest won't get 'em nothing—nor yours, either. I suppose you're Black John Smith. I heard about you in Dawson."

"The supposition is founded on fact," Black John smiled. "I trust you didn't hear nothin' detrimental to my character."

"Only that you're all outlaws up here—and that you're king of the bunch. Well, that suits me. I can look out for myself in any man's camp. I'm a one-man woman—see? And I'm hunting my man."

"Is he s'posed to be on Halfaday?" asked Cush, as he placed a glass of water before the woman.

"He's here, all right—and there's no use in either one of you trying to tell me he ain't. I got the tip straight that he hit up the White River, heading for here five weeks ago. He was to meet me and we was to be married in Seattle in March. When he didn't show up a pal of his tipped me off that he'd skipped to the Klondike. I went to Dawson an' hung around but I couldn't locate him. Then a guy that knew him told me he was hiding out somewheres around Whitehorse—and here I'd come right through Whitehorse, and didn't know it! This guy says Hank got a tip that the police was layin' for him in Dawson, so he didn't go there. I went back to Whitehorse and met a guy that told me he'd hit for here to lay low till the heat was off.

"So—here I am. I'm telling you he done me wrong. But he won't get away with it. No man living can leave little Katie waiting at the church—not even Hank Bedore!"

"It shore looks like this here Hank's in a hell of a fix—wherever he's at," commented Cush.

"What do you mean by that?" demanded the woman, her sloe eyes stabbing at him across the bar. "Do I look so hard to marry?"

"No, no, mom! You got me wrong. Cripes, I've married four different ones that was worst lookin' than you be—an' they was all han'some women, at that—except, mebbe, the third one. What I mean is—this here Hank, he mightn't want to marry no woman—not even you."

"Well, he's going to marry me, whether he wants to or not. I know my rights. I planned the last two bank jobs he pulled, besides helpin' him to crush out of stir—and he don't need to think he can slip off and leave me holding the bag."

"That's right, mam," agreed Black John heartily. "Drink up, an' have one on me. An' if there's anything me an' Cush kin do to help you, you kin count on us."

"Humph," sniffed the woman: "Men always stick together— especially outlaws."

"Yer right, in a way," admitted Black John judicially, "an' then agin, yer wrong. Take it in a matter of private enterprise—like a man takin' a bank, er an express company fer what he could git—if sech transaction was pulled off before he come to Halfaday, it would be all right with us. But in a case that involves the public morals of Halfaday, things is altogether different, an' me an' Cush will be found on the side of rectitude every time. Not only that but we're both firm believers in matrimony—him by experience, an' me as a matter of theory. An' believe me, if after due consideration of the facts, a weddin' is deemed the moralist way out, the offendin' party will either be married er hung—an' don't you fergit it. Take this Hank, now—from a word er two you dropped, I take it he's a man of—er—well, of certain criminal tendencies. In other words, an outlaw—like me, an' the bulk of the boys on the crick."

"**I'LL SAY** he is!" exclaimed the woman, a note of boastful pride in her voice. "And he don't stick to no one line of jobs, neither. Hank Bedore can do anything. He's rustled cattle and horses in Montana, and Idaho, and Saskatchewan. He's stuck up banks in Washington and Oregon. He's robbed depots, and grain elevators, and post offices in Dakota, and a train in Utah. That train robbery was a scream. He got a couple of striking shacks to help him with it, and then rapped 'em on the head and left 'em tied up in the express car along with the messenger." The woman paused and laughed heartily at the recollection. "When the train crew found 'em and seen who they was, they sure used them two shacks rough. And what they didn't do to 'em the law did—they're doing time yet. Oh, it was rich!"

"Yeah," agreed Black John dryly, "this here Hank seems to have a sense of humor."

"You bet he has—and you'd never know it to look at him. He's glummer looking than the bar-keep, here. But the best one Hank pulled was on a preacher over in North Dakota. He blew a depot safe, made a get-away in the preacher's rig, and left the bank bands that were around the money under some hay in the preacher's barn. The dumb preacher got ten years for the job and Hank wasn't even suspected."

"Hank sure likes his little joke, now and then."

"Yeah," agreed Black John again, "no clownin'—jest a sort of subtile humor."

"That's it," the woman said, her dark eyes narrowing slightly, "and I suppose he's laughing up his sleeve at the joke he thinks he played on me—leaving me waiting for him to show up there in Seattle. But he won't get away with that one—not in a thousand years, he won't. I'm no dumb shack, nor yet no preacher. When he tries to put one over on Tacoma Kate, he'll find he's got the wrong cat by the tail.

"He can't do me like that—after me slipping him the gun that he bluffed his way out of the big house with! He was doing a stretch in Walla Walla on account of a couple of dirty crooks turned him in because he double-crossed 'em on a hick town bank job up in the timber country. We'd been living together better than a year, and he'd promised to marry me—but always kept putting it off on one excuse or another, so when he got picked up I went to see him and I told him he could lay there in stir till he rotted for all of me. But he talked and talked, reminding me of a lot of jobs we'd planned and hadn't got around to yet, and how if he was out we could go on with our work, and live high, and he promised faithful that he'd marry me as soon as he got to where I was, if I'd slip him the gat. I done it, and that's the last I seen of him."

"Hum, from a couple of hints you've let drop, it would seem as though he might be jest a bit ontrustworthy. Why would you be wantin' to marry him?"

"Why? Why because he's a damn good, all around man— that's why! He's a damn good meal ticket as long as he tends to business. And besides, his dad's got a swell case of heart disease and a damn good ranch. If I was Hank's wife and anything should happen to him after the old man dropped off, I'd get the ranch—see? A girl's got to look out for herself in this world. When I get him so he can't get away he'll play square with me. He won't dare to do anything else. He's afraid of me—knows I'd carve him up, or put a bullet through him as quick as I'd look at him, if I had a good reason. Once I get him cinched, he'll quiet down and tend to business. Hank's a good man—if anyone understands him. We could get along fine, working together. He loves me, too—he's told me so a hundred different times."

BLACK JOHN nodded. "Jest a couple of hard workin' lovers tryin' to build up a nice quiet little home, eh? Well—like I told you—if there's anythin' me an' Cush kin do to help you, jest let us know."

"First," replied the woman, "I want to know where Hank Bedore is. And don't tell me he ain't on this crick—because I know better."

Black John shook his head. "I don't claim, for shore, that he ain't here. But I'm givin' you my word, mam—if he is, I don't know it."

"He's probably going under some other name," suggested the woman.

"Judgin' from what you've told me, it wouldn't seem on-likely. But the fact is, that there ain't no strangers showed up on the crick fer the past three months, under any name."

"Says you! Well, have it your own way—but little Katie's going to stay right here till she looks over every damn man on the creek—and don't you forget it!" She turned to Cush. "Do you keep a hotel? Can I stay here? I've got money to pay my way."

Old Cush shook his head in vigorous negation. "No, mom, I don't keep no boarders, nor yet no lodgers."

"Where am I going to stay, then?" demanded the woman.

Cush indicated the big man who stood beside her at the bar. "John there—he's got a good cabin. He sometimes puts up newcomers till they kin git located. You might ask him."

"Not by a damn sight—not no wimmin! There's One Eyed John's cabin. She kin move in there. You see, mam," he explained, "this here One Eyed he used to live amongst us till he committed some irregularity that earnt him a hangin'. He left a good cabin, all furnished, an' right handy to the fort. You kin throw yer stuff in there an' stay till you've had a chanct to look the boys over. There won't no one bother you, it's nice an' quiet, an' fer a home lovin' body like you seems to be, it ought to be right cozy. Then, if it happens that you find this here Hank Bedore on the crick, an' you an' him was so minded, you might locate there permanent. I'd sell the place at a reasonable figger, provided you an' him could dig up some money between you.

"It's a good claim, too—you'd ought to do right well—industrious as you appear to be."

"Claim? What would we want with a claim?"

"Why, same as the rest of us—to work it, of course."

"Work! You mean dig gold out of the ground?"

"Well, yes—that was the thought. That's the way the rest of us here on the crick makes a livin'."

The woman laughed disdainfully. "You're a hell of a bunch of outlaws—stickin' up here, breaking your backs on the end of a shovel when there's a thousand rube banks down in the States just begging for someone to come along and take 'em. Work! You wouldn't catch me working—nor Hank, neither. Here I'm twenty-seven, and Hank's past thirty—we've got our future to think of."

"Yeah," Black John admitted, "there's that angle, too. Of course a couple of young folks jest startin' out, that-away, you wouldn't want to make no mistakes in choosin' a career—but at that, you've got to remember that some futures is a damn sight longer'n others."

"His ain't going to be long enough to worry about if he don't marry me when I catch up with him," retorted the woman, grimly. "Is there a priest or a preacher on the crick—or anyone that can marry us?"

"Oh, shore. Jest you leave them details to us. You run down yer man an' we'll see that you git hitched, all right. We could have the weddin' right here in the saloon, with free drinks on the house. We could even have singin', if you was so minded."

"I'll find him, all right," the woman replied grimly. "And in the meantime, how much rent do I pay for that cabin?" Raising a neatly shod foot to the brass rail, she turned back her skirt, unsnapped a heavy rubber band from about the top of a long silk stocking, and drew out a thick packet of yellow-backed bills.

"Cripes a'mighty!" exclaimed Black John, his eyes bulging, while Old Cush, his steel rimmed spectacles back on his nose, leaned as far over the bar as his reach would permit. "You seem to be—er—well provided!"

"I'll say I am. And when Hank Bedore gets back to Washington he's going to find he's short one cache. He didn't think I knew where he cached the sixteen thousand he got out of a lumber company payroll job he pulled a year ago. But the damn fool don't know he talks in his sleep. So when he run out on me in Seattle, I slipped up to Gray's Harbor and dug up the fruit jar he'd planted it in. He'll never know who got it. That's what he gets for not playing square with me."

"That's right," Black John agreed, eyeing the bank notes the woman had slapped onto the bar. "It ain't often, now days, you see two young folks startin' out their married life with sech mutual onderstandin'."

"You talk like some damn preacher," the woman said. "Come on—how much do I owe you for that cabin? I don't suppose there's any grub in it, is there?"

"No, there's no grub. An' that's all it'll cost you—jest what grub you need. The rent's free. We aim to be hospitable here on Halfaday. So you kin put yer money back where you got it."

Peeling off a hundred dollar bill, the woman returned the packet to her stocking, and raised her eyes insolently to Black John, who was watching the procedure with interest. "Well—you know where I keep it, big boy. Any time you think you've lived long enough, just come around and try and get it. Like I told you—little Katie can take care of herself in any man's camp."

BLACK JOHN grinned. "It's as safe where it's at as it would be in the Bank of England, fer all of me. An' as fer Cush, he couldn't quite stretch fer enough to see where you did put it. But that's his hard luck."

The woman laughed. "I'll buy a drink," she said, pushing the bill toward Cush. "And you can take your change out of that for what supplies I'll be a needing. I'll make out a list, directly."

"Revertin' to the subject of money," said Black John, as he filled his glass from the bottle, "how's Hank heeled? I ain't inquirin' in no sperit of inquisitiveness er idle curiosity, but merely with the thought of aidin' an' abbettin' you in yer search fer him. You see, if he's broke, er nearly so, he'd most likely locate him a claim somewheres an' begin takin' out dust. But if he's well heeled, he might jest ease into some abandoned shack along the crick an' sort of lay low. In either case, if he's on the crick, he'll have to show up before very long fer supplies, an' Cush could be on the lookout fer him—but it would help if he know'd whether the man would be spendin' dust, er bills. An' he'll want to know what he looks like."

"Oh, he's heeled all right," replied the woman. "He wouldn't have to work. He might have had other caches, for all I know—but I do know he's got the thirty-four thousand, five hundred that he took that bank for up in the timber country. He had to tell me where that cache was. When he was in stir I told him I was broke, and when I promised to slip him the gun, and some get-away cash, he told me where to find it. There was thirty-five thousand in it, and he told me that if I took more than five hundred out of it, he'd give me the works when he got out. He promised to pick up the balance himself and come right on to Seattle and marry me. And that's all I did take out of it, too. You bet I figured quite a while on what was the best thing to do. I knew already where that Gray's Harbor cache was with sixteen thousand in it, and with the thirty-five thousand in the bank cache, that made fifty-one thousand I could get away with and leave him to finish his five-year stretch in Walla Walla. A girl can't afford to make no mistakes—she's got to do the right thing. Five years, with good behavior time off, ain't such a hell of a while, and I figured that when Hank got out and found out what I'd done, it would be just like him to lay for me and beat me up, or maybe even knock me off—he'd be that mad. But even if he didn't, fifty-one thousand ain't so much, neither, to last you the rest of your life, when you ain't no older than I am. And I figured that with Hank out, the two of us could earn a lot more than that, what with all the hick banks and payrolls we could take, so I just took the five hundred, like he said, and got the gun to him, and better than four hundred in cash—and then when the dirty pup got out, he scrammed on me! Can you beat it?"

"Tch, tch, tch, sech duplicity is way beyond me," said Black John, "after you bein' so square an' upright, too. It jest goes to show that a barkin' dog sometimes bites the hand that feeds him. After usin' you that way, mam, I don't blame you fer marryin' him in spite of hell. He shore needs a lesson. I'll sort of inquire around amongst the boys an' see if any stranger has showed up along the crick onbenownst to me an' Cush. What fer lookin' did you say he was?"

"I didn't say, but you'll be able to spot him, all right. He's kind of slim built, stands about five foot-ten or eleven, black eyes and dark complexion. He's kind of sour looking, and looks at you sort of sideways. Sometimes he wears a short black mustache, and sometimes he shaves it off.

"He's got a bullet scar across the top of his left shoulder where he got nicked in a fight with a posse when he was running off a bunch of horses in Montana.

"I made him quit that horse and cattle game. There ain't enough in it for the risk you take; and besides, banks and payrolls are a lot more genteel."

"Yeah," agreed Black John, "cowstealin' would seem a bit boorish, at that. An' a man, 'specially a young fella, can't afford to jeopardize his social standin'. If you'll order what you want, mam, Cush will put it up, an' I'll help you down to the cabin with it. Then I'll sort of circulate around amongst the boys."

III

WHEN BLACK JOHN returned to the saloon a few minutes later, Old Cush set out the battle and glasses, with an air of vast relief. "Fill up," he invited. "Cripes, John, I'm glad you got back. I've saw a lot of wimmin in my time, takin' it first an' last—an' I married four of 'em. But I never seen one that was as plumb tough as what she is. Don't you have nothin' to do with her, John—take it from me, she's dangerous as a cocked gun."

"Oh, I don't know, Cush," grinned the big man. "Little Katie's got her p'ints. You didn't see as much of her as I did."

"I didn't think you'd holler out, like you done, at the sight of no mere money," replied Cush. "I couldn't see over the bar, an' when I put my foot on this here keg to h'ist me up, the damn thing rolled with me, an' if I hadn't had holt of the bar with both hands I might of broke my neck."

"It would of been an ignominious death—an' would of served you right fer tryin' to palm her off onto me, when she was in-quirin' fer board an' lodgin'."

"I know'd you wouldn't have her over in yer cabin permanent I was jest jokin'."

"You're idea of a joke, an' this here Hank Bedore's seems to be somewhat sim'lar," opined Black John. "But at that, when she went up into her sock after that roll, she had me kind of—of flabbergasted. She didn't have on no—no—"

"Not none whatever?" exclaimed Cush, a scandalized expression on his face.

"None that I could see—an' from where I was standin', I don't think I missed nothin'."

"Well—the damn huzzy! We got to do somethin', John. We don't want no woman like her on the crick. Cripes—if the boys know'd that there wouldn't be no work done on the crick till snow flies!"

"There don't seem to be nothin' we kin do about it. Of course, if this here Hank should show up, we could marry 'em—an' let him do the worryin'."

"John," asked Cush gravely, "dressin' like you claim she don't—ain't that some form of skullduggery?"

BLACK JOHN'S grin widened. "How in hell would we prove it? An' even if we did succeed in gittin' the evidence before the jury—I'm doubtin' that we'd git a conviction."

"An' if we did," said Cush, "it wouldn't hardly seem right to hang her fer it, nohow—much as she ought to be. But even if Bedore does show up, we ain't got no one here that could marry 'em. What did you lie to her fer, when she asked you about it? You know damn well there ain't no priest on the crick—an' the parson won't be back till fall."

"Well, hell, Cush—you're the coroner. You could—"

"Not by a damn sight! A coroner sets on dead men. He can't marry folks."

"He could try. A man never knows what he kin do till he tries."

"Not me. I ain't goin' to mix up in no onlegal proceedin's."

"Ain't you got no milk of human kindness in yer soul? Cripes, Cush, can't you see that young girl's jest a yearnin' her heart out to marry the sweetheart of her youth? An' do you mean to tell me that you'd stand back an' not do nothin' about it? Why, if I was that hard hearted I couldn't never look into her eyes agin."

"I don't never want to look in 'em agin. Them eyes of hern makes the hair prickle on the back of my neck when she looks at me. They remind me of my second wife's. An' neither I don't want to look into the eyes of no jedge when he'd tell me I'm guilty of—of fraud, er whatever kind of skullduggery it would be to marry folks when you didn't have no right to."

Black John heaved a deep sigh of resignation. "Timidity, an' the lack of initiative is responsible fer an unpredictable amount of—"

"Listen," Cush interrupted, "if them big words is meant fer me, you might as well of said 'em on a duck's back, fer all the soakin' in they done. I don't know what yer talkin' about; an' I don't give a damn. So you might's well save yer wind. My mind's made up. I ain't goin' to marry no one, no time, an' no place."

"Ah, well—where there's a will there's a way, as the Good Book says. The matter seems to be put squarely up to me."

"Huh—you ain't no priest, nor no preacher, nor no jestice of the peace. Yuh ain't even a coroner."

"No—but despite all them handicaps an' limitations, I'll succeed. I kin evolve a synthetic priest."

"You kin do what to one?" queried Cush, his brow wrinkling. "Cripes, if you'd talk sense, mebbe I could git what yer drivin' at."

"Listen, then—you remember Meeker, alias John Brown, the one we hung that night fer murderin' Dykes. Well, before he come to Halfaday he robbed the mission at Teslin an' stole a priest's uniform, er whatever you call it, an' later he performed a fake marriage on Dykes an' that woman that thought she was his wife."

"Yeah."

"Well, in the natural course of events, that priest's outfit fell into my possession, I havin' run acrost it amongst Meeker's effects after his demise. So, figgerin' that sometime it might prove useful in an emergency, I packed it up to my shack. Now my idea is that in case this Hank Bedore shows up on the crick, which bein' an outlaw he ondoubtless will, I'll deputize Pot Gutted John to don the outfit and perform the ceremony."

"Pot Gutted would make a hell of a priest."

"Oh, I don't know—he looks well fed, an' he'll shave up nice an' pink, like a priest—an' he kin read. I rec'lect that you've got a prayer book with the weddin' ceremony in it that belonged to one of yer wives."

"It was the last one. The first three wasn't religious."

"An' you've got a song book, too."

"But it wouldn't be accordin' to Hoyle," objected Cush. "This here prayer book is a Piscopalium one, an' priests is Catholic."

"The p'int is well taken, but kin be ignored fer the reason that this Tacoma Kate wouldn't know a prayer book from the Rig Veda, an' I'm bettin' that the finer theological distinctions would be entirely lost on Mr. Bedore."

CUSH SHOOK his head dubiously. "It would take a damn sight more than one of them black gowns to make a priest out of Pot Gutted John. I don't believe he kin read none too good, neither—an' there's quite a bit of readin' to do—what with some prayers that's printed in there, an' all."

"The prayers kin be omitted fer the sake of brevity, an' also because eminatin' from Pot Gutted, they wouldn't git no higher'n the ceilin', nohow. All he'll need to read is the practical part—about him takin' her; an' her him."

"I don't think it'll be no legal weddin'—what with cuttin' it short, an' Pot Gutted not bein' no priest, an' all," opined Cush, stubbornly.

"It'll be legal enough for Halfaday," Black John replied. "You know damn well, Cush, that up here we've abolished a lot of the legal technicalities that clogs the courts, an' gives the sinful more breaks than what they've rightly got comin'. Pot Gutted will look like a priest—an' to all intents an' purposes, he'll be one. An' waivin' a couple of prayers will be inconsequential."

"You mean, Pot Gutted kin stand there an' wave them prayers, an' it would be jest as good as readin' em off?"

"Jest exactly," grinned Black John. "Yer power of preception is improvin'."

"Huh—it's a wonder more of 'em wouldn't do it, then. You know, John, a man feels like hell standin' there gittin' married? The first three times wasn't so bad. The first time we skipped off, an' was married by a jestice of the peace over in Covington. The second time was a jestice of the peace, too. Them jestice of the peace weddin's don't take very long, but that second one seemed quite a while, at that—what with her pa standin' there with the shotgun, an all. I was mighty glad when it was over an the old man oncocked that gun. It give me a sense of relief. But there was times afterward that I wished he'd shot, an' be'n done with it. The third time, I don't rec'lect much about, bein' so drunk I didn't even know we was married till she told me about it next day an' begun askin' me fer money. The fourth time

STRANGE DOINGS ON HALFADAY CREEK

though, was one of them church weddin's. That took a hell of a while, with a lot of folks settin' there lookin' on, an' my shoes hurtin', an' that preacher standin' there in front of us readin' off them prayers like he never would git to the end of 'em. Weddin's is all right. But they've got their drawbacks. But why in hell are you so anxious to pull off this weddin'? What do you care if them two git married; er don't?"

"I'm thinkin' only of the welfare of Halfaday," Black John replied, reaching for the bottle, and filling his glass. "Like you said a while back, that woman is dangerous as a cocked gun. If Bedore should show up on Halfaday, an' there ain't a weddin', she'll butcher him, shore as hell. An' we don't want no murder on the crick—'specially one pulled off by a woman. We'd either have to hang her, which none of us would like to do—er we'd have to turn her loose, an' establish a bad precedent—folks would think we didn't have no guts. An', besides, when they git married, they'll quit the crick fer good. You heard her say we was damn fools to stay here, an' break our backs on the end of a shovel when all them banks down in the States was waitin' to be robbed. Well, the quicker they go, the better fer Halfaday. A woman like her kin raise more hell on a crick than a run of smallpox. An' that double-crossin' skunk, Hank, wouldn't be no credit to any community."

"Mebbe," suggested Cush, "this here Hank won't marry her when he does git here."

"Any objections he might have in the matter could ondoubt-less be overruled."

"Accordin' to her tell, he's got quite a roll on him."

"Yeah. The amount is worth contemplatin'. Them bills she's got salted away in her sock ought to be nest egg enough fer any young couple."

"What do you figger on doin' for a weddin' certificate? There's got to be one signed by the one that marries 'em, an' a couple of witnesses to boot."

"Yeah, I'll git one out of the parson's shack. He done 'em up in a paper an' left 'em on the shelf when he went outside so they wouldn't git dirty. There was other kinds of blanks, too—about baptizin's an' sech like. I was doubtin' their usefulness on Halfaday, but it jest goes to show that most anything kin come in handy on a crick. You an' me kin sign fer the witnesses."

"I ain't goin' to sign nothin'! First thing you know Corporal Downey would be up here wantin' to know what the hell come off."

Black John suddenly smote his thigh with his open palm. "By Cripes, Cush—fer onct yer timidity has give me an idea! We'll hold this here weddin' over in the Alasky Country Club. Downey wouldn't have no jurisdiction if he did come. An' he shore as hell ain't goin' to waste no time pokin' around in Alasky cases. The Mounted has got trouble enough of their own down along the river."

"That's right," agreed Cush. "If we pull the weddin' off over there, I don't mind helpin' out with it—bein' as it's fer the good of Halfaday. But I'm shore as hell glad it's him marryin' that woman, an' not me."

ONE ARMED JOHN sauntered in with a string of fish. "Where's she at?" he asked, glancing about the room, as Old Cush slid a glass toward him and shoved the bottle along.

"Where's who at?" Black John countered, filling his own glass.

"That woman that come up the crick a while back. She was damn good lookin'. I was fishin' in a bend an' I seen her go by."

"Didn't she stop an' talk to you—ask you no questions, nor nothin'?"

"Nope. She never seen me. I squinched down behind a stump. I don't want nothin' to do with no more wimmin. It was on account of one a damn sight homlier'n her that I got my arm shot off. Her husband done it with a shotgun—an' from where he was standin' it was practically a miss. But it teached me a lesson, at that. If I would lose another arm I would have to quit fishin'."

"You've got some nice fish there. What'll you take fer about a half a dozen of them grayling?"

"Dollar apiece, same as always. I ketched 'em way down the crick. There's a fella moved into Olson's old shack. I seen him shovin' up the crick in a canoe, an' when he seen that empty shack he landed an' looked it over, an' then he packed his stuff in, an' draw'd up his canoe on the bank."

"Olson's old shack, eh? What did he have to say?"

"Whatever it was, he's still got it to say. I snuck on without stoppin'. He's kind of dark, like some kind of a greaser, er A-rab, er somethin', an' he had a kind of a mean look on his face. How many of them fish did you say you wanted? I'll be gittin' on' to my shack before dark."

"Leave 'em all," said Cush, counting them and weighing out the dust. "I'll take the balance of 'em."

When the man had gone, Cush glanced at Black John over the top of his steel framed spectacles. "Well," he said gloomily. "Hank's here."

"Yeah, it kind of looks that way," Black John admitted.

"What you goin' to do, now?"

"There ain't nothin' much we kin do, till mornin'. I'll slip over an' tell Katie that I've got good reasons to believe that I've located her light o' love, an' if she'll lay low tonight, I'll contrive to have him up here tomorrow. Then I'll fetch Pot Gutted John over to my cabin an' instruct him in the part he's got to play. You might slip me that prayer book, so I kin sort of mark the parts we need."

Stepping into his living quarters, Cush returned shortly with the book which he turned over to Black John. "I hope things works out all right," he said. "But where there's a woman mixed up in it, I can't help feelin' forebodeful. It's prob'ly on account of them first three wives I had."

IV

EARLY THE FOLLOWING morning Black John strolled casually into the little clearing that surrounded Olson's old shack, located on the bank of the creek several miles below the fort. Lowering the moose rifle from his shoulder, he greeted the man who stepped from the door, water pail in hand.

"Hello, stranger! Jest pokin' along the crick to see if I couldn't knock me off some fresh meat."

The man, slender and dark, wearing a small black mustache, slanted him an appraising glance. "You wouldn't be Black John Smith, by any chanct?"

The big man grinned. "Yeah—by the chance of thinkin' up that name before so many others did that we had to prohibit the use of it on Halfaday. Why?"

"I got the tip in Whitehorse that I better see you. Go on in the shack an' wait till I fetch some water. I've got fresh meat, but that's about all I have got—in case you ain't et. Got lost comin' up here, an' run out of supplies."

"Head up Ladue Crick by mistake? Quite a lot of folks does that."

"No. Missed the mouth of this one an' went to hell an' gone up the White. I ought to be'n here three weeks ago, if I'd had any luck."

"This here tip you got in Whitehorse to see me—was it fer some special purpose; er jest as part of the scenery?"

"Well—the fella claimed you was all outlaws up here on Halfaday, an' you was king of the bunch. Fact is, I'm on the run myself. I was headin' fer Dawson, but this fella tipped me off that the police was layin' fer me down there—so I come up here."

Black John nodded. "It's a common practice," he said. "What do you figger on doin', now you've got here?"

"Well—jest like the rest of you does, I s'pose," the man replied. "Fact is, I've always be'n a kind of a lone wolf—but I expect I could fit into a gang."

"Sech expectation would be plumb futile, as fer as Halfaday is concerned, fer the simple reason that there ain't no gang on the crick to fit into."

"No gang!" exclaimed the man, slanting the speaker a glance of incredulity. "What d'you mean—no gang? What do you guys up here do fer a livin'?"

"We're miners," Black John replied. "We take gold out of our claims."

"You mean—work?" exclaimed the man, a horrified expression in his black eyes.

"Yeah. Up to now there don't seem to be no other way to coax the gold out of the gravel.

"Time a man puts in twelve, fourteen hours a day with a pick, an' a shovel, an' a windlass, he's willin' to admit that the process savors of work."

"Hell—a man don't have to work, does he? Provided he's got enough to live on without."

"Nope. Idleness, *per se,* ain't no offence on Halfaday. But sech idler has got to refrain from any kind of crime, includin' skullduggery, in any form."

"What's skullduggery?" growled the man.

"We ain't never evolved no hard an' fast definition of the term. The way it stands now, it's any offense that I deem hangable, that ain't included under the more glarin' frailties, sech as murder, larceny, an' claim-jumpin'."

"This guy down to Whitehorse told me about yer hangin's up here. He claimed you didn't allow no crime on the crick on account of because you didn't want the police comin' in on you. But I s'posed that you an' yer gang raided' other cricks, er mebbe the boats along the big river, an' then holed up here till the excitement blow'd over. An' I figgered on throwin' in with the gang."

"Sech supposition is erroneous in the extreme. In the first place, sech excitement as would be raised by a raid like you depicted wouldn't never die down, with the Mounted on the job. An' in the second place, like I told you—there ain't no gang."

"Trouble is," sneered the other, "these Mounted Police has got you birds buffaloed. What with the small number of 'em there is, an' all the country you've got to work in, there ain't practically no danger at all. What you fellas need is someone with guts, an' brains enough to show you how to organize. What do you say to me steppin' in an' showin' you what I kin do?"

BLACK JOHN shrugged indifferently. "It's all right with me. Every man is the proprietor of his own neck. I might p'int out, though, by way of precedent, that three, four others has had the same hunch. I don't rec'lect, off hand, jest who they was. But their names er aliases is visible to the naked eye on their slabs, up in the graveyard. Perusal of 'em might give food fer thought."

"You mean—you hung 'em? How in hell could you hang 'em if—"

"The usual method," interrupted Black John, "is to slip a properly constructed loop of rope around their neck, an' then, with the rope throw'd over a rafter, er a handy tree limb, to yank 'em off their feet, maintainin' 'em in sech position till Cush pronounces 'em dead. The procedure is crude, but effective."

"What I mean—if them birds didn't commit no crime on Halfaday, how could you hang 'em?"

"We couldn't. Their crime was committed the minute they started in to organize a gang with criminal intent. It come under skullduggery, an' was treated as sech."

"Well, damned if I'm goin' to work!" exclaimed the man testily. "There ain't no man livin' kin make me work, if I don't want to!"

Again Black John shrugged. "There won't be no one try to make you work. You mentioned havin' sufficient funds to main-tain yerself in a state of leisure. Go to it. It ain't none of our business—jest so you keep out of mischief."

"I've got between thirty-three an' thirty-four thousan' dollars—but that won't last no hell of a while. Damn it!" he cried, in sudden fury, "I might better of hit straight fer Seattle an' married Kate, like I promised her I would! She's got a good head on her, an' all the guts in the world—an' we could of be'n on easy street, takin' small town banks! Instead of that, I hits out fer the Klondike, expectin' easy pickin's with so much loose gold in the country—an' here I find that the police is layin' fer me before I git to Dawson! Then I figgered this Halfaday Crick was a sweet set-up—an' now I'm here, I find out there ain't nothin' to do but work! It's tough luck. I ain't gittin' no breaks."

"Why," suggested Black John, "don't you go ahead an' marry the lady?"

"Marry her! How the hell kin I? If the police in Dawson is layin' fer me, the ones at Tagish an' the passes will be, too—by now. An' besides, I'm three months overdue fer that weddin'. Kate, she'll be on the prod—right. She played square with me when I was in stir—went to a thirty-five thousan' dollar cache I told her about an' peeled off five hundred, jest like I told her to, an' she slipped me a gun to crush out with, an' the balance of the cash—me promisin' her that I'd pick up the thirty-four thousan', five hundred, an' hit straight fer Seattle an' marry her. Well, I changed my mind—see? An' she'll be sore as hell. She packs a pearl handled thirty-eight strapped to her right leg—an' man, kin she make it hum! An' when she's hopped up with coke, I'd ruther face a tiger!"

Black John grinned. "This here Tacoma Kate, now—"

The man's eyes suddenly widened, as he stared at the speaker. "You know her?" he cried. "How the hell—"

"I can't claim to be no old friend of hers," Black John interrupted. "Though I seen quite a lot of her, fer what time she's be'n on the crick."

"Kate—here on Halfaday!"

102

"Yup, she pulled in yesterday, huntin' fer you—that is, if you happen to be Hank Bedore, which seems more'n likely. It seems that after waitin' a reasonable length of time fer you to show up in Seattle fer the weddin', she revisited that cache, an' found out you'd emptied it, so she done some inquirin' around an' some pal of yourn slipped her the word that you'd hit fer the Klondike—"

"What a pal!" gritted, Bedore venomously.

"An' so," continued Black John, "she hit fer Dawson, where she layed around fer a month er so, an' then someone tipped her off that you was around Whitehorse, so she went there an' learnt that you'd hit fer Halfaday. She thought we was lyin' to her when we told her no one that answered your description had show'd up on the crick, an' she voiced the intention of stayin' right here till she'd looked over every damn man on the crick."

"I'm sure between hell an' high water, now," Bedore groaned.

"Oh, I don't know," replied Black John. "The fact is, the lady didn't express no warlike intentions, onless you refused to marry her when she ketched up with you."

"You mean she stills wants to marry me?"

"Not only wants to, but she stated in no oncertain terms that she's goin' to—er else. You see, she ain't no more enamoured of a life of drudgery than what you be, an' she explained that when you an' her got hitched the two of you could live high on what you could git out of them rube banks. She's got a lot of respect fer your bankin' ability, Hank—if you'll pardon the use of yer first name—it's the one she used."

"An' yer sure she ain't sore—sure she won't start in workin' on me with that pearl handled gat?"

"Not if you do right by her, an' marry her like you promised."

BEDORE SEEMED lost in deep thought. Presently he shook his head hopelessly: "It ain't no use," he said. "We couldn't git out of the country nohow—not with the police on the watch fer me."

"You kin git out, all right," said Black John. "There's only one small detachment on the Dalton Trail, an' I kin tell you how to dodge that—it's easy."

"Where's this Dalton Trail at?" asked the man, an eager look in his eye.

"I'll draw you a map after yer married," answered Black John. "You see, I ain't takin' no chances. You might change yer mind agin, an' leave the lady on our hands. An' good lookin' as she is, she'd become a disturbin' factor on the crick."

"I'll marry her, all right!" exclaimed the man. "I'll marry her as soon as I kin—an' we'll git to hell out of a country where there ain't nothin' to do but work! Where's she at?"

"She's sojournin' temporarily in One Eyed John's cabin up near the fort."

"Who's One Eyed John?" queried the man, a look of jealousy flashing into his eyes.

"Oh, he's a fella we hung. You don't need to worry. She's batchin' it."

"How's she heeled? Has she got any money?"

"On Halfaday," replied Black John, "we mind our own business. An' that don't include no research into a visitin' lady's resources."

"Damn if she's goin' to know I've got any, neither. I'll tell her they took me fer my roll in Skagway. S'pose you go on up there an' tell her you located me, an' if she aims to go on the war path, you slip back down the crick an' give me a warnin'. I'll start up fer the fort in a little while, after you git the chanct to kind of feel her out."

"Okay," agreed Black John, "an' there's a foot trail. You won't need yer canoe. I'll go on ahead. An' I might remind you," he added, "that you promised in my hearin' that you'd marry this gal, an' on Halfaday, breach of promise comes under the head of skullduggery. So any evasion of this obligation will earn you a prompt an' thorough-goin' hangin'."

"But—what if she's on the prod?" asked Bedore, a look of terror in his eyes.

"In case she voices any hostile intent, you'll be relieved of the promise, an' given safe conduct off'n the crick. We don't want no murders on Halfaday."

"Well—it kind of looks like my luck had turned, at last."

"Yeah," muttered the big man, under his breath, "one way er another—it shore does." Aloud he added, "So long—I'll be seein' you at the fort."

Circling, he lay in the bush at the edge of the clearing and watched the cabin. Some twenty minutes later Hank Bedore stepped out, glanced about him, and proceeded to bury a paper-wrapped packet under a rock, then strike up the trail at a leisurely pace. Black John shook his head in frowning disapproval. "Holdin' out on his bride," he muttered. "Sech an' amazin' act of duplicity is humiliatin' to behold. It shore beats hell what some folks will do."

A few minutes later he slipped over and, removing the packet from under the rock, thrust a thick roll of bills into his pocket. "Looks like he's short about five hundred from what he claimed he had. Sech will ondoubtless git 'em back to where they kin git to work on them banks. I'll shore be glad when this weddin' is over an' done with. Folks of their stripe ain't no addition to a crick."

V

CROSSING THE CREEK, Black John struck out on a shortcut trail that brought him to the vicinity of Cushing's Fort a good half hour ahead of Bedore.

Pot Gutted John was just finishing breakfast when Black John stepped into his cabin. "Git that priest's outfit together an' hustle over to the Country Club. Don't fergit the book, an' remember to read only them lines that I marked. Git all rigged up to marry these folks. Me an' Cush'll fetch 'em over there in an hour er so. An' don't fergit that white collar goes on hind side before."

"I be'n foolin' with that collar," Pot Gutted John said disgustedly, "an' it ain't goin' to work very good. That there long jacket shoves it clean up in under my ears on account I ain't got nothin' to button it to. There ain't no way to 'tatch it to my shirt to hold it down."

Black John frowned as he regarded the collar the other had picked up off the bunk and was holding gingerly in his hand.

"You ought to washed yer hands before you fooled with it," he growled.

"It looks like hell with them big black thumb smooches on it, but it'll have to do. Take off yer shirt an' we'll rig it onto you somehow. Now git me a piece of string."

The man removed his shirt and produced a length of strong cord which Black John tied about his chest close under his armpits. Buttoning the collar about the man's neck, he attached it to the encircling cord before and behind by means of other pieces of string. "Put on that robe, now—an' mind you keep it buttoned so they can't see you ain't got on no shirt." The man donned the robe and Black John helped him with the buttons. "Draw in yer belly!" he commanded, as he struggled to make the garment meet about the man's enormous mid section. "An' keep it draw'd in er you'll have buttons flyin' all over Alasky. Wait—where's yer dish rag an' I'll see if I can't wash off the worst of them smooches. There—that looks better. Hold still, now, an' I'll rub on some flour to white it up a little while it's still damp." A few moments later he stood back and surveyed the effect. "That looks all right," he approved. "The flour's a little bit thick in spots—looks like a couple of biscuits had stuck to it an' dried. But the chances is, they won't notice. If they do they'll prob'ly think you et in a hurry. Here—hold out yer right hand an' I'll bandage it up. We'll tell 'em it's hurt an' git one of 'em to sign the weddin' certificate fer you, so if Downey er someone would come around investigatin' they couldn't find no handwritin' to match. Remember, now, to git a kind of a be-nevolent an' benign look on yer face."

"What kind of a look?"

"Don't look so damn glum. Hell—it ain't your weddin'!"

"Yeah—but a man can't hold his belly in only so long—an' if them buttons pops off right in the middle of things—I'm goin' to look like hell, standin' there without no shirt on."

"Well, Cripes—you've got pants! One man can't expect to have everything. An' remember when you speak to them two, call 'em 'my children'—an' when it's over don't forgit to kiss the bride."

"Do what!"

"Why—kiss the bride," grinned Black John. "It's customary at weddin's. Take it from me, she's a good looker. It won't be no distasteful chore."

"You go to hell! There's one man runnin' up an' down Halfa-day already with only one arm for kissin' another man's wife. I don't mind helpin' you out on a priestin' job, John—but by God, you kin do yer own kissin'!"

"All right," laughed Black John, "git goin'. But take it easy an', don't work up no sweat, er that collar'll look like a coil of dough."

A FEW minutes later he knocked on the door of One Eyed John's cabin. "All set fer the weddin'?" he asked, when the woman opened the door. "I jest be'n down talkin' to Hank. He'll be along d'reckly. I told him we'd meet him in the saloon."

"All set? I was all set three months ago! What's that damn doublecrosser got to say fer himself?"

"Well, he give me to onderstand that all is fergiven, as fer as he's concerned. I mean—it's all jake with him to go ahead with the weddin'."

"Oh, it is, eh? Didn't he give any excuse for giving me the run-around?"

"Why—he claimed it was—er—owin' to circumstances. I didn't crowd him fer no partic'lars, it not bein' none of my business. He says he's sorry the way things worked out. But I wouldn't be hard on him, if I was you, ma'm. He seems right anxious to marry you—the quicker, the better."

"You say he's up to the saloon?" asked the woman, apparently somewhat mollified.

"If he ain't there yet, he soon will be. I'm expectin' him any minute. We'd better be gittin' up there."

"All right—let's go." The woman turned into the interior for a moment and then joined Black John, and the two proceeded to the saloon where Old Cush set out bottle and glasses.

"Hank Bedore ain't show'd up yet, has he?" Black John asked, when the three glasses had been filled.

"Nope. Ain't no one be'n in this mornin' except Pot Gutted John stopped in a few minutes ago. He looked like—"

"Oh, shore—Pot Gutted!" interrupted Black John, with a vigorous wink at Cush. "I was talkin' to Pot Gutted yesterday an' he told me he was goin' over to the Country Club to see how Father John was gittin' along—said he burnt his hand an' it was all bandaged up. I told him to tell the father that there was liable to be a weddin' on the crick in a few days an' we wanted he should perform it. He told Pot Gutted that he didn't feel able to come down here, but if we'd go over there he'd be glad to officiate. He sent down a blank certificate fer someone to sign fer him, on account of him not bein' able to hold no pen. I've got it here." Producing the document, Black John laid it on the bar before the woman. "Here, ma'm—Cush will give you a pen. Jest sign the name of Father John right there on that line where he put that X with a pencil so we wouldn't make no mistake. Cush, there, he can't write—an' I ain't much of a hand at it, myself."

"Are you sure it will be legal?" demanded the woman sharply. "I don't want nothing wrong with the papers—in case Hank's old man should drop off. I want that ranch."

"You kin take my word fer it, ma'm, it'll be jest as legal as if Father John had signed it hisself. You kin ask him when you git there, an' he'll tell you the same thing. It's on account of his hand—that's all."

The woman signed, and taking the paper, Black John waved it back and forth, to dry the ink, and returned it to his pocket. "Drink up," he invited, "an' have one on me." They drank, and the glasses were refilled. "It ain't every day, here on Halfaday," he smiled, "that we git the chanct to drink with a blushin' bride."

"You can forget the blushing part," said the woman, and her voice hardened. "And if that damn Hank don't show up, there won't be any bride. But if he don't he'll never leave Halfaday— unless the buzzards carry him off!"

"There ain't no buzzards in this country," corrected Cush. "What corpses we don't bury the wolves gits."

"We don't want no killin's on the crick," Black John said. "If he don't show up, ma'm, we'll take the case up in miners' meetin' an' hang him fer breach of promise. But," he added, with a grin, "it won't be necessary. Here he comes, now."

A MAN paused for a moment in the doorway and then advancing to the bar, and stood face to face with the woman. "Hello, Kate," he greeted. "How in hell did you git here?"

"How would I?" she countered, her eyes meeting his. "I don't give a damn *how* you got here. What I want to know is *why* you got here—instead of over to Seattle, like you promised?"

"I couldn't make it, Kate—honest I couldn't. They was crowdin' me too hard. I didn't dast show up around Seattle. They'd of picked me up sure."

"They wasn't crowdin' you so hard you couldn't grab off that money in the cache," she taunted.

"That was different. It wasn't in no town. I grabbed that off an' hit north acrost the line. I come here from Vancouver. I aimed to go to the Klondike an' then send word to you to come up. But in Whitehorse I run onto Screwy Ned, an' he slipped me the office that the cops was layin' fer me in Dawson—so I come here."

"Now you're here—what you going to do? Settle down and dig gold out of the mud?"

"Not as anyone knows of. I thought, if you wanted to, we'd go ahead with the weddin'. By the way—did that screw die? I never found out."

"Sure he died—about a week later. They've got murder on you, now."

"He asked fer it," retorted the other surlily, "hangin' onto his keys like he did—so I let him have it."

"What do you care? There's plenty of more screws."

"Yeah—too damn many. I'd like to knock 'em all off. How you fixed fer dough, Kate?"

"Broke. It took all I could scrape together to trail up here after you. I've got three, four sawbucks left—that's all."

"Who the hell got the sixteen thousan' out of that Gray's Harbor cache, then?" asked the man, a snarl in his voice.

"How do I know? You never told me where it was. How the hell could I have got it? So you had plenty of time to go to Gray's Harbor, too? But you couldn't get to Seattle! You know damn well the cops could never have found you—where I was. You told me you hit north across the line—you didn't say anything about swinging around by Gray's Harbor. You lie every time you open your mouth. I ought to plug you where you stand!"

"Now don't git excited, Kate!" cried the man, a note of fear in his voice. "I'm givin' it to you straight. I couldn't never have made the hide out. There was too much heat. I ain't claimin' you got that sixteen thousan'. I jest asked you—that's all. You was the only one that knew I had a cache up there."

"But I didn't know where it was. Do you think I went up there and dug up all the land around Gray's Harbor hunting for it? You've got plenty without that. I left thirty-four thousand and a half in the other cache."

"Yeah—I had it, all right. But I ain't got it now—only a five-hundred case note that I stuck in my kick for an ace in the hole—that's every damn nickel I've got. They took me fer my roll in Skagway—Soapy Smith an' his crowd. I lasted jest two nights."

"Smart guy, ain't you?" sneered the woman. "Run all the risks of getting knocked off taking banks and payrolls, then cache part of the dough where the first kid that comes along finds it, and let a lot of cheap tinhorns take you for the rest! Well—we've got five hundred and thirty or forty bucks between us. That'll get us back to where we can go to work again—and believe me, I'll handle the dough after this. I'll figure out the jobs, an' you pull 'em—then I'll take care of the money.

"But if the police are watching out for you, how are we going to get back up the river?"

Hank glanced at Black John, who had been an interested listener. "He claimed he knows a trail out with only one police post on it that we can dodge. He also said he'd draw us a map—after we're hitched."

"That's right," agreed Black John. "I'll draw you a map that'll git you out of the country. I always like to help young folks git a start in life. The quicker you two git back to where all them banks is, the better it'll be."

"Well—let's git this weddin' over with," said Bedore.

"Who's goin' to do the job? I don't see no preachers, er priests, er magistrates around here."

"We've got to go over to Father John's," explained Black John. "He's stayin' over to the Alasky Country Club."

"Country Club!" exclaimed Bedore. "What in hell's a country club doin' in a place like this?"

BLACK JOHN grinned. "It's a buildin' we put up over acrost the line so the Yukon wanteds kin have a place to go to when the Mounted shows up on Halfaday. We jest call it the Alasky Country Club on account of it's bein' a nice name. Father John stays over there. I sent word to him that we might be wantin' him fer a weddin', but he says we'd have to go over there on account of him burnin' his hand. It ain't only a little piece up the gulch. We'll be back in an hour. Cush, he'll lock up an' come with us—we'll be needin' two witnesses to make it legal. If anyone wants a drink in the meantime, he kin wait."

The ceremony came off without a hitch, and the four returned to the saloon where Black John drew a map of the Dalton Trail while Cush made ready the supplies for the trip.

"You drop back down the White about sixty mile," he explained, "to where the trail hits the river. Then you leave yer canoe an' hit out afoot up the trail with yer packsacks. I've marked the police station, here on the Chilcat, an' jest before you git to it, you swing off up this draw I've got marked, an' cross a little divide to a crick—an' foller down that to the trail agin. You'll be in American territory, then—an' you keep right on down to Haines."

As the two were about to depart, Black John handed them a sealed envelope. "Don't open this till you git on the Dalton Trail," he said. "It's jest a little weddin' present from one that wishes you all the good luck you've got comin'. So long—you've got a sort of rough trail ahead. You better git goin'."

When they had disappeared around a bend of the creek in the woman's canoe, Old Cush turned to Black John with a snort. "Weddin' present! Fer the likes of them! By Cripes, John—if a woman shows up on Halfaday, no matter how ornery she is, jest so she's good lookin', it's a cinch she's goin' to git money out of you, one way er another. How much did you give 'em?"

"Oh—not much. It would figger somewhere around forty-five er fifty thousan' between 'em."

"Well, be damned!" exclaimed Cush, in disgust. "You ought to have a guardeen! I thought I'd saw some tough wimmin, but

I never seen nothin' like her—here or anywhere's else—not even my third wife."

VI

THE FOLLOWING MORNING as Black John faced Cush across the bar, a couple of drinks and the inevitable dice box between them, the door opened cautiously and a head was thrust into the room. The head was hatless, and swathed in a blood-soaked bandage, while the face that showed beneath it was scratched and gouged into bloody furrows. One eye was blackened and closed, and the other roved swiftly, but comprehensively about the room. As if satisfied with the scrutiny, the man entered hurriedly, closed the door behind him, arid swiftly approached the bar.

"Gimme a drink," he begged. "God knows I need one! Tell me—is she here?"

"Is who here?" asked Cush, as he slid a glass along the bar.

"Kate!"

Black John peered intently into the disfigured face. "Well, damn if it ain't Hank! Don't tell me you've mislaid yer bride, a ready. Cripes, the last time we seen you two, you was floatin' off down the crick in her canoe—happy as two turtle doves, er rattlesnakes, er somethin'."

"Happy—hell! Do I look happy? I'm askin' you—do I?"

"Well—as near as I kin discern, you don't look like anyone that had flew into no ecstasy of joyfulness, at that."

"My God—I'm lucky to be alive! An' it's all your fault!"

Black John grinned, as he surveyed the bandaged head, and the bruised and battered features. "I s'pose different folks has got different idees of luck," he opined. "But yer barkin' up the wrong tree, if you think I assaulted you."

"It was Kate. But it was your fault she done it. It was on account of that weddin' present you give us—a hell of a weddin' present, I'll say—a note tellin' her I've got that thirty-four thousan an' a half out of that cache—an' tellin' me she's got that sixteen thousan' out of that Gray's Harbor cache hid in her stockin'. We opened it when we got down to the cabin where my stuff was, an' she read it out loud."

Black John nodded, his eyes beaming benignly. "Jest as I figgered you'd do. It's made me feel good ever sence, contemplatin' the joy I was conferrin' on you two young folks by disclosin' all them hidden resources that each one thought the other didn't know nothin' about."

"Joy—hell!" growled the man, gingerly fingering his bandaged head. "She hadn't no more'n finished that note till we both jumped at onct. I made a dive fer her leg, figgerin' to git holt of her gun. But she switched legs on me, an' I come up with that package of bills an' the hull top half of her stockin' in my hand. Meanwhile she's went fer her gun, an' got it. I grabs her wrist, an' she ups with her other fist an' socked me one in the eye, an' then started to work on my face with them damn sharp fingernails. God! Like chisels, they was—gougin' an' clawin', an' rippin'. I had to leave go of her wrist to git my other hand up to my face, er she'd of clawed my eyes out. An' then she swung the gun on me an' let me have it. I hear a hell of a roar, an' the next thing I know, I'm in the cabin alone.

"I lay there a while, listenin' to make sure she's gone. Blood's runnin' down my face where a bullet plowed acrost my forehead, an' I bandaged it up. She's gone, all right—an' so is everything else—canoe, grub, blankets, money, an' even my shoes, which she prob'ly jerked 'em off huntin' that five century note I told her I'd stuck in one of 'em—an' then she throw'd 'em away so I couldn't foller her—as if I'd want to! She made a clean sweep, all right—like I said, when she blasted me down with that pearl handled thirty-eight of hem, I had that Gray's Harbor money in my hand that I'd tore out of her stockin'—but when I woke up all I had was the top half of the stockin'—the money was gone!"

"Oh, well," comforted Black John, "you've still got that thirty-four thousan' you lied to her about losin' down to Skagway—an', mebbe, if she's that kind of a gal, yer better off without her."

"Like hell I've got that thirty-four thousan'! She got that, too—the dirty, doublecrosser! I had it cached under a rock at the edge of the clearin'—an' damn if she didn't find it!"

"H-u-m-m, seems like she ain't got no principles at all, the way she carries on. How could she of found that cache, I wonder?"

"Yeah, how could she? It's uncanny the way she finds caches. I never told her about that Gray's Harbor one, neither but she found it. She's smart, Kate is—too damn smart fer me! Mebbe it's the coke does it. I seen her take a couple of sniffs goin' down the crick in the canoe."

"Where do you figger she's gone?" asked Cush, glancing about uneasily.

"She's got that map, an' she's got grub. She's hit fer the outside, damn her—an' she's got that weddin' certificate, too!"

"You might overtake her before she gits to Haines," suggested Black John, "if you hurry."

"Overtake her!" cried the man, his eyes widening in horror. "You mean me?"

"Why, shore. We'll stake you to a light stampedin' outfit. You want to git yer money back, don't you?"

"Listen, feller—I might want to git that money back—but not that bad! I'm broke—an' she's packin' off damn near fifty thousan' that rightfully belongs to me—but believe me, brother— that fifty thousan' ain't no object. One run in with that damn wildcat is enough fer one man in one lifetime! She kin keep the fifty thousan'—but I would like to git that weddin' certificate. When my old man kicks out, I wouldn't want fer her to git the ranch."

"You could apply fer a divorce," suggested Black John.

"Divorce! Hell, man—I can't appear before no court! They've got enough on me to hang me, back there in Washington."

"Well," admitted Black John, "of course, there's that angle, too. Why not fetch annulment proceedin's—jest have the weddin' set aside, as though it hadn't never come off?"

"I'd have to go to court, jest the same."

"No," said Black John. "Not in the Yukon, you don't. We've got a statute here fer the protection of innocent third parties—like yer old man. It differs from the divorce statute, in that the latter is an action brought *ab initio,* in a court of last resort; while the annulment proceedin' kin be instituted *a priori* at its source. This means that both parties to the weddin' is placed in *statue quo,* upon application to the priest that married 'em, an' the permission of any duly constituted authority—like a coroner, er a U.S. marshal. The weddin' becomes quashed forthwith, *pro bono publico,* an' any marital entanglements which the parties of the first part might have got into is thereby dissolved, *per se.*"

"Cripes!" exclaimed Bedore, "I didn't know you was a lawyer!"

"A lot of others don't know it, too. But sooner er later, they find it out."

"But I'm broke. I can't pay no lawyer—an' I dastn't go to no U.S. marshal fer this here permission."

"If I was to act fer you in this matter," said Black John, "without any fee, what would yer future plans be?"

"If you'd do that, an' draw me another map, I'd hit out over the Dalton Trail jest as quick as it would be safe to travel it without no danger of overtakin' Kate."

"It's a deal," Black John replied. "An' what's more, me an' Cush will supply you with a stampedin' pack to make the trip with. I'll slip over to the Country Club, now an' state the case to Father John, an' also to a U.S. marshal I know, that lives in the vicinity, an' the whole matter will be cleaned up in a couple of hours. I'll fetch you back a paper, duly signed by the proper authorities, statin' that the weddin' in question is declared to be null an' void—an' not only that—but it never come off, in the first place. That will give you double liability, in case the authorities ever investigate."

THE DOOR opened, and Corporal Downey of the Northwest Mounted Police stepped into the room. Striding to the bar, he laid a hand on the arm of the cringing man.

"Hank Bedore," he said, "I arrest you at the request of the Washington State authorities, on a charge of murder and escape—an' I warn you that anything you say may be used against you."

"How'd you find me?" asked the man, in a dull, hopeless voice.

"We had orders to be on the watch for you, an' when you didn't show up in Dawson, I came here on the chance of pickin' you up. Then, down on the White, I met a woman who told me I'd find you in Olson's old cabin, on Halfaday. She said you tried to rob her, there, and she had to shoot you. Said she only creased you, she thought, and you'd be all right by the time I got there. When I didn't find you, I came on here."

"Rob her!" cried the man. "I don't s'pose she told you she robbed me of right around fifty thousan'?"

"She didn't mention it," grinned Corporal Downey.

"She's hittin' out over the Dalton Trail with the money, right now," said the man. "if you hurry, you kin ketch her."

Black John grinned. "I wouldn't take what he says too serious, Downey. Fact is, the lady in question did foller this man up here, but me an' Cush both heard him tell her right here in this room that he was broke—except fer five hundred dollars he claimed he had in his shoe. Also me an' Cush both happens to know that the lady was well provided with cash before she met up with this man—so in my opinion, this robbery charge of his should be took with a dose of salts."

Downey nodded, and turned to the prisoner. "Come on, we'll be gittin' back to Dawson. I ain't goin' on any wild goose chase out on the Dalton Trail on your say-so. If you've got any complaint to make, you can make it later. I don't believe, though, that when they get through with you back in Washington, you'll be needin' that fifty thousan'—or any other amount."

When the officer had departed with his prisoner Old Cush refilled his glass and shoved the bottle toward Black John. "I wonder if she will git that ranch in case they hang Hank?" he speculated.

"Oh—yeah—the ranch," replied Black John absentmindedly. "She might, at that. The onderhandedness an' duplicity of wimmin is sad to contemplate. The trouble is, they ain't got no ethics. By the way, Cush, here's a roll I wish you'd stick in the safe fer me—an' don't fergit to give me credit. It should figger up to somewheres between thirty-two an' thirty-four thousan', accordin' to how much Hank spent gittin' here."

BLACK JOHN FILES A CLAIM

"YOU CAN'T TRUST a woman," opined Old Cush, proprietor of Cushing's Fort, the combination trading post and saloon that served the little colony of outlawed men that had sprung up on Halfaday Creek, close against the Yukon-Alaska border. He filled his glass and shoved the bottle toward Black John Smith who faced him across the bar. "Not even if you marry 'em, you can't."

Black John grinned. "Well—you'd ought to know. I never tried marryin' any of 'em, personal."

"I married four of 'em, one time an' another. Trouble is, they'll believe any damn lie another woman comes along an' tells 'em. Take my second wife, now—we was livin' up over the saloon I was runnin' them days. It was on Freeman Avenue in Cincinnati, an' I done pretty well there, an' we was gittin' along all right till one night I closed up along about midnight an' went upstairs an' damned if she wasn't gone—an' all her stuff along with her—an' I ain't saw hide nor hair of her ever sence. Come to find out, my bartender's wife told her I had another woman, an' was keepin' her in a flat over in Covington. Can you beat that?"

"Well—did you?"

"Did I, what?"

"Did you have this other woman?"

"Shore I did—but it wasn't no flat, jest a couple of rooms over a grocery. That's what I was tellin' you—you can't trust 'em; they'll believe any damn lie they hear."

"Sech perfidy is shore sad to contemplate," remarked Black John. "But mebbe you was better off shet of her."

"I don't know," said Cush, wagging his head reminiscently. "The third one was worse—I'd shore be'n money ahead if she'd of skipped out on me. But fer Cripes sake—lookit comin' in the door!"

Black John turned to greet Corporal Downey, of the Northwest Mounted Police, who stood smiling in the doorway. "Hello, Downey—yer jest in time. Cush is buyin' a drink. What fetches you up here—some miscreant took to the bush?"

"A murder an' robbery down in Saskatchewan—Ottawa sent us a couple of descriptions an' wants us to check up on 'em. They're supposed to have headed for the Yukon, but we haven't be'n able to locate 'em along the river, so I swung up here. Any newcomers?"

Black John shook his head. "Nope—none since you was last here. Looks like crime is kind of on the wane. How's things around Dawson?"

"Pretty quiet so far this summer. Guess everyone's too busy to bother with crime."

A comely Indian woman appeared for a moment in the storeroom door, and Cush beckoned to her. "Take this rinse tub out an' dump it, an' fill it up fresh. It's cloudy, an' besides a couple of mice got drownded in it. An' when you git through, set on a couple of extry plates—Downey an' John might's well eat here, an' it's gittin' along to'rds noon."

The three talked for half an hour over their drinks, when a young man burst suddenly into the room and made straight for Corporal Downey.

"You're a policeman, aren't you? I was coming down the White, and I saw you as you turned up this creek. I recognized the uniform, and yelled as loud as I could. I was portaging around that rapids just above the mouth, but the water made so much noise it drowned out my voice, and by the time I'd reached the creek, you'd gone on up. I followed as fast as I could, but I couldn't overtake you."

Black John smiled. "There's damn few men kin overtake Downey on the trail, son—winter er summer—so don't let that worry you none. What's on yer mind?"

"It's a murder—Bob Jorden, our transit man, was shot and killed at his instrument, and it's the third time it's happened, and it's Breedon and his outfit that's doing it so they can get to the canyon first, and they've probably made away with Mr. Teasdale, too, and—"

"Hold on!" interrupted Downey. "Here you've got a man shot an' killed three times, an' two other men, an' a canyon mixed up in it. Suppose you take your time an' tell me what really happened."

"I mean, it's the third time our instruments were shot at, and—"

"Begin at the beginnin'," cut in Downey. "In the first place, who are you, an' where did this shootin' take place?"

"My name's Emerson, and I'm rodman for the Consolidated. There was a stampede to Feather Creek, last fall—it runs into the White a few miles above here, and the whole creek was staked from rim to rim. But it's a little creek, and there isn't water enough in it to sluice out the dumps. The pan washings show rich stuff in the winter dumps—and no water to sluice 'em. So some of the men consulted Mr. Teasdale, chief engineer of the Consolidated, and he sent Breedon up to investigate, and see if he could figure some way to get water into the creek. Breedon was an independent engineer—and a damned crook—because after he'd looked the ground over he collected his pay, turned in an adverse report, and then immediately formed a dummy company of his own—the Feather Creek Flume and Mining Company, he calls it—but it's all his own capital.

"THE CONSOLIDATED had bought up some claims along the creek, but had quit buying when they got Breedon's report—

and then they learned that Breedon was buying in on Feather Creek as fast as he could. So Mr. Teasdale went up there himself and found what Breedon had already found—a lake about twelve miles back in the mountains, that can furnish all the water that will be needed on Feather Creek.

"In the meantime, Breedon had already started a crew surveying a line for a flume to carry the water from the lake. Teasdale got busy and put on a crew and it's a race between the two crews to complete the survey. The outfit that gets a flume to Feather Creek will clean up big—they'll not only have water for their own workings, but they can sell water to the men who have hung onto their claims."

"If the gravel's rich enough, an' these outfits have claims enough on the crick, it looks like they could each put in a flume," observed Downey.

The rodman shook his head. "It wouldn't work, too expensive—but even if the profits would warrant it, they could not get two flumes from that lake. About three miles this side of the lake there's a high rock ridge cut by a narrow canyon—and the flume has to go through that canyon, in some places so narrow that only one flume could be built there. The outfit that first builds through that canyon will have a water monopoly on Feather Creek."

"Is this here canyon dry, 'er does a crick run through it?" asked Black John, with seeming indifference.

"There's a little trickle of water through there—you could hardly call it a creek—not enough for any practical use."

"An' what's all this got to do with a murder?" asked Downey.

"I'm coming to that—you wanted me to begin at the beginning. As I told you, when Teasdale found out what Breedon was up to, he put on a survey crew and, in spite of the fact that Breedon had a start, we were crowding him hard—in fact, at the rate we were going, it was plain to see that we would run our line through the canyon before they did. The lines are running parallel, not over five hundred yards apart, up a broad, basin-like valley.

"**THREE WEEKS** ago Mr. Teasdale had to go to Dawson on some important matter, and he left Bob Jorden in charge of the operation, with orders to push on and beat Breedon's outfit at any cost. He said he would be back within two weeks without fail. Then things began to happen. The second day after he left, our level was smashed by a bullet. The level party kept a mile or so behind the transit party, working out contours, and the levelman had set up his instrument, that morning, and stepped away from it for a moment, when a scattering of shots sounded from the direction of Breedon's line, and a high power bullet made junk out of our level. The levelman and his rodman rushed toward the spot from which the shots came, and some two hundred yards away, about midway between the lines, they came upon Breedon and two of his men just getting ready to skin out a young moose.

"The levelman, Turner, accused Breedon of smashing his instrument, and Breedon pointed to the moose. 'We were killing some meat,' he said, with a grin. 'If one of our bullets went wild and smashed your level, it's just too bad. We're sorry—sorry as hell. If you can prove we did it, I have no doubt that my company will pay for the damage—if you put in a claim and can convince them that it was our fault.'

"Turner carried on with a spare level, and a week passed without any trouble—then exactly the same thing happened to our transit. Bob Jorden had set up his transit, and stepped back from the instrument to look at his notes, when there was a scattering volley of shots from the direction of Breedon's line—and the transit was smashed. Bob and Slim Sparrow, an axman, and I ran over there to find Breedon and a couple of his men just sticking a moose they had shot. Bob Jorden was mad, plenty mad, and what he told Breedon was an earful. But Breedon only sneered, pointed to the dead moose, and told him just what he'd told Turner—that if we could prove that they caused the damage, his company would pay for it, later. This time he even had the crust to say that he doubted that his company would consider two such claims—they would lie outside the probabilities. And on top of that, he hinted that we were probably shooting up our own instruments, and blaming it on them, as an alibi to Teasdale—because we knew we were losing out on the race. Of course, we knew we weren't losing out, and we were furious—but there was nothing we could do about it, except to go back and carry on with our extra transit. We knew, though, that if it happened again we were through, because we had no more instruments." The young man paused and gratefully swallowed the drink Cush pushed toward him.

"**THEN IT** did happen again—only differently, this time. We had the edge on them, and we were holding it until yesterday morning. Bob set up his instrument in a fairly open place, dotted more or less thickly with clumps of scrub spruce and brush. I was ahead with the rod, ready to give him a sight, and Sparrow, the axman, was beyond me swamping out the line. I watched Bob adjust his instrument, and held the rod. He sighted and before he could motion me to shift the rod, there was a roar from the bush in the direction of Breedon's line, and I saw Bob stagger back a step or two, whirl halfway around and crash forward onto his face. I dropped the rod, yelled for Sparrow, and ran toward Bob as fast as I could. As I ran, I glanced toward the other line, and caught a glimpse of a man running through the scrub four hundred yards away. It looked like Breedon, and I'm quite sure he was carrying a gun."

"Do you know it was Breedon? An' are you dead sure he was carryin' a gun?" asked Downey.

The other hesitated. "This is a mighty serious thing, Corporal," he said gravely. "A man's life may hang on my testimony. As I told you, I was running when I saw this man. He was running, and he was three or four hundred yards away, with clumps of scrub growth between, so that I only caught glimpses of him. I believe that man was Breedon—it looked like him, and I am almost positive he had a gun in his right hand. But I wouldn't like to state positively either that the running man was Breedon, or that he had a gun."

Downey nodded. "Go on," he said. "What about Jorden?"

"Bob Jorden was dead when we got to him," replied the other, his voice faltering slightly. "Bob was one of the finest fellows I ever knew—the best friend I had in the world. And there he lay—dead—with the blood flowing in a thick red stream from his temple. It made me sick, then furious—if Breedon had showed up then, I could have killed him with my hands. Then Sparrow came up. He, too, had seen the man running. He thought it was Breedon, but he couldn't be sure. Sparrow's coming sort of calmed me down. I sent him to notify Turner, and I hit for the tents, threw some grub into a pack sack, and beat it for the river.

"There were some boats and canoes on the White, at the mouth of Feather Creek, and I jumped into a canoe and hit out for Dawson—for the police. I camped last night on the river, and this morning, when I was making that portage just above the mouth of this creek, I saw you. As I told you, I yelled and yelled, but I couldn't make you hear. The noise of the rapids drowned out my voice. So I followed you here—hoping to overtake you."

"I'd prob'ly have heard it if you'd fired a shot," said Downey.

"I had no gun. But I'm sure glad I found you. It has saved me a long trip to Dawson."

"I'll say it has," said Downey. "I know Breedon. He's a go-getter, an' not too particular about how he gets what he's after, either. Used to be chief engineer for an outfit that went bust on Indian River. That is—the company went bust. The talk is that Breedon came out of it with half a million or so, personally. It's results that count with Breedon—not methods. He's a dead shot with a rifle, too. Won a match in Dawson this spring.

Shoots a .300—only one in the country, far as I know. An' it's either got a defective chamber, or his ammunition is defective.

"I noticed, at the match, that all his empty shells was split up about an eighth of an inch from the bullet end. It kind of looks like he'd got himself in bad. We'll hit out for Feather Crick right away."

"You better eat first," said Cush. "The klooch must have dinner about ready. I'll have her put on another plate."

"That's right," seconded Black John, "an' while she's doin' it, I'll slip over to my cabin an' throw some grub in my pack sack. I've heard about them diggin's over on Feather Crick, but I never be'n there. Don't even know where Feather Crick is— prob'ly one of them little cricks that runs into the White way up, an' prob'ly wasn't named till last fall when the flurry was on. I'll go along with you."

"Good," said Downey. "I'll be glad of your help."

"W-e-e-l," drawled the big man, "I wouldn't go so far as to offer to help none. I ain't no policeman—an' I'd kind of hate to establish a bad precedent. But I won't hinder, Downey—I won't hinder. Bushwhackin' a man mindin' his own business is a mighty low form of skullduggery."

"I hardly believe that Breedon would deliberately kill a man under the circumstances, ruthless as he is," opined the officer. "But if he shot the man while trying to put his instrument out of commission, it isn't going to help his case. A homicide resulting from the commission of an illegal act is murder, no matter what the killer's intention was."

"Yeah," grinned Black John, "I always claim a man ought to keep his acts as legal as the circumstances permits. I'll be back in a minute—I hear the klooch rattlin' them dishes around."

II

ON THE AFTERNOON of the second day thereafter, the three reached the survey camp to find that Turner, the levelman, had taken over the transit and was pushing the line on, leaving the level work to be caught up later.

The weather had held cool, and the body of the dead transit man lay as it had fallen, the men having covered it with a blanket.

An examination of the body showed that the lethal bullet had entered the man's left temple, passed behind the left eye, and come out at the corner of the right eye, smashing the bone, slivers of which were visible at the edges of the wound of egress. Downey spent considerable time examining the wounds, using a pocket magnifying glass, and making notes in a small notebook.

"You can bury him now," he said, returning the book and glass to his pocket, and proceeded to examine the ruined instruments, again using his glass. He glanced at Turner.

"Can you set up your level on the exact spot where this ruined one stood when it was struck by the bullet?"

"Certainly I can, and I can show you the head and the hide of the moose they claimed they were shooting at when they smashed the level."

The instrument was set up, and the four proceeded to the spot where the head, hide, and offal of the moose lay. Downey carefully searched the ground in the vicinity of the spot, and succeeded in finding two empty shell cases, a .300, and a .303. The .300 shell showed a split about an eighth of an inch long at the bullet end, and Downey pointed out to the others that from the point where he picked it up, the level was in plain sight, offering a fair target for a good marksman, at a range he later stepped off as one hundred and seventy-eight yards.

Turner was then allowed to proceed with his surveying while the rodman, Emerson, returned with Downey and Black John to the point where the transit had been struck. Using the damaged instrument, Emerson set it up on the spot it had occupied at the time it was smashed, and then led the way to the remains of the second moose. Once again Downey searched the ground, this time finding three empty cartridge cases—a .300, a .303, and a .30-40. As before, the cartridge case was split exactly as the other had been, and as before, the point where it was found presented an unobstructed view of the instrument—this at a paced range of 165 yards.

"It was Breedon's rifle that fired these shells, all right," said Downey as he pocketed them. "It was good shootin', but not too good for a marksman like him. Now," he said to Emerson, "we'll have you set up the transit exactly where it stood when Jorden was shot."

When this was accomplished, Downey stood for a long time as his eyes took in every slightest detail of the terrain. "Where were you standin' when you heard the shot?" he asked.

EMERSON POINTED along the line. "You'll find a stake at the exact spot," he replied, and led the way, pausing about half way between the instrument and the stake to point in the direction of the Feather Creek Flume and Mining Company's line.

"I must have been about here, running toward poor Jorden, when I saw the man I think was Breedon running through the scrub. It was way across there—near that leaning dead spruce—the one with the three limbs sticking out to the right. I saw him pass that tree, and he was visible for maybe twenty or thirty yards before he disappeared in the scrub."

Again Downey studied the terrain. "It would be a long shot from there," he said. "But men have been killed at longer range than that."

"It might be," suggested Black John, "that the long range was what made him miss—I mean, if he was shootin' at the transit. If a man was squintin' through that eye-piece, his eye would be right down clost—an' Breedon wouldn't have had to hold more'n just a hair to the right to throw a bullet an inch or two off at that range."

Downey shook his head. "A lot farther than that, John—he wasn't shooting at the eye-piece. You noticed, I suppose, that both those instruments were hit in the middle, where the compass, and bubble tubes, and vernier arc, with the different thumb screws and all make a pretty fair sized target. That bullet would have been a foot or more off, to have struck Jorden where it did."

They proceeded to the stake and again Downey looked carefully around. "Now where was this axman?" he asked.

"Sparrow was a little farther along—there at the edge of that little clearing. He was cutting out a clump of brush. There was an Indian family camping there. A man and a squaw and three kids."

"Siwashes? Where?"

"There in that little clearing beside that spring. They had their tepee set up right square on the line. Jorden had told 'em a couple of days before that they'd have to move. The man was a surly cuss, couldn't understand any English—or pretended he couldn't. We were going to pull his tepee down after the next set. He'd had plenty of warning—he understood we wanted him to move, whether he understood the words, or not."

"Where are these Siwashes now?"

"I don't know. They were still here when I left to go for the police. Sparrow might know—he or Turner."

"Well," said Downey, "I guess that's about all you can help us with."

"Aren't we going over where I saw that man running and hunt for the empty shell—like we did at those other places?"

The officer shook his head. "No," he replied, "we wouldn't find no shell. I'll look around here for a bit, and you go find Sparrow, an' tell him I want to talk with him."

Emerson looked up quickly. "Good Lord, Corporal, you don't think Sparrow had anything to do with it?"

"No," Downey replied dryly, "from what I've be'n able to figure out, Jorden was shot with a gun—not an ax. By the way, if I remember right, you said that both the other shootin's—the ones when the instruments were hit—there was a volley, or a scatterin' of shots. But this last time, when Jorden was killed, you heard only the one shot—is that right?"

EMERSON TOOK time to think. "Why, yes," he answered. "I hadn't thought of it before, but that's so. I heard only one shot—and then I saw Jorden stagger back and fall."

"All right—go fetch Sparrow. I'll be right close here somewhere—if you don't see us when you get back, just yell."

When the man had gone, Downey examined the clearing, and the few sorry bits of refuse discarded by the Indians—a filthy rag, a bit of rotten rope, and a couple of pieces of paper—pages torn from an old magazine.

Black John glanced at the pages. "Bet I know what Siwash was camped here," he said.

"Who?" asked Downey.

"Name's Saul Nootka. He's from the Stick Village."

"Sticks!" exclaimed Downey, "You mean, on the American side?"

"No. These Sticks live on this side—about thirty or forty miles up a river that runs into the White from the south a few miles below here. David's Village, they call it. They moved there quite a few years ago because they was afraid of the Chilkats. There's a priest up there tryin' to convert 'em—guess he ain't had no hell of a lot of luck at it, though. Seem like them Sticks converts hard; they've got some kind of a heathen religion of their own. This here Father Cassat ain't a bad fella—he stops into Cush's now an' then."

"What makes you think it was Saul Nootka who was camped here?"

"Well, I recognize this magazine. It's one that laid around Cush's saloon till everyone on the crick had read it. This Saul Nootka done some packin' fer Cush, before the snow went off, an' Cush give him that old magazine an' another one."

"What for? He can't read, can he? Emerson said he couldn't even understand English."

Black John grinned. "He savvys English all right—when he wants to. But he can't read—none of them Sticks kin. He wanted paper to wad his gun with, so Cush give him the old magazine."

DOWNEY POCKETED the paper as Emerson returned, accompanied by Sparrow, the axman, who corroborated Emerson's story of the killing, in every particular.

"An', now," said Downey, "when did these Siwashes that was camped here go?"

"They must of started bustin' camp right after I went to tell Turner about Jorden gittin' shot. When I come back, they was jest pullin' out. They hit fer the river, the man an' the woman carryin' packs—an' the biggest kid, too. An' him not more'n six er seven year old, by the looks of him."

"Do you know whether the man was here at the camp at the time the shot was fired that killed Jorden?"

"No, he wasn't. I seen him take his gun an' hit out through the bush about half an hour before. He was always comin' an' goin' with a gun er a fish net. I yelled at him an' told him he better come back an' move his stuff out of our road—but he never let on he heard me, jest kep' on a-goin'. Guess when he heard that shot, an' found out a man had be'n killed, he got to hell out of here."

"That's all," Downey said. "You can go back to the job." He turned to Emerson. "I want to go on up an' have a look at that canyon an' this lake you're figurin' to tap for water," he said. "If you know the way, you better come along with us. I'd kind of like to see about how hard you was crowdin' Breedon's outfit in the race—it might be material evidence."

"Sure, I'll take you there," agreed Emerson, "it's only about four miles from here to the canyon, and about three from there to the lake."

The canyon was, as Emerson had said, hardly more than a transverse crack in the huge rock-ledge that crossed the projected survey lines at a right angle. In one place, it was wide enough for only one flume of sufficient capacity to furnish the water necessary for the Feather Creek diggings. Black John seemed mightily interested in that spot. When they had passed through the canyon and reached the more open rock country beyond, he paused and gazed long and earnestly to the north, and to the south. Downey waited, while Emerson continued on toward the lake.

"Do you know," the big man said, "this here canyon an' of course the lake beyond, lays in American territory."

"What makes you think so?" asked Downey.

For answer, Black John pointed to a couple of peaks to the northward, and another to the southward. "Them peaks," he explained, "are on the line. We're a good two miles into Alasky, right now."

"That won't make any difference with their project," said Downey. "They can make the proper arrangements with the American authorities. An' it don't affect my jurisdiction of this case—Jorden was killed on the Yukon side of the line."

"Oh shore," agreed the big man, "it prob'ly won't make no difference to no one. I was jest commentin' on the fact—that's all."

A short time later, the three stood on a rock ridge that formed the eastern shore of a considerable lake.

"There she is," said Emerson. "She's deep, too—look at that color. Enough water for forty creeks like Feather."

"How the hell you ever goin' to git through this ridge?" asked Black John. "Tunnel?"

EMERSON LAUGHED. "Hardly," he answered. "A tunnel through here would take time, and a mint of money. We'll bring the water over the top of it—syphon."

"Syphon, eh?" said Black John. "I don't know nothin' about syphons, except I've seen Cush syphon licker through a rubber tube out of a barrel into the bottles. But if you kin syphon the water over this ridge, why is it so damn important to run yer flume through that canyon? Why couldn't the outfit that loses out on the canyon jest syphon the water over the top of that other ridge, same as this one?"

"The expense would be prohibitive," Emerson explained. "Syphons of this size are expensive we've got to carry the water from the lake over the top of this ridge through pipe. From there on we'll run an open flume. Pipe of that size runs into money—to syphon water over that other ridge, would mean laying a pipeline clear from the lake—unless they damned the canyon and made a reservoir behind the ridge. And the outfit that was running their flume through the canyon would never stand for that."

"H-m," replied the big man, "I can't see why a man would pick out engineerin' to make a livin' at—he's got to know too damn' much."

"We'll be goin' back, now," said Corporal Downey. "I want to have a talk with Breedon."

"And don't forget to question him about Mr. Teasdale, Corporal," urged Emerson. "He was due back here a week ago—and I know he'd have been here, unless something has happened to him. This is a mighty important job—and he knows he's needed here. In the light of what happened to poor Jorden, I'm afraid Breedon's done away with Mr. Teasdale, too."

With Emerson leading the way to Breedon's camp, Corporal Downey spoke to Black John. "I've got to arrest Breedon, an' I can't be bothered with havin' him on my hands. It looks to me like there's more to this case than appears on the surface—an' I've got some more investigatin' to do around here. I was wonderin' how it would be if I'd appoint you a special constable to take him down to Dawson, an' tell Constable Peters to lock him up till I work this thing out?"

Black John shook his head emphatically. "No, sir—not me! I ain't no policeman—an' never will be. Cripes, Downey—the boys on Halfaday would find it out, an' I'd be through. They wouldn't never have no confidence in me no more, if they found out I'd throw'd in with the police. Why don't you deputize one of them Feather Crickers to take him in?"

Downey shook his head. "I don't know any of 'em—wouldn't trust 'em. This Breedon's a smooth one, and accordin' to reports, he's got plenty of money. He'd bribe the man to turn him loose, sure as hell—especially if he could convince him that Feather Creek would never get water as long as he was in jail. I don't know how in the devil I'm goin' to handle this."

"Why, hell, Downey, I'll take this here Breedon down to Dawson fer you an' turn him over to Peters—if that's all you want. Be glad to."

Corporal Downey glanced at the other in surprise. "What! I thought you just said you wouldn't?"

"You don't hear very good," grinned Black John. "All I said was that I wouldn't be no policeman—special constable, or even special commissioner, er no other kind. But that ain't sayin' I wouldn't take Breedon to Dawson, if it'll help you out any."

"But how about the authority?"

"Authority!" laughed Black John, doubling his fists and flexing his mighty arms. "It looks like Breedon's the only one that's got to worry about that. I ain't never laid eyes on the gent, but if I can't take him to Dawson, he's got to be a hell of a lot of man. Is it important that I should deliver him to Peters all in one piece?"

III

THE THREE ARRIVED at the camp of the Feather Creek Flume and Mining Company just as the crew had finished supper. Breedon greeted the officer with a hilarity that seemed a bit forced, as his glance shifted to the others.

"Hello, Corporal! Out looking over the country? Anything we can do for you?"

"Yes," replied Downey, "you can do some explainin'—maybe."

Breedon's eyes shifted to Emerson, he frowned. "Oh—you mean about these damn fools claiming we shot up their instruments? The idea's ridiculous, on the face of it. Think of it, Corporal—two wild bullets smashing two different instruments at two different times! Does it sound reasonable—I'm asking you?"

"No," replied Downey, "it don't. But I wasn't thinkin' of wild bullets, Breedon. I was thinkin' of damn well placed bullets—bullets fired by an expert marksman—such a marksman as—well, as you, yerself, fer instance. Bullets that hit exactly where the man that fired 'em wanted 'em to hit."

"What do you mean?"

"I mean," replied Downey dryly, "that you done some good shootin'!"

"Look here, do you mean to infer that I shot up those instruments! And that I did it deliberately?"

"Yeah—that was the idea I was strivin' to put acrost."

The other flushed angrily. "By God," he blustered, "I understand that you're a policeman, and all that—but that don't give you any license to come here and accuse me of deliberately destroying property on the say-so of any damned irresponsible whipper-snapper that runs to you with a pack of lies!"

Downey grinned. "You might be a good engineer, Breedon, but you sure as hell ain't up on what you call a policeman's license."

"A private citizen has some rights in this country."

"Yeah, but such rights as he's got don't include shootin' up other folks property with a rifle."

"I suppose," Breedon replied sarcastically, "that you're prepared to prove these charges?"

"That's right," replied Downey crisply. "Your rifle's a three hundred, ain't it, Breedon?"

"Well, what if it is?"

"I'd like to take a look at your shells. Like to look at all the other rifles in this camp, too—an' the ammunition."

"Help yourself," replied Breedon, with a show of indifference. He turned to his men, all seven of whom had been interested listeners. "Trot out the other two rifles, boys, and the ammunition. The officer wants to look at 'em." Stepping into a small tent, the man reappeared, carrying a rifle, and a partially filled box of ammunition. "Here's my gun, and the shells. It's a three hundred."

DOWNEY GLANCED at the gun the man held in his hand and nodded. He took the box of ammunition and glancing into it, thrust it into his pocket. "These shells split up from the end a little ways when they're fired, don't they, Breedon? I noticed that at the shoot you won down to Dawson, this spring?"

"Defective ammunition," grunted Breedon. "It never did that before."

Downey glanced at the other rifles, examined the ammunition that the men submitted to him, and returned it. "This all the firearms an' ammunition you've got?" he asked.

Breedon nodded. "Yes, just the three rifles. I suppose the boys showed you all the shells. I told 'em to."

"That's all of 'em," volunteered one of the men.

"I notice," said Downey, "that the three hundred bullets is copper jacketed, an' the others—the three-o-three, an' the thirty-forty is nickel."

"Well—what of it?" asked Breedon.

"The bullets that smashed both them instruments was copper jacketed," Corporal Downey replied. "They left little snooches of copper on the brass where they tore through. Besides that, in both cases where them instruments was smashed, I found an empty three hundred shell that had been ejected from your rifle at a point from which the smashed instrument presented a good fair mark."

"So what?" demanded Breedon insolently.

"So you done the shootin'," Downey replied.

Breedon laughed nastily. "Smart cop, aren't you? I suppose you've examined all the ammunition in Teasdale's outfit, too, eh?"

Downey shook his head. "No," he replied, "I didn't go to all that bother. I didn't see no use in it."

"I'll tell you the use in it," growled Breedon. "They shot up their own instruments—shot 'em up so they'd have an alibi for themselves when Teasdale comes back."

"Where's Teasdale gone?" interrupted Downey abruptly.

"Why—I don't know. How the hell should I know where he's gone? Dawson, I suppose."

"How did you know he was gone?"

"Saw him go, and haven't seen him since. It's like this—when Teasdale left, the Consolidated had a pretty fair chance of completing their line before we did. Since he's been gone, we've gained on his outfit till we're practically sure of beating them.

"They know that, and they know that Teasdale will want to know the reason—so they shoot up their instruments, and claim we did it."

"That's a lie!" cried Emerson hotly. "We're right now a good two days ahead of you—and you know it!"

Corporal Downey silenced him and turned to Breedon.

"You claim they shot up their own instruments," he said. "Did you hear any shots from their direction at the time these instruments was smashed?"

"No, I can't say I did," Breedon answered. "Both times there were three of us shooting at a moose, and more or less confusion."

"How many men have you got on this job?"

"Eight, including myself."

"How many do you need fer the work you're doin'?"

"I need every damned one of them. We're really short-handed, as it is. We've got to get our line finished ahead of the Consolidated."

DOWNEY NODDED, "An' yet you've got plenty of time fer moose huntin'. You, the boss of the outfit, take two men off this job you're in such a hell of a hurry to finish, an' spend quite a bit of time huntin' moose."

"We're short of grub, and the men have got to eat," snapped Breedon. "The reason there happened to be three of us, each time, is that when one of us sees a moose, he calls to the others and we run for the rifles and kill him."

"An' each time you manage to git a Consolidated instrument along with the moose."

"And I tell you they shot their own instruments!" retorted Breedon. "As I said, I, personally, didn't hear any shots from their direction, but one of my men told he did—both times." He turned to one of the men. "It was you, Johnson, who told me you heard a shot from their direction, each time they accused us of shooting their instruments."

"That's right," answered a man—too glibly, thought Corporal Downey. "Both times whilst you fellas was shootin' them moose, I heard a shot from over on their line."

"What's your job here?" asked Corporal Downey, eyeing the man.

"I'm level rodman."

"What time of day was it when you heard these shots?"

"I don't know exactly—along in the morning sometime."

"You was workin' when you heard 'em—on your regular job?"

"Sure I was."

"An' the others—the ones that was shootin' the moose—was they on the level crew, too?"

"No, the boss, there, an' the others was in the transit party."

"An' the level crew, do they work right along with the transit crew?"

Breedon glanced toward Emerson, who was an interested listener, and hastened to answer, "No, the two parties don't work right together. The level party keeps behind the transit men."

"How far behind?"

"Well—far enough so they don't interfere with each other's work."

"How far?"

Breedon, aware that Emerson's eyes were on him, flushed, "Well a mile or two behind."

Downey turned on the man Johnson with a grin. "You've got damn good ears—fer a man your size. Both them moose was shot within a hundred an' eighty yards of their line, an' you, standin' a mile er two away, each time heard another shot, that you could tell was even nearer their line than that." He turned to Breedon, "You ought to coached some man who was nearer the shootin'."

Breedon bristled angrily. "Do you mean to infer that Johnson is lying? And that I told him what to say?" he demanded.

"Yeah," Downey answered, "puttin' it bluntly, that's exactly what I mean."

BREEDON'S ANGER flared. "Oh, you do, eh? Well, if you want to get tough about this thing, copper—I can get just as tough as you can! Suppose our bullets—yes, even the bullets from my rifle—did smash their damned instruments, what of it? Bullets that miss their mark go wild—and a wild bullet could hit an instrument.

"If one wild bullet could, two could—or a dozen, for that matter. Of course, it's too damn bad, for the Consolidated—tough luck. Coincidence, I believe, is the word for it, isn't it?"

"No—habit is the word," replied Corporal Downey.

"Even if you can prove my bullets ruined their instruments, you could never prove they were fired intentionally—so what are you going to do about it?"

"I'm goin' to arrest you to start out with, an' then—"

"Arrest me! By God, you can't arrest me on any trumped up charge, like this! These birds shooting up their own instruments, and then preferring charges against me, to get me arrested and jerked off the job so they can win, is too thin! If they can prove my bullets wrecked their instruments, they've got recourse in a claim for damages—and that's all that they've got. I know my rights! I won't stand for an arrest—and my men won't stand for it, either." His eyes swept the faces of his men, whose glances shifted uneasily to Downey's uniform, then dropped sheepishly.

"Don't be an ass, Breedon," said Corporal Downey quietly. "These men have got some sense, if you haven't. Stick out your hands, now, an' we'll try these on."

One glance told Breedon that his men would have nothing whatever to do with interfering with an officer of the Mounted in the discharge of his duty. For only an instant he hesitated, then thrust out his hands.

"I'll get you for this!" he shouted, his voice trembling with fury. "I'll have you busted—kicked out of the police! Damn you—how much is the Consolidated paying you for making this pinch? They can afford to pay plenty—to get me off this line. You can't take me off. Damn you—I demand bail!"

"I ain't authorized to accept bail in any case," replied Downey quietly. "An' besides, murder ain't a bailable offense."

"Murder!" cried Breedon, the fury in his eyes giving way to a look of bewildered surprise. "What do you mean—murder?"

"You're under arrest for the murder of one, Robert Jorden, transit man for the Consolidated. An' it's my duty to warn you that anything you say may be used against you."

"It's a lie!" shouted Breedon. "I've seen Jorden alive since those shots were fired!"

Several of the men, who had been seated on the ground, leaped to their feet.

"I seen him, too!"

"And so did I."

"Me, too!"

"That's too thin—don't fall fer it, Corporal!"

"If he ain't on the job, he's hidin' out somewheres!"

"It's a trick of the Consolidated to git Breedon off this job!"

CORPORAL DOWNEY held up his hand for silence. "The man is dead," he replied. "I examined his body. He was sightin' through his instrument which was pointin' west. He was shot in the left temple, which means that the bullet came from the south—from the direction of your line—an' he was killed day before yesterday mornin'—not when them moose was killed."

"Day before yesterday," Breedon repeated, in a voice that held no trace of anger—only a numbed incredulity. Then suddenly his eyes widened. "Day before yesterday—did you say day before yesterday morning, Corporal?"

"That's right," answered Downey.

"About the middle of the forenoon?" asked Breedon eagerly.

Downey turned to Emerson, who nodded. "Yes," he answered, "it was along about the middle of the forenoon."

"Then, by God—I heard the shot that killed him!" Breedon cried. "And so did Small, my transit man, and his rodman, Pelly! I had gone on ahead of the transit, ahead of the rodman, and I heard a shot from the direction of their line. The first thing that occurred to me was that someone of the Consolidated crew had taken a shot at our transit, in retaliation—"

"Retaliation fer what?" interrupted Downey.

"Why, retaliation for our—" he paused, and his face flushed.

"Yeah—yer what?"

"All right, damn it!" cried Breedon, "In retaliation for my shooting their instruments! I did it—and all you've got on me is malicious destruction of property, or some such petty offense! You'll never pin this murder on me—because I didn't fire a shot day before yesterday. As I was saying, when I heard that shot, I thought they were shooting at our transit, so I ran toward it as fast as I could go. When I got there Small was setting up as though nothing had happened—and nothing had. He said everything was okay, as far as he knew; said he heard the shot, and so did Pelly, so we concluded that they were shooting themselves some meat over there."

"Did you have a gun with you?"

"Yes, I always carry my rifle when I go ahead in the hope of getting some meat." He paused, and looked Downey squarely in the eye, and there was the ring of sincerity in his words as he added, "I did shoot up their instruments in the hope of delaying their work, as I told you. But I did not fire a shot that day—and I certainly did not shoot their man. If he was murdered, I hope you find the murderer—and that's straight. You can forget what I said about being in the pay of the Consolidated. That was foolish—I apologize. I was so angry I hardly knew what I was saying, and didn't give a damn. But if you'll turn me loose, I'll certainly help you get to the bottom of this murder in any way I can."

DOWNEY SHOOK his head. "Can't do it, Breedon. As for what you said—about me takin' money from the Consolidated, or any other outfit, I didn't pay no attention to it—it was too damn silly. But I can't turn you loose. Besides this charge of malicious destruction of property, there is the matter of Teasdale's disappearance to be cleared up. You might not know nothin' about that, either—but I ain't takin' no chances."

The man shrugged. "I suppose I'm slated for Dawson then," he said. "Is it asking too much that I be given a couple of hours before we start, to line up the work here so it can go on without me?"

"No objection to that. Take all the time you want. Emerson can go back to his own camp now. I've got some more investigatin' to do around here. This man will take you to Dawson." He indicated Black John. "We'll camp here tonight. You'll be startin' for Dawson in the mornin'."

142

IV

WITH A NOTE to Constable Peters in his pocket, and another to Chase, general manager of the Consolidated, in which Corporal Downey inquired as to the whereabouts of Teasdale, the missing engineer, Black John set out early the following morning for Dawson.

Sullen and uncommunicative, Breedon sat in the bow while Black John in the stern seat, skilfully guided the canoe down the swift waters of the turbulent White River. No halt was made for lunch, the only landings being those necessitated by the numerous portages around whitewater rapids. Late in the evening Black John beached the canoe at the head of the rapids just above the mouth of Halfaday Creek, drew it onto the bank, built a fire, and prepared supper. He removed the cuffs from Breedon's hands and the meal was eaten in silence. When it was finished both men lighted their pipes.

Breedon was the first to speak. He blew a thin plume of tobacco smoke into the air, and allowed his gaze to rest patronizingly upon the bearded face that showed indistinct in the play of the firelight.

"I don't know who you are, my good man, nor how much Corporal Downey is paying you to do his dirty work for him." He paused, and Black John nodded.

"That's right," he agreed, "an' if you was to start in an' tell me all the rest of the things you don't know, we'd be settin' here till God knows when."

"What's that?" asked the man sharply, as he peered more intently into the speaker's face.

"You heard it. I didn't notice no evidence of deafness when you was talkin' to Downey."

"Who are you?"

"Smith the name is. John Smith."

"Do you realize who I am?"

"Yeah—yer the party that laid in the bush an' shot the surveyor, when he was squintin' through his transit."

"It's a damned lie! I didn't shoot that man."

"You ought to tell the judge about it then. It looks like Downey figgers you did."

"Downey's a damned fool! He'll never convict me of that shooting, because I didn't do it. But laying the question of my guilt or innocence aside, how much is he paying you to take me to Dawson?"

"Why—damn if I know. There wasn't no price agreed on. I figger he ought to pay me goin' wages."

"How long will it take to reach Dawson?"

"Well, the way the water is, if we stick to the rivers, we ought to fetch Dawson in five, six days. But we won't stick to the rivers. We'll take a cut-off trail I know—acrost Laude Crick, an' acrost Sixtymile, an' down Miller Crick, that'll save a day er so, an' put us right acrost the river from Dawson, an' we kin ferry over."

"That'll be four or five days, then—say four or five ounces."

"Yeah, that is onless he figgers that this bein' police work, sort of, he'll pay police wages—the police don't git no ounce a day."

"But it won't amount to more than, say sixty or eighty dollars, at the most?"

"Somewheres around there—if he pays goin' wages."

Breedon smiled. "I guess you and I can deal," he said.

"Oh, shore," Black John agreed. "I've got a little dust saved up, an' if you've got anything in the way of property that you want to dispose of before they hang you, I'll take it off'n yer hands—if the price is right."

"You ain't goin' to have a chant to spend no hell of a lot, nohow—bein' in jail that-a-way."

"Listen," said the man, sharply. "I'm not going to be in jail. That's what I want to talk to you about."

144

"Me? Hell, it won't do you no good to talk to me. Talk to the judge."

BREEDON SMILED thinly. "What I mean is—suppose I were to offer you a hundred dollars, cash, to turn me loose?"

"You mean—not take you down to the jail in Dawson?"

"Exactly. You'll earn more that way than you will by taking me in—and your job will be finished, right now. Just turn in and go to sleep, and when you wake up, I won't be here. You can tell Downey I got away."

"But you ain't got away. If you git away after you git in the jail, that ain't none of my business."

"Listen," said the man impatiently. "Can you get this through your skull? I'm offering you one hundred dollars, cash, to turn me loose."

The other shook his head. "Downey wouldn't like it," he said. "I told him I'd take you to Dawson an' turn you over to Constable Peters at the police detachment."

"And I'm offering you a hundred dollars to forget it."

Black John shook his head. "Nope. I couldn't do that—it wouldn't be honest."

"Two hundred, then?"

"Nope."

"Five hundred?"

Black John shook his head.

"A thousand, then, damn it! A thousand dollars in cold cash, just to let me walk away from here."

"I can't do it—it ain't honest."

"Two thousand?"

"Nope—if I was to take two thousan' it would be twict as onhonest as if I took a thousan'. I won't turn you loose fer no money—so your might as well fergit it. What was that deal you was talkin' about? You got a claim, er somethin' you was wantin' to sell?"

His answer was a string of unreasoning curses, at the conclusion of which Black John stood up and stepped toward him, the handcuffs in his hand. "If you ain't no murderer, you kin shore swear like one—I guess I'll' put these here handcuffs back on you."

"Get away with those irons," cried Breedon. "You're not going to put them on me."

"The hell I ain't," replied Black John. "Stick out yer hands—an' hold 'em still till I git these things shet. I ain't handy at it, like Downey, an' if I've got to paste you one in the jaw, you won't wake up till you git in that cell in Dawson—if ever."

Only for a second did Breedon hesitate, as his glance swept the huge form, then he thrust out his hands, and Black John slipped the cuffs onto his wrists. "Of all the damn fools I ever saw—you take the cake," growled Breedon. "I'll give you one more chance—how about five thousand?"

"Honesty is the best policy," iterated Black John smugly. "I don't want to git put in no jail."

Nearly a day's run below the mouth of Halfaday Creek, Black John landed, concealed the canoe in the bush, and with the manacled and protesting Breedon in front of him, struck out on a well defined trail that led to Sebastian's village, on Ladue Creek. A light drizzle set in during the afternoon and in the early evening when they reached the village, old Sebastian, the chief, tendered the use of a vacant cabin. When Black John declined the offer with thanks, and proceeded to build his supper fire in the open, in the lee of the cabin, Breedon's ill temper flared high.

"What's the big idea in camping out here in the rain when there's a stove in there under a roof?" he demanded. "What the hell are you afraid of—smallpox?"

"This rain don't amount to nothin'," replied Black John. "It ain't no more'n a heavy fog. The blankets'll keep most of it out, and I'd ruther sleep damp than lousy. If the sun comes out tomorrow we'll be dry by noon."

Breedon peered in through the doorway. "There are bunks in there with good dry spruce twigs a foot thick in 'em, and I'll be damned if I'm going to sleep out in the rain! I'm not afraid of a few minor discomforts."

Black John shrugged indifferently. "Help yerself, but if them minor discomforts gits to bitin' you where you can't reach to scratch with them handcuffs on, don't blame me."

BREEDON TOSSED his blankets onto a bunk, and sat in the doorway out of the drizzle while Black John prepared the meal.

Indians appeared, looked on in stolid silence, and passed on to have their places taken by others. One, a sullen-faced three-quarter-blood whom Black John had warned repeatedly to stay off Halfaday, persistently remained. Out of the tail of his eye, Black John had seen the man exchange glances with Breedon, and he noted that, as others came and went, this man, known along the river as Sammy Cobb, kept gradually but persistently edging toward the doorway until he was finally squatting close against the jamb, not an arm's length from Breedon. Paying no apparent attention to the two, Black John went on about his business of preparing supper, nestling the tea pail against the coals, baking his oatmeal bannocks in one pan, while he fried the fresh moose steaks he had obtained from Sebastian in another. Nevertheless, the fact that swiftly whispered words passed between the two, did not escape him, nor did the deft passing of a bill from Breedon's hand to Sammy Cobb's escape his notice.

When the food was ready, he unlocked one of the cuffs, handed Breedon his portion on a plate, and seating himself close by, proceeded to devour his own portion. There were no further communication between Breedon and Cobb, and presently, the latter rose and sauntered away to disappear into the damp dark.

The meal over Breedon stretched and yawned. "I'll turn in, if there's no objection," he growled, and proceeded to spread his blankets over the spruce mattress of a bunk. "You're a damned fool to sleep out there in the rain," he added, "when you could just as well be in here where it's dry."

"Mebbe," admitted Black John, "but as the fella says, time'll tell. The wind's come up an' it ain't goin' to rain very long, no-how—I'll take a chanct of sleepin' jest outside the door." As he spoke, he examined the single window of the room, ascertaining that, Indian fashion, the sash was nailed tightly shut. This done, he paused before the other, who was seated on the edge of the bunk removing his boots. "Git yer pants off now—er whatever yer goin' to take off—an' slip between yer blankets, an' stick yer hands up here.

"There's a loop of chain steepled to this stanchion where they prob'ly kep' a dog, an' I'm runnin' the cuff chain through it—jest in case someone would come along in the night an' try to turn you loose."

THE MAN sneered. "There's no one here but a lot of damn Siwashes—and none of them give a damn whether I'm loose or not."

"Prob'ly not," agreed Black John, "but you can't never tell what a Siwash'll do—especially if you pay 'em enough. Seems like they ain't got no ethics."

"What do you know about ethics?" asked the man, shooting the other a keen glance.

"Not much—except some has 'em, an' some ain't."

"I suppose," sneered Breedon, "that you pride yourself on the fact that you've got them—turning down that five thousand."

"No," Black John replied, "I can't say as I take no pride in what ethics I've got—seems like they're jest part of me, like my whiskers."

"Whiskers are easy to get rid of. I notice you didn't say like your eyes, or your right hand."

"No, I wouldn't like fer the loss of 'em to cripple me none," retorted Black John, as he dropped the loose cuff through the loop of chain and snapped it onto the man's wrist. "Good night—I'll spread my bed jest outside the door."

Along toward morning he was awakened by the voice of Breedon. "For heck's sake, come in here and loosen my hands! This is intolerable!"

"Was you hollerin' to me?" asked Black John, turning down the edge of a damp blanket.

"Of course I'm calling to you! Who do you suppose I mean?"

"I didn't know."

"Come in here—I'm being devoured alive!"

"You're all right," replied Black John. "It's jest them minor discomforts you claimed you wasn't afraid of. They git lively along about this time of night, but they won't bother you none in the daytime."

Despite the man's cursing, Black John drew the blanket back over his head and went to sleep, and in the morning when he awoke soon after daylight, Breedon was still cursing.

"I give you fair warnin'," reminded the big man. "Like the old sayin' is—you made yer bed, an' you ain't got, no kick comin' if you had to lay in it. Peters, he'll delouse you when you git to Dawson. They git a lot of dirty prisoners."

The man glared venomously, but said nothing. The village was already astir, and a few of the curious paused to stare at the white men. Black John saw Sammy Cobb pass without stopping, and noted that, although Breedon saw him, he gave no slightest evidence of it. He pondered this as he turned the flapjacks in the pan. If Breedon had expected Cobb to release him during the night, he certainly showed no hint of anger or disappointment that the breed had not even made the attempt. He had distinctly seen Breedon slip the man money. If it wasn't for his release, what was it for? The two had certainly had no chance to lay any elaborate plans for release farther along the trail, in the few whispered words they had managed to pass. And Black

John knew Breedon well enough to know that, had the breed double-crossed him, he would have been furious.

HE UNLOCKED the prisoner's handcuff, and handed him his plate. The meal proceeded in silence, and it was nearly concluded before the probable answer dawned on Black John. The lips beneath the heavy black beard broke into a broad grin, just as Breedon laid his plate aside, and pressing his back against the door frame, moved his torso violently from side to side.

"What's so damn funny?" growled the other angrily.

"Bless the Duke of Argyll," grinned the other, with seeming irrelevance.

The remainder of the trip to Dawson passed without incident, except that Breedon's inhabited blankets and clothing gave him no end of annoyance.

"How'd you make out?" asked Peters, as he locked Breedon in a cell.

"Fine," grinned Black John, "barrin' a couple hundred minor discomforts Breedon picked up along the trail. But he'll tell you about them—he ain't talked of nothin' else fer the last three, four days."

Returning to the office, Peters read the note the other handed him. "Downey wants him booked fer murder," he said. "That'll keep some lawyer from gittin' him out on bail until Downey has a chanct to investigate this Teasdale matter. But like he says—Teasdale may be right here in Dawson, his delay in gittin' back to Feather Crick, havin' nothin' to do with Breedon."

"Yeah," Black John agreed. "I'm goin' over to the Consolidated, now. I've got a note here that Downey wrote to Chase."

"Chase'll be glad to see you," Peters said.

Black John left the police detachment, but before going to the office of the Consolidated, he stepped into the recorder's and filed a discovery location on a small creek which he described as Canyon Creek, lying in unsurveyed territory a few miles to the westward of Feather Creek.

Paying the fee, he pocketed the paper and proceeded to the Consolidated, where he was immediately shown into the office of the general manager, Chase, who greeted him warmly.

Chase read the note, and leaped to his feet. "Good God," he cried, "Teasdale never returned to Dawson! We supposed he was on Feather Creek pushing that flume survey. It's a cinch that Breedon's outfit will beat us, now."

Black John shook his head. "No, it ain't no cinch, Mr. Chase. Breedon, he's in jail, right here in Dawson, with a murder charge agin him."

"Murder!"

"Yeah. There's be'n hell a poppin' up there in the Feather Creek country, an' Downey's up there straightenin' things out. Breedon, he shot up a couple of yer instruments, hopin' to delay yer crew so he could beat 'em to that canyon. But they went ahead with some extry ones they had, an' it seems like they ain't lost no time to speak of. Then yer transit man got murdered, an' Downey arrested Breedon fer that. I fetched him down here to Dawson, so Downey could go ahead an' work up his evidence. Of course, Breedon claims he never done it—an' mebbe he didn't. It's accordin' to what Downey finds out."

"But Teasdale!" cried Chase. "What has become of Teasdale?"

"Downey's workin' on that, too."

"We've got to have more than one policeman working on it. Teasdale has to be found. I'll offer a reward, five thousand dollars—no ten thousand—for information that will lead to the recovery of Teasdale, dead or alive—and another five thousand for information that will lead to the arrest and conviction of the person, or persons who are responsible for his disappearance! I'll post the reward right now—and take measures for advertising it not only in Dawson—but throughout the whole territory."

BLACK JOHN nodded. "That would set everyone working on the case that could git him a grubstake together, an' who didn't have no other means of support," he said. "But you got to re-member, most of 'em would be chechakos who don't know the country, an' don't know nothin' else, neither. The police won't go after the reward—they'll do their damndest, anyhow—an' the sourdoughs has all got business of their own to look after. Publication of a fifteen thousan' dollar reward will send all the riff-raff of the country scatterin' into the hills, an' they might mess things up so no one would ever find Teasdale."

"But how else can we find him? Have you any better plan to offer?"

"Well," grinned Black John, "I ain't no general manager or nothin', an' ain't supposed to be as smart as one, but I know the country pretty good, an' I've got a hunch. On top of that, I ain't so damn busy, right now, that I can't take time to make a play fer that fifteen thousan'—provided it's a bony-fido offer—"

"It's a bona fide offer, all right!" interrupted Chase. "Do you want me to put it in writing?"

"No—yer word's good with me."

"What's your plan?"

"It ain't much of a plan—that is, there ain't no complex angles to it. It's jest that you withhold publication of this here reward fer, say eight days, an' I'll slip out in the meantime, an' fetch Teasdale back here, an' the man that kidnapped him, along with him."

"You mean—that yon know where he is? That you can go and get him?" cried the astounded Chase.

"Well—like I said, I've got a hunch. I don't know nothin' fer shore, and all I kin say is that I seen a man the other day that might of be'n the one that's got Teasdale."

"But—could you make him talk?"

"Yeah," said Black John, "I ain't handicapped, like the police is in sech matters. Yeah, I kin make him talk—an' talk fast."

"I've got more confidence in you than in anyone else," Chase replied. "Go ahead. And if I don't hear from you at the end of eight days, shall I publish notice of the reward?"

"Shore," grinned Black John. "An' if I don't show up in eight days, you might add a couple thousan' to it fer the discovery of my remains, too."

<h1 style="text-align:center">V</h1>

ON THE FOURTH night thereafter, Black John skulked in the deep shadows of Sebastian's village, and scrutinized the faces of the natives that passed back and forth between the various cabins that were strung for a distance of a quarter of a mile along the south bank of the creek. Two hours vigil had failed to reveal the face he sought. He considered going to old Sebastian, the head man of the village, and asking for the man he wanted. This procedure had its drawbacks. While Sebastian was very friendly with Black John, yet he was a chief who also must consider the interests of his people, and he would ask numerous questions. Black John knew that should he fail to satisfy the old man of the justice of his business, he would be met with evasive answers, and a profession of ignorance as to the man's whereabouts, that would delay matters until Sebastian found means to warn him that he was in danger—in which case the man would take to the hills, where he could remain hidden for months.

Despite this, John was about to head for Sebastian's cabin when footsteps sounded, and he drew deeper within the shadow of the scrub spruce that stood within arm's reach of the footpath over which the approaching man must pass. The man was visible, now. Black John's muscles tensed. In the starlight, he caught a glimpse of a dark face. The next instant his arm shot out, and the huge fingers closed about the throat of the unsuspecting traveler. Jerking him into the deep shadow of the spruce, Black John held him as he struggled frantically, his hands tearing at the mighty wrist, and his eyes bulging in horror as they stared into the bearded face. The man's lips parted and his tongue lolled between yellowed teeth, as his struggles grew feebler. Then, suddenly, the grip on his throat relaxed and he stood sucking great draughts of air into his tortured lungs, his eyes still on the bearded face. Seconds passed as he stood there, weak and wobbling, then with a low choking sound, half moan, half sob, he turned toward the trail. Before he could take the first step, a huge fist crashed against his jaw, and he dropped like a poled ox, his legs and arms twitching feebly.

REACHING DOWN, Black John grasped the inert form by the neck of the shirt, and the seat of the pants and swung it to his shoulder. Then he walked rapidly down the creek, avoiding the trail. Fifteen minutes later, he halted and deposited his burden upon the ground at the foot of a big spruce tree which threw out a large limb some eight or nine feet from the ground.

Stepping to the creek, he scooped up a double handful of cold water which he dashed into the unconscious man's upturned face, then, from about his middle, he uncoiled a fifteen foot length of rope, one end of which terminated in a loop formed by a properly constructed hangman's knot.

The man's eyelids fluttered open, and he moaned. Presently he stirred uneasily, and struggled to a sitting posture, his eyes staring up at the figure that stood towering above him, its fingers, plainly visible in the bright starlight, slowly widening out the loop in the end of the rope. He stared at first apathetically, as one in a daze, then, as realization of the import of the silent figure seemed to dawn upon his befuddled senses, he uttered a whine of terror, and again his eyes seemed to bulge from his head in a stare of horror.

"Well, Sammy," a deep voice was saying, "you've come to the end of yer rope—this end here, the one with the loop in it."

"No, no! You no kin hang me!"

"Can't, eh? You seen us hang that hooch-runner that was sellin' licker in the village, that time. I rec'lect that you was one of the Siwashes that took in the sight."

"Me—I ain' sell no hooch!"

"No—you done a damn sight worse than that, you murdered a white man, killed him."

"No! Me, I'm ain' keel no w'ite mans. You mus' got to mak' de—w'at you call de miner meet'!"

"Miners' meetin', eh? Well, Sammy, this here's a miners' meetin'—a one-man miner's meetin'—an' yer charged with, an' convicted of murderin' one, to wit, Teasdale, up on Feather Crick, er thereabouts—an' it's the verdick of this meetin' that you be hung to that there limb that's stickin' out between you an' them stars."

As he spoke, Black John slipped the noose over the breed's head, and tightened it snugly about his neck, the man offering no resistance whatever, so great was his terror. "You rec'lect that hooch-runner, don't you—how he spun around, first one way an' then the other, when we pulled him off the ground, an' how his feet kep' doublin' up an' kickin' out agin—an' how his eyes damn near bunged out of his head, an' his tongue hung out, an' he begun to turn kind of blue around the gills? Well, Sammy, yer goin' through all them motions yerself in about three minutes. Stand up, now, so I kin git this rope throw'd over the limb."

The man made no movement to obey. His eyes were fixed in a glassy stare. His lips moved but no sound issued from between them—he was literally speechless with terror. Black John continued, and coiling the rope, tossed it over the limb as he talked. "All right, Sammy—if you'd ruther git hung settin' down than standin' up, it's all the same to me. This here hangin' is goin' to learn you not to kill no more white men."

The Indian suddenly found his voice. "No! No! No!" he screamed. "I'm ain' keel no w'ite mans!"

Black John heaved on the rope, jerking the man clear of the ground. As the noose tightened about his throat both hands flew upward and grasped the rope above his head, relieving the strain on the noose. "No keel 'um!" he shrieked. "W'ite man ain' dead!"

Black John eased up on the rope, and as the breed's feet touched the ground his clawing fingers loosened the noose. "Leggo that rope!" bellowed the big man, and the other's hands dropped to his sides.

"How the hell do you expect me to hang you, an' you pullin' on your end of the rope with yer hands? Cripes—anyone would think it was you that was tryin' to hang me! What' d'you mean—the white man aint dead? Listen, Sammy—yer a damn thievin', lyin', no-count Siwash that's guilty of every known form of skullduggery, an' you know I know it, so there ain't no use lyin' to me, 'cause I wouldn't believe nothin' you say. You seen that white man I was takin' through here the other night, an' you seen his hands was chained together with the police irons—well when he got to Dawson he told the police all about it—how he hired you to guide this other white man to Dawson. He paid you some money, an' he promised you some more. But he says that instead of guidin' this man to Dawson, you up an' killed him, an' robbed him—"

"No—no! I ain'—"

"Shet up! Don't lie to me! I seen him pass you some money, tight there in the door of the shack, that night. Well, when the police found out you'd killed this white man, they sent me up here to hang you, bein' as I was hittin' fer Halfaday anyhow, an' you bein' nothin' but a damn Siwash, they didn't want to bother to do the job theirselves. When I send in yer ears they'll pay me a hundred dollars fer my trouble. So if you'll quit yankin' on that rope when I git you hauled up, I'll go on with the hangin', an' be gittin' back to Halfaday. You've be'n more bother to hang already than two white men."

As the big man prepared to heave on the rope once more, the other blurted. "W'ite man's lie! I got de man. He no keel. He no hurt."

"You mean you've got this white man alive?"

"Sure—got um 'live."

"Where?"

"Een de cabin—trap camp—on de li'l crick."

"How far?"

" 'Bout fi' mile—mebbe-so seex mile!"

BLACK JOHN glowered. "Listen—if yer stallin' fer time, it ain't goin' to do you no good. If that white man ain't in that cabin when you take me there, I'll hang you shore as hell. If he is, yer lucky, 'cause the police wouldn't want I should hang even you fer a man you didn't kill—savvy? If this man's alive, we'll turn him loose, an' you'll go along with me to Dawson an' tell the police all about how that man I took to Dawson the other night hired you to kidnap this other white man an' hide him out. That'll git you out of this murder trouble, an' give you a chanct to git even with him fer tryin' to save his own neck by gittin' you hung."

"I tell um—you bet! You see pret' quick de w'ite mans ain' keel."

"All right—we'll git goin'. But first I'm goin' to tie yer hands behind yer back so you can't pull no monkey work. An' I'm leavin' this noose around yore neck, too, an' keepin' hold of the other end of the rope, so don' try to pull no fast ones on me, er you'll wake up in hell with yer tongue stickin' out."

Following on down Ladue Creek for a mile or so, the breed turned up a small feeder. At its mouth he paused and faced Black John appealingly.

"De rope mak' de hurt on ma neck—too mooch, w'at you call, de scratch."

"That ain't nothin' to what it's goin' to feel like if that white man ain't in that cabin," retorted Black John, drawing a huge cotton bandanna from his pocket. "You Siwashes ain't nothin' but a bunch of damn sissies, nohow, but seein' I'm leavin' that rope on till you git clean down to Dawson, I wouldn't like fer yer neck to git filed down to where it wouldn't hold up yer head. Hold still, an' I'll fix it. I wouldn't want folks should think I hadn't done everything I could think of fer yer comfort."

Some four miles up the feeder a trapper's tiny cabin nestled snugly against the foot of a rock wall at a point where the thick growing scrub entirely concealed it from view. It was well built of logs—even the door being of spruce logs ingeniously and strongly dowelled together, and secured on the outside by means of a heavy hasp and staple through which was driven a sturdy hardwood pin. The cabin was windowless, the only ventilation being afforded by the stovepipe hole on the roof, and a narrow slot between two of the logs through which the breed had passed the prisoner's daily ration of food and water. Stooping, Black John called through the slot, and was immediately answered by a voice from within:

"Who's there—a white man? For God's sake get me out of here!"

"Jest a minute," replied Black John as he knocked the pin loose with a blow of his belt ax, and shoved the door open. The next moment he drew back from the stench that assailed his nostrils as an unkempt and unshaven figure leaped through the doorway, and stood blinking in the bright starlight—sucking great draughts of pure air into his lungs.

"I've lost track of the days—but it must be a month I've been shut in that damned hole."

Black John nodded. "Yeah, it must be nearly a month. But yer out now."

THE MAN'S eyes rested for a moment on the face of the breed, and with a growl of rage, he leaped toward him. Black John interposed his huge bulk. "Hold on now, Teasdale—jest take it easy. The breed's hands is tied behind him. You wouldn't want to hit a man with his hands tied—there wouldn't be no satisfaction in it."

Teasdale subsided. "You're right," he said. "When I saw that damned devil I—went berserk, I guess. You seem to know who I am. Who are you—and how did you happen to find me?"

Black John, speaking rapidly, soon acquainted Teasdale with the sequence of events that had transpired since his abduction. When he had finished, he grinned. "An' I suppose you've got a story of yer own to tell?"

"My story's short," Teasdale replied. "I started for Dawson for a conference with Chase, and this man offered his services as guide. I engaged him, and the second night out we camped at some point on the bank of the White. I awoke towards morning to find myself trussed like a turkey—wound, blankets and all, in turn after turn of babiche line. It was an ingenious job—how he ever managed it without waking me, I don't know—and the procedure that followed was equally ingenious. My demands to be turned loose were met by grins. As the guide prepared breakfast I laid my plans for escape—I knew that there were numerous portages downriver, some of them long, and I didn't believe the breed would bother to carry me over them. He would loosen the lashing, and I'd watch my chance to overpower him. But when we were ready to pull out, instead of loosening the entire lashing, he merely loosed the part that secured my legs leaving my arms bound. He had used two lines—one for the upper part of my body, and another for the lower.

"The blankets about my feet he got rid of by the simple expedient of cutting them in two at my waist. Also, I found that we were not going to hold to the river. At first I refused to budge, but a few prods with the point of a belt knife got me going. We walked all day, part of the way on a trail which we left during the afternoon, reaching this cabin in the early evening.

I was searched, and everything I possessed was removed from my pockets. I was then thrust into the cabin, with my arms still bound. The door was secured and, punching out the chinking between those two logs the breed told me to press my back against the opening and he'd cut the line. There never was one damned minute from the time I was trussed up till I was locked in here, that I had a chance to put up a fight."

"Pretty slick," agreed Black John. "Some of them breeds is smart. We better turn in now an' git us some sleep. We'll give the breed a dose of his own medicine, an' let him do his sleepin' in that stinkin' shack. Me an' you'll sleep outside—you kin have my blanket. It ain't cold, an' I'm used to sleepin' out. In the mornin' we'll be hittin' fer Dawson."

"Not me!" exclaimed Teasdale. "I'm hitting for Feather Creek. My conference with Chase can wait—in view of what's happened up there, I know I'm needed on the job."

BLACK JOHN regarded the man with a smile. "There ain't no barber shops on Feather Crick, is there? You look from here like a shave an' a haircut an' a good hot bath wouldn't hurt you none."

"To hell with that! I've got to get back. I'll beat that damned Breedon out, if it's the last thing I ever do! You take this scoundrel to Dawson—I'll give you a note to Chase, and he'll pay the reward, all right—"

"I ain't worryin' none about the reward," replied Black John. "An' neither I don't believe you've got to worry none about beatin' Breedon out. When I left there a little better'n a week ago your boys had a couple days' jump on Breedon's outfit, in spite of their handicaps. Besides that, I've got a document here that might interest you. Wait till I lock Sammy up, an' git a fire lit an' you kin look it over."

A few minutes later, Teasdale was perusing the claim grant. He looked up. "What's this got to do with running those lines?" he asked.

"Well, this here Canyon Crick is that little dribble of water that seeps down through that canyon yer both headed fer. It ain't so much of a crick, as cricks go—in some of the shallow places it wouldn't float a burnt match. But what I claim, a crick's a crick—no matter what the size of it—so I named it Canyon Crick, an' filed a discovery claim on it that takes in the canyon from rim to rim."

"But good Lord, man—that canyon floor is pretty much hard rock and this is a placer claim! The chances are that whatever gravel there is there is perfectly barren of gold."

"Well," replied Black John, "that would be the man's hard luck that ondertook to mine it. I wasn't thinkin' of sinkin' no shaft. It jest occurred to me whilst I was lookin' at it, that if a man filed a claim there, he could mebbe sell it to one of you two competin' outfits."

Teasdale stared for a few moments at the paper. "A hold-up, eh?" he frowned. "Well, it won't work. Even if you do hold that claim, we can get water rights across it."

"That's right. If you don't want it, mebbe Breedon'll buy it. If lie gits title to it, though, an' lays his flume through there first, you're goin' to have a hell of a time gittin' in your flume. There ain't room fer only one flume at this point, an' you know it—that's why yer racin' to beat him. The way it is now, you've got to show yer survey line from one end to the other before you kin git a flume franchise. If either one of you'd had sense enough to file that narrow pass, an' build yer section of flume acrost it—on yer own property, you could have took yer time about completin' yer survey."

FOR SEVERAL moments Teasdale sat silent. "By God, I believe you're right. A man can construct any flume he sees fit on his own property without any flume franchise, and then if the other outfit sought the legal right to cross the property with their flume, they could get it, all right—but with our flume in, it would be a physical impossibility for them to build theirs."

"That," agreed Black John, "was the thought that was lingerin' in my mind."

"What will you take for this claim?"

"I wouldn't like to set no price right now. What with comin' up here to git you loose, I ain't had time to give it no thought. I'll jest wait an' see what Chase thinks about it."

"But Chase has never been up there—he doesn't know the physical aspect of that canyon."

"Breedon does," replied Black John. "If Chase don't want it, I might sell to him."

"Sell to Breedon!" exclaimed Teasdale a horrified expression on his face. "Listen—if my boys were a couple of days ahead of the Breedon outfit a week ago, I'll have to take a chance on their holding their lead. But even if they should lose it, if we have title to this claim, and should start right in laying our flume, it wouldn't do Breedon any good. By God I will go with you to Dawson!"

VI

SOON AFTER BLACK JOHN'S departure with the prisoner on the morning after Breedon's arrest, Corporal Downey proceeded to the place where the dead transit man had been killed. Standing upon the exact spot occupied by the man at the time he was shot, the officer carefully scrutinized the terrain. The distance to the dead spruce past which Emerson saw the man running that he believed to be Breedon was fully four hundred yards. As is the wont of lone men, Downey voiced fragments of his thoughts in a low, muttering voice. "Emerson claimed he started runnin' as quick as he heard the shot, an' he'd run mebbe fifty, sixty feet when he seen the other fella runnin'. If the other fella started at the shot, he wouldn't have covered any more ground than Emerson—which would still make the range better'n three hundred an' fifty yards. Too far for even a man that can shoot like Breedon to try to hit an instrument, when with all the cover there is between here an' there he could have slipped up to a dead sure range. An' besides, if Breedon had fired that shot, he'd never have admitted runnin' with a gun in his hand."

Downey's eyes shifted to the nearer terrain—open, rocky country thickly dotted with clumps of stunted spruce, and thickets of berry bushes. Walking at a right angle to the trail in the direction from which Emerson said the shot had come, he began carefully to examine the ground on the far side of each clump and thicket that could have screened the assassin from sight of his quarry. From clump to thicket, and thicket to clump he went, dropping to hands and knees for a closer scrutiny of the ground. An hour passed before he found what he sought—a few blades of coarse grass broken off at the ground, and pressed into the dry earth by the feet of someone who had stood for a considerable time on the spot. Passing around the clump, he again examined the ground minutely, crawling backward and forward upon hands and knees. Finally, when he had reached a point some fifteen feet from the clump, a low exclamation of satisfaction escaped him and he picked up a small object from a bunch of coarse grass—a scorched and badly tattered bit of paper.

Carefully he smoothed and flattened the frayed fragment upon his knee, and drew from his pocket the pages of the old magazine. While few if any complete words were discernible on the fragment, it was evident at a glance that the paper and the type of such letters as were visible on the fragment were identical with the paper and type of the magazine pages. Pocketing his evidence, Downey retrieved his pack sack and struck out for the White River where he had left his canoe at the mouth of Feather Creek. Following Black John's directions, he dropped back down the White some twenty miles, and headed up a small river that flowed in from the southward. Ascent of this river proved impractical by canoe and concealing the craft in the bush, Downey shouldered his pack and struck on up the creek, following a dim trail that time and again lost itself among the rocks, to be picked up later higher up the river, now on one side, now on the other.

FOR THREE days he continued without seeing a soul, and save for the dim and illusive trail, without evidence that human beings had ever passed that way.

On the evening of the third day he emerged from a rocky, steep-sided gorge onto a little flat, a half mile long, and possibly a quarter of a mile wide between the rims. Pausing in the mouth of the gorge, he surveyed the dozen cabins of mud and pole construction, and an equal number of skin tents. Smoke from the supper fires rose on the still air, and Corporal Downey could see people moving about among the buildings.

Advancing to the village which straggled along the right bank of the river, he was greeted by the stolid stares of dark, flat faced squaws who tended the supper fires, and of their equally stolid husbands and offspring who lounged before the cabins and tents. Stovepipes protruded from some of the roofs, but these were evidently for winter use, the natives preferring to do their cooking in the open in summer.

Apathetic, fly-tortured dogs, lean with the summer starvation, accorded the officer scarcely a glance as he picked his way among them toward a cabin at the upper end of the village, which he took to be that of the priest, as it was flanked on one side by a garden plot, and on the other by a structure, larger than the others, the roof of which was surmounted by a rude wooden cross.

The door of the cabin opened at his approach and a man stood in the doorway. He was a large man whose features, save for a thin, well shaped nose, and dark, brooding eyes, were entirely concealed by a curly chestnut beard. His long black robe was clean, but wrinkled, and showed evidence of much wear. The dark eyes held no hint of welcome, and Downey instinctively sensed a barrier of unspoken antagonism, though the priest's words were civil enough as he answered the officer's simple greeting. "Good evening. Are you Father Cassat?"

"Good evening, my son. I am. Will you come in and partake of my poor hospitality? I have little to offer, and a poor enough place in which to entertain a man of the police, but such as I have is yours—and moose stew is sustaining after a hard day on the trail."

"Moose stew is better than I would have had," smiled Downey, as he slipped the pack sack from his shoulders, and set it beside the door.

"Bring it inside," advised the priest. "The dogs are very hungry."

"I never saw Siwash dogs that wasn't about starved in the summer. The Siwashes can't seem to get it through their skulls that they'd have better an' stronger dogs when winter comes an' they need 'em, if they'd keep 'em at least half-fed in the summer— better puppies, too."

"Ah, yes. I try to teach them by example. I keep my own dogs fed and housed during the summer, and even protect them in some measure by means of smudges, from the flies. But the lesson goes unheeded. The natives are simple souls, giving no thought for the morrow."

The priest lighted two candles and placed them upon the table, after which he filled two bowls with stew from a pot on the stove, and set cups and a pot of tea upon the table, together with chunks of heavy bread which he broke from a slab.

THE MEAL was eaten almost in silence. At its conclusion, Downey filled and lighted his pipe, while the priest attended to his simple dishwashing duties after declining Downey's offer of assistance. When he had finished, the officer tendered his tobacco pouch, and taking a pipe from a shelf, the priest filled it, and drew great draughts of smoke deep into his lungs, exhaling it with deep sighs of satisfaction.

"I have had no tobacco other than some miserable stuff mixed with sawdust and whatnot, that the Indians have, for nearly a month. I am out of sugar, too—as you undoubtedly noticed when you drank your tea. I will journey to Halfaday Creek next week and procure some."

"I can let you have enough to last you till then—tobacco an' sugar both," offered Downey. "I'll be goin' back soon."

"Thank you, my son—but do not make yourself short. I have become used to privation—if going without the non essentials can be called privation." They smoked for a time in silence, then the priest said, "I am sorry to see you here, my son—though I knew it would be only a matter of time till the police would come."

Downey nodded. "Yes," he said, "it's a serious matter. But—I don't seem to understand you, Father. Most of the priests—all of 'em that I've run acrost, play along with us. If a Siwash is guilty—an' they know it—they advise him to give himself up."

"My son," answered the priest, "I have given the matter much thought. There have been times when my silence has troubled my conscience, and I have wrestled with it, even as Jacob wrestled with God. I have approached it from the angle of my duty to the State—to the upholding of its laws. And I have approached it from the angle of my duty to my people—which I conceive to be my duty to God. For years I have had this matter on my mind, and for years I have remained silent."

"What?" asked Downey, leaning forward and eyeing the man through the tobacco smoke that fogged the dimly lighted room.

"Ah, yes, it has been a sore problem with me—and a great trial. But despite the law, I can see no harm in it."

"No harm in it!" exclaimed Downey. "An' what do you mean by years?"

"Twelve years, now, I have labored among these people, and I believe that I have met with some measure of success. They have renounced their heathen beliefs, and some have embraced the true faith. There are only a few of them—some ninety souls, in all. They are law-abiding, and they are happy, because for the first time in their lives, they are living without fear—fear of their lives, and of the lives of their women and children at the hands of the fierce and consciousless Chilkats. I know that my small handful of Sticks, here, are Alaskan Indians, and as such, belong on the American side of the line. But they are doing no harm here, they are molesting no one, and they are living in peace. I knew that it was only a question of time till the police heard about us, and would come and drive us back across the line—back to the former precarious existence, close against the country of the Chilkats, back to the land of fear."

"You mean," asked Corporal Downey, his lips twitching to keep back a smile, "that you think I came up here to shoo you an' yer Siwashes back across the line?"

"Why—certainly. I knew that sometime it had to be."

The young corporal threw back his head and laughed—a good full-throated laugh that rang through the little room, and caused the dark eyes of the good priest to widen with wonder. "If that's all that's troublin' you, you can forget it—for all of me," he said. "Remember, I ain't givin' you Government permission to stay here. I ain't got the authority to do that. But I'm givin' you an unofficial tip—just man to man between us—don't you do no more worryin' about these Siwashes of yours gittin' shoved back across the line. In the first place, no one down on the big river knows they're here—an' no one would give a damn, if they did know. We've got our hands full, what with the country fillip' up like it is with chechakos, tryin' to stamp out crime an' run a few other Government departments, to boot—without botherin' to sift through the back country an' find out if there's a few Siwashes squattin' somewheres they hadn't ought to be. You just set tight, an' keep yer mouth shut, an' mebbe in a hundred years er so the police will find time to look your outfit up. By that time they'll have been here so long that they'll have the right to stay."

THE PRIEST rose, stepped to Downey's side and taking his hand, looked deeply into his eyes, "Do you mean, my son, that my people do not have to move? That you are not here to drive us back across the line?"

"I mean that, for all of me, you can stay here as long as you like. I'll never bother you, without orders to. An' like I told you, there ain't much chance of such orders bein' issued for a long time to come."

"Thank God for that!" breathed the priest fervently. "But if not that, what brings you here?"

"Do you know a native named Saul Nootka?"

"Yes, Saul Nootka is one of my people."

"Is he here in the village?"

"No, he is not here just at the moment. Saul and his wife and children started out this spring to hunt and fish among the rivers and creeks that flow into the White River above here. Three or four days ago they returned to the village, saying that the hunting was not good because many white man had come into the Feather Creek country. Saul left his family here, and struck out alone, saying he was going back for a while to the country of the Sticks to visit his father who still lives there, and who is very old. Why do you ask?"

"He killed a man on Feather Creek, an' I've come to get him."

"Killed a man! Surely you do not mean—murder!"

Downey nodded. "Yes, Father—it looks like a murder." In as few words as possible, Downey acquainted the priest with the facts as he knew them, the good father listening intently, a troubled expression on his face. When Downey had finished the priest spoke.

"There is something you have overlooked, my son."

"What's that?"

"I do not know. From what you have told me, it looks as though Saul shot this man. But I cannot believe that he shot him in anger, because the man ordered him to move his tent. Saul is a good man. He would not kill in anger."

"Can he speak English—understand it?"

"Yes, he worked for a short time upon the river, somewhere near Fort Egbert, I believe, chopping wood for the steamboat company. He had picked up a smattering of English. And he works occasionally for Mr. Cushing, on Halfaday Creek."

"I can't figure no other reason for him shootin' Jorden than because Jorden had told him he'd have to move. Of course, Jorden might have be'n pretty rough about tellin' him, cussin' him out, or maybe threatenin' him."

The priest shook his head. "No—if Saul shot the man, he had some reason other than merely being cursed or threatened. Of that I am sure."

"But what could it be, Father?"

"I do not know. I do know, however, that there are cloisters in the minds of the primitive peoples that no white man, no matter how close his association with them, may ever enter. I know, also, that their interpretation of our words and our acts is sometimes at wide variance with the meanings we wish to convey."

"No matter what his reason was," Downey said, "if he's crossed the line, I've got no authority to follow him. We'll have to take it up with the American authorities."

The good priest smiled. "The American authorities will pay scant heed to your request for his arrest. He is in an out of the way part of the country, and I doubt that they will even try to locate him. It is best, my son, that you yourself should question him."

"But—how?"

"I shall send for him."

"But will he come?" asked Downey, doubtfully.

"Yes, he will come. I shall send one of the young men for him tonight. Within ten days or two weeks, he should return."

"We might question his wife," Downey suggested.

Again the priest smiled. "It would be useless. Her loyalty to her husband would forbid her to speak. She would simply proclaim ignorance of any shooting, and beyond that veil of professed ignorance we could not penetrate. I know my people—their virtues, and their shortcomings."

"You're sure he'll come, if you send for him?" persisted Downey. "I hate to waste ten days or two weeks if I don't get results. If you're sure, though, I'll wait. There's been times that it's taken me longer than that to run down a murderer."

"He will come. I pledge you my word that you will be permitted to question Saul Nootka in this very room. Wait here, and I shall start a young man on his trail."

THE ENSUING days passed not too monotonously for Corporal Downey. He hunted moose in the hills with the priest, and observed with interest his self-imposed labors toward the welfare of his people, a simple, docile folk, whose respect and affection for the good father seemed genuine. And during the evenings there were long talks, in the course of which Downey's own respect grew for this man who was devoting his life to the welfare of this little band of unimportant folk, whose very existence was unknown even to the Government upon whose soil they made their home.

"How," asked Father Cassat, on the tenth evening, as the two sat talking together, "did you ascertain that Saul Nootka was the man who was encamped upon this survey line? Did he tell these surveyors his name?"

"No, it was Black John Smith who identified him through the pages of the old magazine he had discarded. He recognized it as one Cush had given Nootka for gun wadding."

"Ah, yes—Black John," repeated the priest with a smile. "A strange admixture of good and of evil."

Downey nodded. "His ethics are open to question. But in the long run it seems to me John does a lot more good than he does harm."

"I am inclined to agree with you, my son. A rough man, but a strong one. Had he not chosen the path of the outlaw, he might have exerted a powerful influence."

"He exerts a powerful influence, as it is," Downey replied with a grin. "An' among a bunch of men that, if it wasn't for him, would be the toughest men in the Yukon to handle. From the angle of the police, we're mighty glad he's on Halfaday."

A knock sounded on the door, and Father Cassat rose and opened it. A middle-aged Indian stood in the doorway, a smile on his wide, flat face.

"Come in, Saul," invited the priest. "There is a man here who wants to talk to you."

The man stepped into the room, and seeing Downey's uniform, nodded good-naturedly. "Hello, p'lice—you com' for git me? Me, I keel de man's oop by Fedder Crick. Som' tam p'lice com'—you bet."

Downey eyed the man in surprise. "Why did you kill him?" he asked.

"Keel um so he no kin keel ma 'oman—ma li'l babies."

"He wouldn't have killed your wife and babies! What do you mean?"

THE MAN nodded vigorously. "Sure—w'at you say, dam' right he keel um. Com' wan day, say, 'God dam' you Siwash git to hell out ma line.' Me, I'm not got hees line. He say 'you no git out tomor' I'm keek you tent to hell.' Me, I'm got ma tent beside de li'l spreeng for git de water. Plent' room w'ite man's go wan side—go nudder side. I'm ain' say nuttin'. I'm ain' move ma tent. Nex' day com' mans wit' ax cut down brush. Com's man w'it painted stick. Com's man wit talk-fas' gon—she de mans w'at tell me I'm got hees line. Me, I'm tak' ma gon an' go out in bush an' watch. Mans set oop de talk-fast' gon, an' aim it rat on ma

171

tent w'ere is ma 'oman an' ma li'l babies in dere. Den heem wait till de nudder mans cuts de brush so kin git good sight on tent. Den heem sight de talk-fast gon som' mor'—an' me—I'm shoot heem on de head, so he no kin shoot ma 'omen—ma li'l babies all to hell."

"Good God!" exclaimed Downey. "He thought the transit was a gun of some kind—a machine gun, prob'ly. But how could he know about machine guns."

"Fort Egbert," suggested the priest. "He cut wood near Fort Egbert."

The man nodded vigorously. "De talk fas' gon go put put put; put put put—mor' fas' lak you kin count. Me—I'm see de—w'at you call so'ger man's set oop de talk-fas gon on de t'ree leg—lay down on de bey, sight de gon, pull de trig—put put put; put put put. Me, I'm ain' want ma 'oman an' ma babies to git keel."

Downey sat for some seconds in silence. "It's too damn bad," he said. "The poor devil thought he was doin' right. If Jorden had used some sense in gettin' him off the line, he'd be alive today. After cussin' him out like that, no wonder Nootka thought he was goin' to shoot. You're dead right, Father, about the white man's acts an' his words sometimes registerin' all wrong in these people's brains."

"Yes. What will you do now?"

"There ain't only one thing I can do—take him in. He ain't no more guilty of a murder than you or I, but these Siwash homicides, especially where the victim is a white man, can't be passed over. He'll have to stand trial—and when the jury hears the evidence, I believe they'll turn him loose."

"But if they do not turn him loose?"

"Then he'll be sentenced. But the sentence will never be carried out—I'll see to that. It will go on the records, and then in a short time the man will be paroled, or maybe pardoned in full."

"You promise to see to this?"

"I promise, Father. I know the judge who will handle the case. The police are interested in justice—not in convictions."

The priest nodded. "I believe you, my son, and I will promise that his family shall not want while he is away."

Corporal Downey departed in the morning with his prisoner, who accompanied him without complaint after Father Cassat had explained to him in his own tongue the reason for the journey. They followed down the river on foot to the point where Downey had cached the canoe, there the Indian took his place in the bow, and Downey took the stern. Two days later, they stepped into Cushing's Fort to be greeted by Old Cush.

"Hello, Downey—step up an' have a drink! Hello, Saul—hit fer the kitchen an' tell the klooch to fix you up a bowl of stew."

The Indian looked questioningly at Downey who nodded. "Sure—go ahead. But, come back in here when you've finished."

"What you doin' with the Siwash?" asked Cush. "An' where in hell's Black John?"

VII

IN DAWSON, AFTER filing charges of kidnapping against Breedon and Sammy Cobb, Teasdale sought a barber shop, leaving the breed at police detachment dictating a statement to Constable Peters, under the watchful eye of Black John. Sammy's story was that Breedon had hired him to offer his services as guide to Teasdale, and if they were declined, to follow him and abduct him before he could reach Dawson, and hold him for a month. If they were accepted, the task would be easier. For this service Breedon paid him a hundred dollars, with the promise of another hundred at the end of a month. The bill that Black John had seen pass from Breedon to him was the promised hundred, which Cobb had demanded when he saw Breedon in irons. The wily breed was taking no chances of losing the second hundred.

Teasdale returned in an hour and Black John accompanied him to the office of the Consolidated, where they received an enthusiastic welcome from Chase.

"And now," continued Teasdale, as he finished recounting his adventure to the general manager, "this man here seems to have hit upon a scheme that occurred neither to Breedon nor to me. You'll remember that in my preliminary report, I mentioned a certain canyon through which the flume must pass, which is at one point so narrow that only one flume could possibly be constructed through it. It was this that made the completion of our survey ahead of Breedon of such vital importance. The outfit that first received the franchise would have a water monopoly on the Feather Creek workings. No matter if a second franchise were to be granted later, it would be a physical impossibility to construct a flume that would reach the lake without an unwarranted expenditure of money. I'm ashamed to have overlooked so obvious a solution, but as you know, Breedon's report while he was in our employ made no mention of such a canyon, and since then I've been so busy trying to push our survey on ahead of his that it never occurred to me to file a placer creek claim that would take in this canyon from rim to rim at that point."

"Does a creek flow through the canyon?" asked Chase.

"Oh, yes—at least a dribble that by courtesy can be called a creek."

Chase turned to Black John. "So you filed this claim?" he asked.

Black John nodded. "Yeah—it looked to me like a good proposition."

"Swell placer claim, eh?" grinned Chase.

The big man returned the grin. "Well, I wouldn't know about that till I'd had time to git down through the hard rock. But it shore is a swell flume right of way."

A clerk came in and laid a thick packet on the desk in front of Chase, who picked it up, and handed, it to Black John. "Here's your fifteen thousand," he said, "for returning Teasdale as per agreement. Now—how much do you want for your claim?"

"Well, like I told Teasdale—I ain't set no price on it."

"How does fifteen thousand strike you?"

"Not very favorable."

"Twenty-five thousand, then?"

"That's better, but I wouldn't like to make no snap decision. S'pose you jest put that offer in writin', an' give me a couple of hours to think it over. It's two o'clock now—I'll be back here at four."

"He'll go straight to Breedon with this offer—and of course Breedon will raise it!" objected Teasdale.

"Well," grinned Black John, "I'm hopin' he will."

"It's a virtual hold-up!" Teasdale exclaimed. "It's unethical in the extreme!"

BLACK JOHN'S grin widened so that white teeth flashed beneath the black beard. "Now, I'm glad you fetched up that subject of ethics. D'you rec'lect last year, on Squaw Crick, how the Consolidated—"

Chase interrupted, clearing his throat roughly. "I guess we can pass over the ethics of the matter," he said hastily. "The fact is, Black John is in a fine position to bargain, and there doesn't seem to be anything we can do about it." He turned to the big man. "Sure, I'll make that offer in writing. Take it to Breedon, and see what he'll do. If he won't raise the offer, come back here and get your money. If he does, come back anyway, and give us another bid. All I'm asking is that you'll give us a break."

Black John nodded. "I'll promise to give you a break, all right. So if you'll make out that offer I'll git goin'."

After visiting the office of an attorney, he proceeded to the police detachment where, knowing that Black John was working with Corporal Downey in some way, Constable Peters readily gave him permission to interview Breedon in his cell. The big man stepped into the cell room to be greeted by a string of curses that caused Sammy Cobb in an adjoining cell to grin with appreciation. Black John also grinned.

"Fer a man that's goin' to git hung fer murder, it looks like yer kickin' up a hell of a fuss over a little thing like a kidnappin' charge."

"I'll never hang for murder," cried Breedon. "Damn you, I didn't kill that man!"

"In sech case, you might be interested in a business deal. I rec'lect, back there on the river that first evenin', you mentioned some kind of a deal you wanted to make—but, somehow, you never got around to explainin' it—"

"Never explained it! If you weren't just a plain damned fool, you'd have known that the deal I referred to was the offer I made you to turn me loose!"

"Oh," exclaimed Black John, with a child-like smile, "that's what you was drivin' at? Turnin' down a deal like that wasn't foolishness; it was honesty. There's a difference, Breedon, that mebbe some folks wouldn't see. But I've got a deal here that might interest you."

Producing his claim grant, he thrust it between the bars of the cell, and as Breedon glanced at it the big man explained the facts as he had already explained them to Teasdale. Then, he showed him Chase's offer of twenty-five thousand dollars, cash.

Breedon glared at him. "So now you come to me with this, and if I should make you an offer you'd make me put it into writing, and then run back to Chase with it, and get a higher one from him—and come back to me—"

"Yeah," agreed Black John, "an' one of you would be bound to go higher'n the other one—an' I could sell out to the one that did."

"It's a damned hold-up," cried Breedon, "and I won't stand for it!"

"All right, jest give me back the paper, an' I'll go an' git the twenty-five thousan' off'n Chase."

"Look here," Breedon said, "if I'd offer thirty, Chase would offer thirty-five—then I'd have to go to forty, and so on. Now I'll tell you straight, man to man—neither one of us can go over fifty thousand, at the outside. If we went over that we'd lose money.

"You would, eh?"

"Absolutely—I'm giving it to you straight."

"Well, of course, I wouldn't want to see no one lose no money."

"Of course, not. You're an honest man; I've seen enough of you to know that—not overly smart, but honest. Now I'm perfectly honest and candid in telling you that fifty-thousand is absolutely the limit that either Chase or I could go on this deal. So, if I brush aside all quibbling with small raises of Chase's offers, will you sell me this claim at the top figure—fifty thousand dollars, in cash?"

Black John considered the proposition. "You got that much on you?" he asked at length.

"No, certainly not. But it's right here in Dawson. I can give you an order for it. I have more than that in the Tivoli safe—spot cash. What do you say?"

Black John hesitated. "Yer shore Chase wouldn't go no higher?" he asked.

"Absolutely sure. I'm giving you my word of honor."

"Oh. Well, in that case yer prob'ly right. Yes—I'll take the fifty thousan', an sign a transfer of the claim. But there's one thing I ought to tell you—I don't figger it would be plumb honest not to—an' that is—it's jest possible that this here canyon is acrost the line."

"What do you mean across the line—what line?"

"Why, the boundary line must run along in there somewheres. It might be in Alasky, an' in sech case, this paper wouldn't be no good—you can't file an American claim in Dawson."

"There's no boundary mark through there; what makes you think it's over the line?"

"I didn't say fer shore it's over the line. If it was, the recorder wouldn't of give me the papers. He don't know, an' a common man like me ain't s'posed to know more than a recorder. I jest said, mebbe."

"Well, I haven't completed the survey, but I don't believe the line runs very near there. If it does, damned if I'm going to pay fifty thousand for a worthless paper."

"All right—I jest thought I'd warn you. It ain't no more'n right that I should. No hard feelin's. I don't blame you none. I'll go an' sell the claim to Chase."

"But—Chase won't buy it, either."

"YEAH. HE ain't sech a good business man as you. He's willin' to take a chanct. I stopped in an' got a lawyer to make out a paper that Chase'll sign. I give him twenty-five dollars an' it didn't take him only a little while—no wonder lawyers gits rich. This here paper releases me from any responsibility—like fraud, er obtainin' money under false pretenses, er havin' to return the purchase price, in case the claim don't lie in Canadian territory. The purchaser assumes all the risk, an' the deal stands—no matter where the claim lays."

"And you say Chase will sign that?"

"Oh, shore—he's willin' to take a chanct."

"Well, by God, if he can afford to take a chance—I can! I know Chase, worked under him long enough to know that he comes pretty near to knowing what he's doing all the time. You take the transfer on to me, and I'll sign your release."

The papers were signed, Black John pocketing the release, and an order on the Tivoli for fifty thousand dollars in cash. When the business was concluded, he started for the door.

178

"Hold on!" cried Breedon. "You forgot to give me the transfer."

"No," the other replied, "I didn't fergit." He called loudly for Constable Peters, who stepped into the room. Black John handed him the transfer. "In case I ain't back here inside an hour to git this paper back," he instructed, "you turn it over to Breedon. It ain't nothin' but a claim grant—you kin read it."

Breedon sneered. "Don't trust me with it, eh?"

"Well, I'd hate fer you to have that there transfer, an' then find out you ain't got no fifty thousan' in the Tivoli safe."

"I trusted you with the order for the fifty thousand without first having the transfer in my hand."

"Oh, shore," replied Black John, "but you got to look at our reputations—I ain't no damn kidnapper."

Proceeding to the Tivoli, Black John collected the money, the packets of big bills being paid over without comment. Then he proceeded to the office of the Consolidated.

"Well," asked Chase, "what's the answer? Do we have to go to thirty-five thousand?"

"Nope," Black John replied, "the deal's closed."

"Closed! What do you mean?"

"Breedon, he bought the claim. Paid fifty thousan' fer it, cash money. When he explained to me how no one could go no higher'n that without losin' money on the deal, I didn't see no use wastin' time runnin' back an' forth. Besides, I wouldn't like fer you to lose no money—"

"But damn it, we'd have paid a hundred thousand, if we'd had to!"

"Yeah, but accordin' to Breedon, you'd of lost money. I wouldn't give a damn if the Consolidated would lose the money, but it might git you in bad. I kind of like you personal, ever sence that time I—"

"But I tell you we wouldn't have lost money. That Feather Creek flume might well be worth a million. That's a hell of a trick to play on me—when you promised to give me a break!"

Black John grinned. "I give you a break, all right—you might not know it, but I did—when I sold out to Breedon."

"What do you mean?"

"Meanin' that what green apples Breedon eats won't give you no bellyache. All I'm goin' to tell you is that if your boys up there beat Breedon's outfit to that canyon, you won't have to worry none about that claim. Breedon's a damn crook. He's goin' to be disapp'inted in that claim. I'll be goin', now."

CHASE LOOKED for a moment squarely into Black John's eyes. "I don't understand this deal," he said, "but somehow I believe you are giving me a break. Where are you going?"

"Back to Halfaday."

"Can I go with you?" asked Teasdale. "I've got to get back to the job."

"Shore," replied Black John. "Git yer outfit ready. I'll be pullin' out as quick as I kin git holt of a canoe."

Just below the mouth of Halfaday Creek, some seven days later, the two met young Emerson and two members of the Consolidated crew, coming downriver.

"The line's finished!" cried the young man. "We beat 'em to the canyon by two days. We'll get the franchise. And—say—we found that the lake and the canyon, too, are over in American territory."

"You don't say," drawled Black John, with a wink at Teasdale, who stared at him for a moment, and then threw back his head and laughed uproariously.

The engineer turned back to Dawson with the others, and Black John continued up Halfaday. Drawing out his canoe at the landing, he climbed the steep bank and stepped through the doorway of Cushing's Fort. Corporal Downey grinned broadly, as he pointed at the newcomer.

"Speak of the devil, an' up he pops. There's Black John now, Cush—you was just askin' for him."

"Jest in time fer a drink, John," said Old Cush. "Me an' Downey was about to h'ist one."

"Did you get Breedon to Dawson all right?" asked Downey.

"Oh shore. He wasn't no trouble—after he found out he couldn't bribe me. It shore beats hell, Downey, how crooked some folks is. Seems like they ain't got no ethics, at all. Do you know what he done—offered me five thousan' dollars to turn him loose. Jest as if I'd take money off'n him—fer doin' a trick like that! I'd say the sooner he's hung, the better."

"He ain't goin' to hang," said Downey. "The fact is, he didn't kill Jorden. It was the Siwash, Saul Nootka that shot him. I suspected him and went to the Stick village you told me about, and Nootka explained why he did it—the poor devil thought the transit was a Gatling gun, an' that Jorden was goin' to shoot up his wife an' kids with it. I've got him under arrest."

"Well—I'll be damned, But howcome you suspected him?"

"It was the wound in Jorden's head. When I saw that the bone where the bullet came out was splintered, I knew he had been shot with a soft lead slug, an' not a high-power bullet. Then I found where the killer had stood behind a clump of spruce, an' I found the waddin' out of his gun—an' the waddin' checked with the paper in that magazine you said Cush had given to Nootka."

"Good work," approved Black John.

"Common sense," grunted Downey. "Did you find out anything about Teasdale?"

"Yeah, I located him an' took him down to Dawson—an' that damn breed, Sammy Cobb, along with him. Breedon had hired Sammy to kidnap Teasdale an' hold him fer a month. Teasdale's got kidnap charges filed agin both of 'em. That's what took me so long—goin' back after Teasdale, when I found out he hadn't been to Dawson."

"Good work, John," approved Downey in turn. "How much do I owe you? Just make out a bill for your time, an' I'll O.K. it, an' you can stop in for the money next time you're in Dawson."

"Hell, Downey—you don't owe me nothin'! You know we always work hand in glove with the police, up here on Halfaday. Besides, I've had a lot of fun. I always like to see a damn crook like Breedon git what's comin' to him."

"But you're entitled to pay for your time," objected Downey.

BLACK JOHN grinned, and reaching into his pack sack tossed a thick packet of bills onto the bar. "I didn't lose nothin'," he said. "When Chase found out Teasdale was missin', he offered ten thousan' dollars reward fer him, an' another five thousan' on top of it fer the one that could cause the arrest of his murderer or abductor, if any. An' I copped off both them rewards."

"Fine!" exclaimed Downey. "I feel better about that matter of wages, now."

"Yeah, an' I feel even better'n that." Reaching again into his pack he tossed packet after packet of bills onto the bar. "Fifty thousan' dollars better." He turned to Cush, who was staring at the money in astonishment. "Jest stick that stuff in the safe, an' give me credit fer sixty-five thousan'," he said, "an' I'll buy a drink."

"But," asked Downey, "where did that come from?"

"I sold a claim."

"What claim?" asked Cush. "An' who'd you sell it to?"

"Oh a claim I took up when I was down to Dawson. I sold it to Breedon." He turned to Downey. "You rec'lect that narrow place in that canyon that both them outfits was racin' to run their line through first—well, I filed a claim on that place, that took in the canyon from rim to rim. Then I sold it to Breedon, so he could go ahead an' lay his flume on his own property, an' it wouldn't make no difference, if the Consolidated did git the franchise—there was only room fer the one flume anyhow."

"But," Downey exclaimed, "that canyon is over in American territory!"

"Yeah," grinned Black John, "but the recorder didn't know it, an' neither did Breedon. Of course," he added, "Breedon's bound to find it out, sometime. An' when he does, he ain't goin' to like it much."

Downey's eyes puckered into a frown. "An' then, what'll happen to you?"

Black John grinned. "Nothin'. You see, I give him warnin' that it might lay acrost the line, an' made him sign a, release that a lawyer draw'd up, freein' me from any claim or action agin me no matter where that claim laid. You see he know'd Chase was biddin' on the claim, too. I showed him Chase's offer in writin'. An' when I sort of hinted that Chase was willin' to take a chanct on the claim bein' in the Yukon, Breedon signed the release—'cause he didn't dare to turn it down."

"Huh," observed Cush, as he stowed the packets of bills in the safe, "if I'd of been him, I'd of wanted a damn sight more'n jest a hint from you that Chase would take a chanct on that claim layin' in the Yukon—before I'd of put out no fifty thousan' dollars. Huh-huh, it shore beats hell what some folks kin put acrost."

"Oh, I don't know," said Black John. "You see, he know'd I was honest 'cause I turned down that bribe. What I claim, the reputation fer honesty don't hurt no one." He appealed to the officer. "Does it, Downey?"

"Well, I'll be damned!" breathed Corporal Downey.

"Yeah? Oh, well, here's mud in yer eye. It always kind of tickles me to see one of them damn crooks git what's comin' to 'em."

FATHER JOHN

BLACK JOHN SMITH swung the canoe from his shoulders and returned down the mile-long portage trail around the Fish Rapids of the upper White River for his packsack. Half an hour later he deposited the pack beside the canoe, split a handful of kindlings from a dry spruce stump, lighted a fire, hung his tea pail above the flame, and proceeded to slice a liberal portion of bacon into a frying pan.

A light canoe rounded a bend upriver and rapidly approached the head of the rapid. It beached at the portage landing and a man stepped out and dragged the canoe clear of the water. He was a small man whose frail build suggested undernourishment. Black eyes peered with burning intensity from a face of waxy pallor. From beneath the brim of a flattish black hat silvery hair cascaded almost to the shoulders of a long black robe caught up at the belt by a thick woolen cord from which dangled an ivory cross.

Black John rose to his feet, his bearded lips parting in a smile as his eyes rested momentarily upon the thin, well-formed nose, and the delicately chiseled lips that stood out in sharp contrast to the rugged outline of the country, with its towering mountains, and its rock-ribbed canyon into which the waters of the river plunged with a low roar in a welter of foaming whitewater. For he knew this little priest as a man mighty in spirit as he was frail in body.

"Hello, Father! Jest in time to help me git rid of a bang-up fryin' of bacon an' beefsteak. I'm shore glad you happened along. It's kind of lonesome for a man to be eatin' supper all by himself."

THE THIN lips smiled. "Beefsteak, did you say, John? You mean moosesteak?"

"Not by a damn sight! I've be'n down to Dawson an' I laid in enough honest-to-God beefsteak to last me clean to Halfaday. What I claim, if a man's got to chaw moosemeat most of the year he's entitled to fill up on beefsteak whenever he kin git it. I'll bet it's quite a while sence you've et any beefsteak."

"Not so long as one might think. Last fall in Montreal and in Ottawa I had beefsteak, and also many other good things which one is denied in the outlands."

"That's so. Me an' Cush heard you'd gone outside last fall. Figgered you'd quit. Convertin' them Stick Siwashes must be a hell of a job, at best."

"You knew I had not quit," the little man replied, and again he smiled as his intense black eyes met the twinkling eyes of blue.

"Shore, we know'd you hadn't quit, Father. I was only kiddin'. But I never even got a raise out of that one, did I? How's things on Feather Crick?"

"Not good. The forces of evil are at work among my people."

"The devil kind of got the jump on you while you was gone, eh? Tell you what you do, Father—chase him over onto Halfaday an' we'll call a miners' meetin' an' convict the son-of-a-gun of some kind of skullduggery an' hang him."

"I wish I could do just that. Only this time there are two devils."

"Chase 'em both over. Hell—two, er a dozen—it's all the same to us! Did someone move in on Feather Crick while you was away?"

"No. When I returned, late in the fall, my people were as I had left them. It is a long story. A condition has fallen upon them for which I fear I myself am to blame."

"I'll bet you're the only one that would figger it that way. But let's fergit the damn Siwashes till after supper." Fumbling in his packsack, the big man drew out a black bottle and a tin cup into which he poured a liberal potion. "Throw this into you while I fry up the steak. After we've et we'll fill up our pipes an' you kin tell me all about it. You know damn well, Father, that if me er Cush kin do anything fer you, all you've got to do is to holler."

Stepping to the river the priest diluted the liquor with water and returned to the fire to sip it slowly as the beefsteak sizzled in the pan. Billows of savory smoke surged into the big man's face as he held the frying pan over the coals. He turned his head away, coughing, and, reaching for the bottle, took a deep long pull at it, rasping the dregs from his throat. "Never seen a damn campfire yet that the smoke didn't git in yer eyes, no matter which way the wind blow'd!"

The little priest smiled. "Do you know, John, you've never grown up. You are just a little boy."

"Huh?" The big man peered across the fire in startled surprise.

The smile widened. "Yes—just a wayward little boy who blusters and swaggers and says 'hell' and 'damn' where he thinks it will shock people. But it does not shock me in the least. Deeds rather than words mark the true measure of a man. And those of us who know you best realize that, despite much that is to be deprecated in your make-up, in your heart there is more of good than of evil."

"Well—I'll be damned!"

"Possibly. That is not for me to say. Nor is it for me to either countenance nor condone your loose code of ethics."

The big man laughed. "Dig yer dishes out of yer pack, Father. I ain't got but the one set with me. We want to git at this steak while it's hot. No wonder yer so damn little an' skinny—launchin' into abstract theological problems instead of beefsteak! Hold yer plate, now, while I fork this slab of meat onto it."

The meal over, Black John tossed the other his tobacco pouch, and producing a porcelain pipe bowl from his pack, the little priest fitted a long wooden stem into it, filled the bowl, lighted it with a coal from the fire, and puffed contentedly while the big man washed the dishes.

Lighting his own pipe, Black John glanced across at the priest: "What's this here two-devil business that's botherin' you? Mebbe it ain't as bad as you think. Anyways, it won't hurt to git it off yer chest. What I claim, there can't nothin' happen, outside of earthquakes an' high water, that you can't do somethin' about if you go at it right."

The priest slowly shook his head. "There is nothing you or I can do, John. This is a matter for the police."

"Yeah?—Well, listen—there's be'n several times when things has popped up on Halfaday an' vicinity that a person would say, offhand, was matters for the police—but which, in fact, was adjudicated an' disposed of in a highly satisfactory manner without no police interference whatever. S'pose you jest start in at the beginnin' an' spill me an earful."

"Well—as you know, for upwards of twenty years I have labored among the Stick Indians, and by dint of hard work and vast patience, have succeeded in gathering into a little community on Feather Creek, some ninety souls. I have encouraged them to trap, and to fish, and to hunt in the proper seasons. And to lay by food for the winter instead of living the hand-to-mouth existence of the scattered Indians of the mountains. I have also induced them to plant small gardens. And in about one year in three we harvest enough of potatoes and other vegetables to last us far into the winter. One year we ripened some barley. We have built log houses and a church. But we are very poor, and existence is hard, even in the good years. However, we are better off than many others. And I have continued to look after the welfare of my people, both temporal and spiritual. Some men of the police, notably Inspector Jarvis and Corporal Downey, know of my work among these people and approve it."

"Shore they do, Father. So do me an' Cush. You're one missionary that had sense enough to look after the temporal part before you tackled the spiritual."

"Last fall," continued the priest, ignoring the interruption, "I traveled to Dawson and spoke to these men, asking them if it would not be possible to secure treaty money for my Indians, and they suggested that I go to Ottawa and take the matter up with those in authority there. They both provided me with letters commending my work, and recommending that any aid possible be accorded me.

"I therefore journeyed to Ottawa and to Montreal where I held many conferences with those high in authority of both the Church and the State. I shall not burden you with the details—suffice it to say that in the face of what appeared at first to be insurmountable difficulties and objections, I finally succeeded in convincing the proper persons of the crying need of my people, and of the justice of bringing them within the treaty bounty.

"The result was that early this spring a treaty party arrived on Feather Creek and paid the bounty which, with certain back payments that I had convinced them had accrued, amounted to one hundred and seventeen dollars for each of the ninety members of my community.

"Now, one hundred and seventeen dollars is not wealth. But, as I pointed out to my people, if they should continue to hunt, and to fish, and to trap, and to plant their gardens as they have done in the past, this money, if frugally and judiciously expended, would go a long way toward alleviating their suffering for many years to come.

"They are, for the most part, a docile folk. And I had hoped that they would see eye to eye with me in this matter. In order to conserve their competence I suggested that they turn their money over to me to hold in trust for them. In other words, I would act as their bank, doling out the money to them as seemed expedient for their welfare.

"**BUT, OWING** mainly to the subversive advice of four men among them—men who speak English, and who have worked on the fishing boats of the coast, and the steamboats of the Yukon, they refused to turn over their money to me. A few allowed me to keep part of their competence—but pitifully few. I am holding only four hundred and twelve dollars out of the ten thousand five hundred and thirty dollars that they received.

"Word of the payment had evidently become noised about, for two weeks ago I noticed that many of my people were drinking liquor. Most of the men, many of the women, and even some of the children were becoming drunk nearly every night. I had seen no white men about, nor could I find any, though I searched diligently. Questioning proved of no avail as the men would not talk, and those of the women who might have told me of the source of this liquor feared to do so.

"Finally one woman, the wife of one of the four who speak English and the worst drunkard of them all, came to me and told me that two white men were selling the liquor, and that their camp was at the mouth of a small feeder, some three miles below the village.

"I visited the place immediately, but the men had evidently just departed from there. I believe that inasmuch as these men knew of the treaty payment they must also know the amount of money paid. I believe that they risked only a small stock of liquor on this first tentative venture, and obtained only a relatively small part of the treaty money. And I believe that they will return. Having found out that the Indians will buy their liquor they have hastened to Dawson or to Whitehorse for a new supply. The woman told me that they charged two dollars a quart for the liquor, and that it was three parts water."

Black John, who had listened to the recital without interruption or comment, removed the pipe from his lips and spat into the fire. "You done wrong in not havin' the treaty money paid over to you in the first place, instead of to the Siwashes," he opined.

"Ah, but I tried to do that! I foresaw what might happen if these people came suddenly into possession of this money. And I tried to impress upon those in authority the importance of allowing me to handle the fund as the trustee of my people. But they said it could not be done. Each Indian must receive his allotment personally, and receipt for it personally, with his or her mark. And so it was done."

"Uh-huh. Jest another evidence of the damn fool way Governments do things. Some ten-dollar-a-week clerk back there in Ottawa—an' it might jest as well have be'n in Washington, er Paris, er Berlin, accordin' to what country was involved—sets there an' figgers an easy way of doin' a thing so it'll work out nice with his filin' system—an' that's the way it's got to be done—come hell er high water! There ain't no sech thing as takin' into account the special requirements of an individual case, er of listenin' to advice from someone that knows somethin' about what's got to be done—hell no! The formula's be'n worked out—an' the system'll be followed, no matter if it wipes out a band of Siwashes, er sinks a battleship! Because if it ain't done that way the ten-dollar-a-week clerk back there in Ottawa might ball up his file. An' that's Government efficiency!"

"I fear there is much truth in what you say, John. But nothing can be accomplished by sitting here and recounting the short-comings of the Government. It seems that once a certain routine has been established it becomes as unchangeable as the law of the Medes and the Persians."

"Yeah," agreed the big man dryly. "An' you kin take notice that there ain't a Mede left—an' damn few Persians! Mebbe if their laws had be'n more flexible they'd have survived. Govern-ments could learn a lot by studyin' hist'ry, if they wasn't so damn dumb. What do you figger to do about it?"

"Why, I am hastening to Dawson to impress the police with the importance of taking immediate action in the matter. They must prevent these men from returning to Feather Creek with a further supply of liquor."

BLACK JOHN frowned. "You'd be all right, Father, if you could git in touch with Corporal Downey er Inspector Jarvis. But I doubt that you kin reach either one of'em quick enough to do any good. I jest come from Dawson, an' I know that Jarvis has gone down to Eagle, an' Downey's somewheres upriver. We come up together till I branched off at the mouth of the White. He was goin' on up to investigate a murder somewheres up the Pelly. There's half a dozen rookies in Dawson under Constable

Blake. But I'm doubtin' that Blake would detail a man to go back with you on account of bein' left short-handed in case someone would spit on the sidewalk, er discharge a firearm on Sunday."

"But he *must* send someone! This is a matter of life and death to a great many natives. My labor of twenty years may be rendered useless within the course of a few days if those men are allowed to return to Feather Creek with liquor. It is a matter of the utmost importance. Surely this Constable Blake will realize that!"

"Yeah? Well—try it an' see. On yer way back you might stop in to Cush's an' tell me what luck you had."

"But he must be made to realize the importance and the urgency of this matter! What else can I do? What would you advise?"

Black John gazed into the fire for several moments in silence. "Was one of these damn hooch runners tall an' the other one short?" he asked abruptly. "An' was the tall one carryin' his left shoulder a little higher'n his right, an' stickin' his head kinda forward, like he was lookin' over a fence?"

"I do not know what they looked like. I did not see them, and the woman did not describe them to me."

"Did they see you?"

"That I cannot say. I do not believe that they have seen me, as the woman told me they did not venture onto Feather Creek beyond the mouth of the feeder. The Indians went to them for their liquor."

"W-e-e-l-l," drawled the big man, after refilling his pipe, "mebbe it would be jest as well fer you to go on down to Dawson. Like I said, I don't believe you kin git it through Blake's skull that yer predicament is anything more than an interestin' incident. But yer luck might be that either Downey er Jarvis'll git back to Dawson within the next few days. I don't believe yer hooch runners are on their way to Dawson er Whitehorse, either one. I've be'n four days on the White, an' if they'd be'n comin' down, I sure would of met 'em."

"But where else could they obtain the liquor?"

"They might buy it from Cush. His place is the clostest to Feather Crick, an' it would save 'em a lot of time an' hard work."

"But Cushing would not sell them liquor to trade to the Indians. I'm sure of that."

"Not if he know'd what they was goin' to do with it, he wouldn't," Black John agreed.

"But they might have some story cooked up about what they wanted it fer. I happen to know that Cush has got a lot of surplus liquor on his hands owin' to a deal he put over when Jake Cavanaugh went broke in Whitehorse. Mebbe he'd jump at the chanct to git red of a couple of bar'ls at a profit. After all, he ain't so wide between the ears. A good smart lie might fool him. While you're down to Dawson I'll jest sort of poke around upriver an' see what I kin do."

"But, John—what can you do? You are not of the police. You know you have no authority."

"No? Well—mebbe yer right. But we've got laws on Halfaday that's workable because they're more er less flexible. We ain't like them Medes an' Persians. We aim to survive."

II

THE TWO BREAKFASTED early the following morning and in the first gray of dawn Black John helped the little priest portage his outfit around the rapid, and pushed on upriver. Ascending Halfaday Creek he reached Cushing's Fort, the log trading post and saloon that catered to the wants of the little community of outlawed men that had sprung up close against the Yukon-Alaska border, shortly after dark.

Avoiding the front door he entered by way of the kitchen, passed through into the storeroom, and glued his eye to a slit in the wall by means of which one might see and hear whatever was going on in the barroom where at the moment a stud game was in progress and three or four men stood drinking at the bar.

After a few moments of scrutiny he reentered the kitchen and passed on into the proprietor's private apartment where he removed his coat and pacs, lay down on the bunk, and was soon fast asleep.

Hours later he was awakened by the opening of the door as Cush entered, lighted the glass bracket lamp, and turned to stare in open-mouthed surprise. "What the hell you doin' here?" he demanded. "You drunk, er somethin'?"

Black John sat up, swung his feet to the floor, and reached for a pac. "Nope. Jest ketchin' me a little sleep. I've had a hard day. Come clean on up from the Fish Rapids."

"What time did you git here?"

"Little after dark. What time is it now?"

Cush consulted a thick silver watch. "It's half past two. I jest closed up. Some of the boys was playin' stud. But why the hell didn't you come in the saloon when you got here?"

"I was tired an' in no mood fer revelry."

"Huh—first time I ever seen you too tired fer deviltry! But if you was so damn tired, why didn't you go to yer own cabin instead of crawlin' into my bed?"

The big man laced his pacs and put on his coat. "I wanted to speak with you in private," he grinned. "When I got here I stopped an' took a squint through the peekhole an' seen that a couple of strange faces was in our midst. Fetch the lamp an' we'll go out an' have a snort. It's customary fer the house to set 'em up when a newcomer arrives, ain't it?"

"Yeah, but you ain't no newcomer on Halfaday—an' never was." Picking up the lamp, Cush led the way to the bar, set out a bottle and two glasses, and made an entry in his well-thumbed day book.

"Hey!" Black John cried. "If you ain't buyin' the drinks, we'll shake fer 'em! What the hell you chargin' 'em up agin' me fer?"

"Bed rent," grunted Cush, as he filled his glass. "An' it's about time you was gittin' back, what with them two strangers showin' up on the crick an' pesterin' me to sell 'em three hundred gallon of licker."

"Got quite a thirst, ain't they?"

"Huh—you know damn well they ain't no two men is gain' to drink no three hundred gallon of licker."

"Time an' diligence would accomplish it."

"They claim they's a new stampede on somewheres they call Loon Crick an' they aim to sell the licker to a feller that's goin' to start a saloon there. But I ain't never heer'd of no Loon Crick, nor neither I ain't heer'd of no new stampedes. What I figger, they aim to peddle it to some Siwashes, somewheres. So I be'n stallin' 'em off till you got back. I know'd you'd be along pretty quick."

"I assume that these men have demonstrated their ability to pay fer this liquor?"

"If you mean have they got the money, they have. They banked—"

"Twenty thousan' dollars in used mixed bills," Black John interrupted.

"Twenty thousan' nine hundred an' sixty," Cush corrected.

"H-u-u-m, so their Feather Crick venture netted 'em nine sixty, eh?"

"What do you know about 'em? An' what do you mean about Feather Crick?"

"Downey happened to mention a certain bankin' irregularity in which a cashier was killed an' twenty thousan' dollars changed hands without benefit of a check book somewheres down in Alberta. The Feather Crick incident was what you might say, a sequel."

"Does that mean they cleaned up that nine sixty sellin' hooch to them Siwashes on Feather Crick?"

"That's Father Cassatt's story—an' I believe him."

"I mistrusted them damn coots was up to somethin' like that! An' here they want to buy three hundred gallon more!"

"Well—why don't you sell it to 'em? You've got a lot of that Cavanaugh liquor on hand that you could git rid of at a profit. It don't stand you no more'n five dollars a gallon delivered right here. You as good as stole it."

"What—an' have 'em peddle it out to them Siwashes? Not by a damn sight! I don't need no profits that bad. Father Cassatt's worked like hell up there amongst them Siwashes, an' I wouldn't do nothin' to hinder him. I like the little cuss. What we'd ort to do is hang them two, instead of sellin' 'em any licker!"

Black John shook his head. "It wouldn't be ethical, Cush. You see, Feather Crick, by no stretch of the imagination, could be included within our jurisdiction. An occasional hangin' here on Halfaday has a salutory effect on the remainin' citizens, an' thus tends to uphold the morality of the crick. But if we was to indulge in an orgy of promiscuous hangin's over a wide spread area it might arouse onfavorable comment in certain sources. This Feather Crick venture has no Halfaday angle whatever. The only way the case could properly be brought within our jurisdiction would be to tie it in somehow with Halfaday—like, for instance, if these men should purchase liquor here, an' pack it to Feather Crick, an' sell it to the Siwashes. In sech case I'd feel jestified in sort of talkin' a hand in the game, an' seein' what could be done about it."

"If you'd quit talkin' like some damn preacher, er lawyer, er somebody, an' come right out an' say what you mean, mebbe someone would know what yer talkin' about," growled Cush. "What yer tryin' to git at, I s'pose—if I was to sell 'em this licker, an' they was to pack it over to Feather Crick an' sell it to them Siwashes, then we could go ahead an' hang 'em?"

"That's the thought."

"But how would we git holt of 'em? S'pose they cleaned up over there an' kep' right on a-goin'?"

"Where would they go to? They'll come back, all right. They think Halfaday is a place where a criminal is safe, er they wouldn't be here."

"That's right," Cush agreed. "They be'n askin' about you. Claim they want to hook up with you. That's how I be'n stallin' 'em along. Told 'em you was liable to show up any minute. But they're hell bent to get back to Feather Crick an' clean up on them Siwashes. They claim their hurry is 'cause this here fella that was aimin' to start that there saloon on this here Loon Crick might buy his licker in Dawson er Whitehorse if they didn't git it there pretty quick."

"They'll come back, all right," Black John said. "How much did they offer you fer the licker?"

"Eight dollars a gallon."

"Hum—le's figger a little. Them Feather Crick Siwashes got ten thousan' five hundred an' thirty dollars in treaty money, an' these fellas evidently got nine hundred an' sixty of it. That would leave ninety-five hundred an' seventy still on Feather Crick. Three hundred gallon, after it's cut, would give 'em twelve hundred gallon of trade liquor, which at eight dollars a gallon would come to ninety-six hundred dollars. They've got it figgered down pretty clost, all right. Why don't you go ahead an' sell it to 'em? Of course, you could make a lot more sellin' the stuff over the bar by the drink, but this way you'll make a quick turn-over an' nine hundred dollars profit on the deal—an' it'll give us a chanct to teach these boys a lesson."

"Why can't I claim I can't only spare thirty, forty gallon—er mebbe fifty? That would hook 'em up with Halfaday jest the same as if they got the hull three hundred."

"Nope. I want 'em to git every damn nickel of that treaty money away from them Siwashes. I've got my reasons."

"Huh," grunted Cush. "If I didn't know damn well you don't favor sellin' hooch to Siwashes no more'n what I do, I wouldn't have nothin' to do with it. But if you've got some reasons fer gittin' all that money, I'll play along with you, even if the difference in sellin' that there three hundred gallon by the bulk instead of over the bar will cost me a sight of money.

"It'll be worth whatever it costs to git the chanct to hang them damn cusses. But I shore hope nothin' goes wrong. It would be hell if they was to git away with that Siwash treaty money."

"They ain't apt to," Black John replied. "I'm hittin' out at daylight fer Feather Crick. It's only about forty mile, straight acrost. The way these fellas'll go, down Halfaday an' up the White, it's a lot further. Father Cassatt's gone on down to Dawson to try to git the police on the job. He promised to stop in here an' let me know what luck he had. If I ain't back by the time he gits here, you hold him till I do come. Don't tell him where I've gone. Tell him I'm out moose huntin'. In the meanwhile, there'll be a new priest lookin' after the welfare of them Feather Crick Siwashes."

"What priest is that?" Cush asked.

"His name is Father John."

"You mean—you? Cripes—you'd make a hell of a priest! An' besides Father Cassatt ain't half as big as what you be. If you tried to git into one of them black dresses of hisn, you'd look like you was runnin' around in a shimmy!"

"You fergit," replied Black John, "that I still possess that robe that was stole off'n a priest on Tagish some time back. You rec'lect we rigged Pot Gutted John out in it onct. If it fit him, it'll shore as hell fit me."

"Huh, you've got the damndest way of goin' at things—but it gen'ly works," Cush admitted grudgingly. "What'll I tell them damn cusses about you not showin' up? They're plumb anxious to meet up with you."

"They'll meet up with me, all right," replied the big man, grimly. "Tell 'em I sent word by a Siwash that I was stayin' down to Dawson fer another week er ten days. That'll give 'em a chanct to clean up that Feather Crick job an' git back here about the time I do."

"They've heer'd how you hang folks, up here—an' they're anxious to git on the good side of you. They call you the King of the Outlaws—the man that held up an army. Someone's shore be'n feedin' 'em a lot of crap!"

III

IT WAS LATE in the evening of the second day thereafter when Black John reached Feather Creek. Under cover of darkness he slipped into Father Cassatt's cabin, close beside the little log church surmounted by its wooden cross. He went to bed without making a light, and in the morning donned a long black robe which he drew from his packsack, and stepped out to stand before the church.

A young Indian woman who was passing stopped and stared at him in wide-eyed surprise. Raising a hand, Black John beckoned to her and when she stood before him he said solemnly: "Ora pro nobis, sister," not to mention other matters. The young woman continued to stare at him uncomprehendingly. "Do you savvy English?" he asked. But still she stood dumbly staring at him. He tried to jargon. *"Mika kumtux Boston wawa?"*

She continued to stare for a moment, then turned abruptly and hastened toward a small group of cabins that were visible down the creek. She entered one of the cabins from which two men presently emerged and walked toward him. When they halted before him Black John spoke.

"There's a couple of men here that savvy English," he said. "Father Cassatt told me there was four of you—men that have worked on the river, an' along the coast. I'm here to sort of look after things till Father Cassatt comes back. Go git them other two an' fetch 'em here. I've got some things to tell you fer yer own good."

One of the men turned away, halted, and pointed in the direction of the cabins where two other men were approaching. "Dem com'," he said. "Natla tell um new pries' wan' see um."

When the two had joined the others Black John led the way into Father Cassatt's house. "Now about this here hooch business," he began abruptly, and noted the sullen look that crept into their faces. "Regardin' the drinkin' of hooch there's two schools of thought—one holdin' it to be wrong; an' the other can't see no harm in it. Father Cassatt's a good man. He's your friend—don't never think he ain't. An' he's a friend of mine, too. He thinks you men hadn't ort to drink hooch—an' mebbe he's right. He's gone down to Dawson to git the police to come up here an' arrest the two men that's be'n sellin' hooch to you.

"But me—I don't see no harm in a man's takin' a drink now an' then when he needs one. So bein' as I'm in charge of this here parish while he's gone, I'm slippin' you boys the word that them two men are on the way up here with a fresh batch of hooch. They're got three hundred gallon—a big batch, this time." He paused for a moment, noting that the faces of the four had brightened perceptibly. "Now, you boys know that by the time you git this liquor it's be'n cut by addin' three quarts of water to a quart of whiskey fer a gallon. When it's cut there'll be twelve hundred gallon, an' they'll git two dollars a quart fer it, which is eight dollars a gallon. But they won't have time to git rid of much of it before the police comes. The police'll arrest 'em an' pour out all the hooch on the ground—so you won't git none of it.

"Now, if I was you boys an' wanted that hooch, I'd git to these men when they first hit the crick, an' I'd buy the three hundred gallon before the police gits here. You'll have to pay thirty-two dollars a gallon fer it—but that's the same price you've be'n payin'—when you come to figger that three quarts out of every four in a gallon is water. If you buy it straight you kin cut it yerselves, er drink it straight, whichever you like. About half whiskey an' half water makes a good drink fer wimmin an' kids—an' is favored by some men. Anyways, you could cut it to suit yerselves—them likin' it strong could put in less water.

"But like I said, you'll have to work fast to git it at all. So if I was you I'd hustle around an' git hold of every dollar you kin git yer hands on, an' buy up them three hundred gallon, an' cache 'em somewheres before Father Cassatt gits back here with the police."

When the big man had concluded, the four held a whispered conversation. One of them asked, "W'en de mans com' wit' de hooch?"

"They'd ort to be here tomorrow er next day. They might even make it tonight. They'll take it to the same place they took the other batch. So if you'll show me where the place is I'll sort of hang around there an' let you know when they git here. In the meanwhile, you kin be gittin' that money together. An' remember, you better git every dollar you kin. This is yer last chanct. You won't git another break like this agin—if you live to be a hundred."

There was no trace of sullenness on the smiling faces of the four, as one of them said, "You good pries'! You no say we no kin drink de hooch!"

"Well, like I said, it's the way a man looks at it. Come on— one of you show me where this place is, an' the other three kin git busy collectin' that money."

Black John accompanied one of the Indians to a campsite in a thick growth of young spruce near the mouth of a feeder that ran into Feather Creek about a mile above its confluence with the White River. The Indian returned hastily to join the others in the collection of the money, and Black John took a more leisurely pace back to the priest's house.

Toward noon the next day the big man lay in the spruce thicket and watched two sweating white men and six natives remove thirty ten-gallon kegs from four canoes and pack them to the campsite where they set up a small tent. When the natives had disappeared in the direction of the village, he stepped abruptly into the tiny clearing where the kegs were piled before the tent.

The two men stared in angry surprise as the taller of them— the one with the outthrust head and the high left shoulder— jerked a nickel-plated revolver from his pocket and leveled it. "What the hell d'you want around here?" he demanded. "Beat it, before I put a bullet through you!"

The big man held up his right hand, palm foremost. "Put up your pistol, my son," he uttered, in a deep soothing voice. "I come to you in peace—not in war."

Seeing that he was unarmed, the man lowered the pistol. "What do you want?" he growled.

"Merely a few words with you—words that may prove of profit to you and to me."

"What d'you mean—profit to you?"

"It is thus. I know that you have come here to sell liquor to my people. I know that you have been here before. I know that you charged them two dollars a quart, which is eight dollars a gallon, for liquor that was three-fourths water. And I know that you took from them a matter of nine hundred and sixty dollars. That made me very angry and I dispatched a young woman whose husband was drinking heavily to notify the police who should arrive here within a day or two to arrest you and to destroy your liquor.

"But now that you have arrived before them, it seems there is nothing I can do to prevent you from selling your unholy wares. Such being the case I can see no reason why I, also, should not make some slight profit on the venture. I have great influence among my people, though I have not yet succeeded in persuading them not to drink liquor. But they follow my advice in many things. I see you have here thirty kegs of ten gallons' capacity each. Now it will be impossible for you to dilute and sell, piecemeal, any considerable portion of this liquor before the police arrive and arrest you and destroy the remaining liquor. But if you could sell it all, just as it is, in one quick transaction, you would save all the labor of diluting it, yet you would make the same profit. You could also leave here and be well away before the police arrive. My people still have more than nine thousand dollars of their treaty money. Now if I should advise them to bring this money here and buy this liquor, how much would you be willing to pay me for my part of the affair?"

"You mean, you'll tell 'em to buy it in a lump, an' let us git out of here? It'll cost 'em thirty-two dollars a gallon."

"Yes, I understand that. That is my proposition."

"How much do you want?"

"It strikes me that a thousand dollars would be none too much to ask, in view of the fact that it eliminates any chance of your arrest, besides doing away with a great deal of labor and delay."

"Hell—let's pay it to him!" exclaimed the short, stocky man. "We sure as hell can't afford to be picked up by the Mounted! We'd still make plenty on the deal."

"Okay," the other agreed. "When kin you pull it off?"

"At noon, tomorrow. I will bring the Indians here with the money."

"How many of 'em?" asked the tall man suspiciously.

"There are only four men among them who speak English. I shall bring those four."

"Okay—but they ain't to come heeled."

"Heeled? I do not believe I understand you, my son."

"They ain't to fetch no guns along, nor neither no revolvers. We ain't takin' no chances."

"Very well. It shall be as you say. I shall personally vouch for your safety until you are well away from Feather Creek."

"Okay—be seein' you tomorrow noon."

JUST BEFORE noon on the following day Black John, clad in his long black robe, and accompanied by the four English-speaking Indians, stepped into the little clearing. The tent had been struck and loaded into the canoe. Only the thirty kegs remained in the clearing. Each Indian produced a huge roll of money which the two men took and eagerly counted before slipping them into an open packsack.

"You've only got nine thousan' an' ninety-one dollars here," announced the tall man, as he figured with the stub of a lead pencil. "An' that only pays fer two hundred an' eighty-four gallon—we'll call it two hundred an' ninety, fer good measure. We won't bust a keg. We're takin' one keg back with us, at that."

Black John stepped close to the tall man as he was about to fasten the straps of the packsack containing the money. "Have you forgotten my thousand dollars?" he asked in an undertone.

The tall man thrust his face even farther forward as he fixed the black-robed one with glittering narrowed eyes. "No, we ain't fergot that thousan'—by a damn sight. But you kin fergit it. Yer a hell of a priest—sellin' yer Siwashes out fer a thousan' dollars! The only differences between you an' this here Judas Ishcariot it tells about in yer Bible is that he got his thirty pieces of silver—but you ain't got yer thousan'—by a damn sight!" Pulling the revolver from his pocket he covered the five, calling to his partner over his shoulder, "Grab up the pack, Shorty, an' hit fer the canoe. Then take yer rifle an' stand these birds off till I git in!"

The man called Shorty pushed the canoe into the water, deposited the packsack amidships, and took his seat in the stern while the other backed down the slope, pistol in hand. Stepping into the light craft, the tall man shoved off, and a moment later the outfit disappeared around a bend, borne by the swift current.

The instant they passed from sight Black John leaped high into the air with an unearthly bellow and came down swinging an ax which he had concealed beneath his long black robe. Swinging the ax about his head, he whirled to confront the four astounded Indians, eyes glittering, and white teeth gleaming behind his black beard as his lips drew back in a hideous grin.

"Priest! Priest!" he screamed in a high falsetto. "Ha, ha, ha! They think I'm a priest! I'm a crazy man! I'm a devil! I cut men up an' eat their hearts. Y-e-e-o-w!" He leaped toward the astounded Indians swinging his ax aloft. "I'll eat your hearts an' drink the warm blood. W-a-a-h-o-o!"

The four stood not upon the order of their going. They fled down the slope toward the village, and as they went crashing through the underbrush Black John stood emitting a series of wild weird yells that echoed from the hills like the screech of a banshee. Then he deliberately smashed in the heads of the twenty-nine kegs, and grinned as the liquor gushed out and soaked into the ground. When the last drop disappeared he removed the long robe, rolled it up and placed it in his pack-sack and struck out for Halfaday Creek.

IV

STEPPING INTO CUSH'S saloon just on the edge of darkness the following evening, he was greeted by Father Cassatt who had arrived only an hour before.

"Hello, John! Cush tells me you have been moose hunting. Were you successful?"

"Never even seen a moose. But I didn't expect to see you here. Thought you was hittin' fer Dawson to tell the police about some hooch runners polutin' yer Siwashes."

"I was fortunate in running onto Corporal Downey at the mouth of the White. He was going down to Dawson with a prisoner. You remember you told me he had gone up the Pelly to investigate a murder. He got his man, and was taking him to Dawson. He promised to hasten to Feather Creek as soon as he got his man behind bars in Dawson. So I returned, stopping here as I promised to let you know what luck I had with the police, and also to procure some much-needed supplies."

"You was lucky, to run onto Downey," Black John said. "You prob'ly wouldn't of got no action out of Blake till 'long about groundhog day."

"Yes, I was lucky. But even so, should those men return to Feather Creek before Downey could get there they would do much harm. And I greatly fear they may be there even now. Cushing tells me he sold three hundred gallons of whiskey to two men only the other day. He said they told him they intended to resell it to a man who contemplated opening a saloon at a place they called Loon Creek. I have never heard of a Loon Creek, nor have I heard of any new stampede. I fear that this liquor is even now being sold to my people, and that they will have little, if any, of the treaty money left by the time Corporal Downey gets there."

"Yeah, but if Downey gits holt of the money, he'll turn it back to the Siwashes."

"True. But these men may be able to obtain the money and be gone with it before he gets there. Is there not something you can do, John? You remember you promised me you would look around and see what you could do. Can you not accompany me to Feather Creek tomorrow?"

Black John shook his head slowly. "No, Father, I don't believe I could do you no good by goin' over there. You see, some of them Siwashes of yourn might recognize me, an' whatever influence I might have over 'em would be impaired by my reputation. It might even affect your hold on 'em—consortin' with an outlaw, that-a-way. They might think that I ain't no companion fer a priest to cultivate."

"I do not believe that any of my people have ever seen you— much less would they know of your reputation."

"I don't know about that. You claimed that four of 'em could talk English, an' had worked along the river. Them four might of seen me somewheres. An' a reputation is like news—the worse it is, the faster it travels. If I thought I could do you any good over there, Father, I'd go in a minute—but I don't. You better stop overnight with me, an' we'll sort of talk things over. If we kin figger out some way to handle this case before Downey gits here, we'll go to work on it. It's too late to start out tonight, anyhow. A night's sleep in a bunk'll do you good."

IT WAS nearly noon the following day before the supplies the priest ordered were put up, and a man engaged to help him take them by canoe to Feather Creek.

As they were about to start, two men entered the saloon, and Black John stepped swiftly into the storeroom, unnoticed by the newcomers, who swaggered to the bar and loudly demanded a round of drinks. As Cush set out bottle and glasses, the taller of the two reached into a packsack and withdrew several rolls of bills which he tossed onto the bar.

"Nine thousan' an' ninety-one dollars," he announced. "Count her up, Cush, an' stick her in the safe along with the rest of our dough!"

Cush counted the money, handed the man a receipt, and introduced Father Cassatt as a priest who was in charge of a band of Siwashes over on Feather Creek.

The men stared at the priest in open-mouthed astonishment, grunted an acknowledgement, glancing inquiringly at each other as they turned to the bar and poured their drinks. After downing them the tall man cleared his throat.

"Ain't Black John Smith got back yet?" he demanded. "I want to meet up with him. I've got a hunch him an' us kin do business."

Cush nodded somberly. "Oh, shore. John's back. He's out in the storeroom."

"He is, eh? We're lucky."

"Yeah?"

"Sure. Figgered we might have to wait around here fer a week 'fore we seen him. Holler fer him, will you?"

Raising his voice, Cush called, "Hey, John! Couple of fellas wants to see you!"

The next instant a huge form stood framed in the storeroom doorway, paused there for a moment, and advanced slowly into the barroom.

"My God, the priest!" cried the tall man.

"Ah, yes. So you're the brethren that was inquirin' fer Father John? I trust that sight of me will be a balm to yer souls, if any. What wouldst thou?"

Every bit of color had drained from the faces of the two as the hand of the tall man flew to his pocket and came up grasping the nickel-plated revolver which he leveled at the advancing figure. There was a lightning-like movement, a loud report, and the tall man pitched forward onto his face as his pistol clattered upon the floor.

The short one jerked his hands upward and held them high above his head. "Don't shoot!" he whined. "I'll fork over the thousan'. Toss it out, Cush. I'll make it two thousan'. Fer God's sake, don't shoot! It was Slim's idee—holdin' out on you. I wanted to pay. I'll show you I'm a good fella. I want to do what's right!"

BLACK JOHN'S pistol disappeared from sight as the torrent of words poured from the man's lips. "Why, shore, my son, I sort of figger you'll do what's right. I don't hardly ever make a mistake in sizin' up a man's character—do I, Cush? An' like he said, you kin toss out the money—every cent of it that them two had in the safe. Slim's dead, an' Shorty, here, he won't be needin' his half much longer. He claims he wants to do what's right, an' he prob'ly would—if he lived long enough to. But in his case the sands of life is dribblin' pretty damn fast into the oblivion of eternity, as a poet would say." Reaching for the rolls of bills which Cush placed upon the bar, Black John tossed them onto the card table beside which stood Father Cassatt, who stared uncomprehendingly from the men to the money, as the short man suddenly shrilled:

"Hey, that's my money! What the hell?" He leaped toward the little priest just as Black John stepped forward, placed a huge hand against his face and sent him crashing backward against the bar.

"Listen, you!" the big man roared. "If you want to lay claim to them funds you'll be given the chanct to do so immejitly after the verdick of the miners' meetin', which will be immejitly precedin' the hangin'."

"Miners' meetin'! Hangin'!" gasped the man. "What do you mean?"

"Meanin' that sellin' hooch to Siwashes constitutes the sin of skullduggery of Halfaday, an' as sech is hangable to a remarkable degree. Of course, an astute attorney fer the defense might claim that the offense wasn't committed on Halfaday. But the chances is the argument wouldn't prevail, the act havin' be'n instigated right here in this room, when the goods was bought, an' the profits figgered. Thus, *ab initio*, accordin' to our code, the essence of the crime was committed within our jurisdiction. The whereabouts of its mere consummation, accordin' to the doctrine of *pro bono publico*, is therefore a matter of no moment."

"But," faltered the man, "you can't hang me fer jest sellin' hooch to Siwashes!"

"The hell we can't! We kin try damn hard. An' up to now we ain't had no failures. Even if we didn't hang you, the law would. Corporal Downey's hot on yer trail fer a murder down in Alberta. But bein' as it's hot weather, an' what with the boys all busy on their claims, an' takin' into consideration yer avowed intention of right doin', an' all, I'm constrained to give you a break—sech break consistin' of a packsack full of grub, an' a bit of advice. Cush'll furnish the grub, an' I'll contribute the advice, which is that you shoulder the pack an' head up that gulch, yonder straight fer the Alasky line. Pick 'em up an' lay 'em down, lively an' long. It's a rough country, an' no trail. But it's better than hangin' from a tree, 'cause you might git through. Others has tried it, an' mebbe some of 'em reached the Tanana. We don't know; none

209

of 'em ever come back. If they did git through they know'd damn well they'd be'n somewheres by the time they got there. You've got sixty seconds to make up yer mind, at the expiration of which, Cush'll cut a len'th of rope an' I'll start tyin' the knot."

"I'll go! I'll go! I've heard tell how you hang folks, up here. Gimme the pack-sack. I'll go!"

After the man had departed, Black John turned to the priest. "Count it, Father," he said, indicating the money that lay on the table, "an' then stick it in yer pack."

The little priest counted the bills. Then turned a puzzled face toward the big man. "I—do not understand. This money—where did it come from?"

"Oh, that's the money them damn scoundrels got off 'n yer Siwashes fer the hooch they sold 'em."

"But—here is twenty-seven thousand six hundred and fifty-one dollars!"

Black John grinned. "Well—ain't you satisfied? Listen, Father—if the Government was damn fool enough not to let you handle the Siwashes' money fer 'em, I ain't. Take it, an' use it fer their good."

"But—I do not understand," repeated the bewildered little priest. "Here is seventeen thousand one hundred and twenty-one dollars more than the Indians received from the Government in the first place!"

"Why shore! That's accrued interest, plus the profit on the deal. Hooch runners makes a big profit."

"But—where did it come from? No matter how great their profit, they could not have obtained more money than the Indians had!"

"Listen, Father, I ain't got no time to enter into no intricate an' abstruse financial discussion, nor neither to bother my head tryin' to figger out the ramifications of a hooch runner's profits. I ain't no fiscal wizard, an' never will be. I'll p'int out to you, though, that the ways of sech rowdies is devious an' onder-

handed to a disgustin' extent—so much so that even if they'd
of kep' a set of books it would require the services of a good
auditor to figger 'em out. You've got the money—an' money
talks. It's there—no matter whether you kin figger it out er not.
In your hands that money kin do a lot of good fer them Siwashes of yourn. So take it, an' spend it as you see fit. I promised
you I'd sort of look around an' do what I could—an' I done so
to the best of my ability."

The little priest smiled as he deposited the money in his
packsack. "It seems, John, that you are a very able man. As you
say, in my hands this money will do a vast amount of good for
my people. But, John, there is a thing I do not understand." He
paused and pointed to the corpse. "When you appeared suddenly in the doorway, why did that man cry out, 'My God! The
priest!'? What did he mean by that?"

Black John grinned: "Why—damn if I know, Father. Onlest
it was jest a sort of natural mistake owin' to the similarity in
the way we talk, er our general appearance, er somethin'."

The priest smiled. "You flatter me as to appearance—but not,
I hope, as to language. I've often wished I were a large man. I
have always been frail of body."

"But ye're mighty in spirit, Father—er you'd never had the
guts to stick it out up there amongst them Siwashes!"

The little man made a deprecatory motion with his hand. "It
is the Lord's work. I am proud to be doing it. One more thing,
John—what did the other one mean by his reference to paying
you a thousand dollars? Have you had dealings with these men
before?"

"Well, no—not what you'd say, personal dealin's. I onct acted
as their agent in a small matter, an' they wasn't exactly punctilious in the matter of remuneration. In fact, they wrongfully
withheld an agreed stipend. An' by the way, Father—you rec'lect
that place you was tellin' me about where them damn hooch
runners was sellin' that licker at the mouth of that feeder on
Feather Crick? Well, if you was to look around good when you

git back, you might find a matter of twenty-nine ten-gallon kegs. The heads is stove in, but the staves is all good. Yer Siwashes might think they come pretty high, fer the shape they're in—but they'll come handy to salt down fish in, if you rence 'em out good. So long, Father; an'jest remember—us sourdoughs always sticks together!"

MAIL ORDER TO HALFADAY

LYMAN CUSHING, PROPRIETOR of Cushing's Fort, the combined trading post and saloon that served the little community of outlawed men that had sprung up on Halfaday Creek hard against the Yukon-Alaska border, laid aside the month-old newspaper he had been reading and set a leather dice box, a bottle, and two glasses upon the bar as Black John Smith stepped into the room stamping the mud and sodden snow from his feet. "Looks like winter's ketched up with us at last," he said. "But, at that, it's helt off fer quite a while."

"Yeah," Black John agreed, crossing the floor and hoisting a foot to the brass rail.

"She's a wet snow, now. But the wind's swingin' into the north, an' I'll bet that by this time tomorrow we'll know winter's here, all right." Picking up the box he cast the five dice onto the bar. "Beat them four treys in one."

Cush gathered the dice and threw three fives. "Horse on me," he admitted, and cast them again. "How does them five deuces suit you?" he asked as he shoved the box across the bar.

"Horse apiece," Black John announced as he failed to beat the deuces and gathered the dice into the box. He rolled them out and grinned at Cush. "See them three little fours? I'm leavin' 'em in one, because the law of averages says you can't shake two good hands in succession—an' you jest throw'd five deuces."

"Huh," Cush grunted, as he rolled out the dice. "There's three sixes that beats 'em, an' that proves this here law of averages yer allus talkin' about ain't worth a damn, an' never was. If a man's luck's runnin' he wins; an' if it ain't he don't. An' on top of that the drinks is on you." He filled his glass and glanced at his watch. "Two o'clock. I s'pose some of the boys'll be driftin' in pretty quick. There wouldn't hardly be no p'int in their workin' with this wet snow soggin' up their clothes."

As though in answer to his prediction the door opened and a man whom both recognized as Jake Moore, the trader's helper at Selkirk, thrust his head and shoulders into the room. "Wher'd d'ye want this damn box?" he demanded. "An' next time you order licker have 'em ship it to Dawson, er else put it up in smaller boxes."

"It ain't licker," Cush replied. "You kin fetch it in here an' set it there in the corner."

"Whatever it is we've had a hell of a time gittin' it here. We fetched it down the big river an' part ways up the White in a polin' boat, but from the Fish Rapids on it was a packin' job. It tuk me an' six Siwashes eight days, an' what with payin' 'em an' feedin' 'em, it'll cost you forty-five ounces." The man turned and issued orders to several natives and by dint of much pulling and pushing on the part of the Indians, and profanity from the white man, the large box was finally placed in the indicated corner of the barroom. "Be'n two inches wider acrost we couldn't of git it through the door," growled the man, scowling at the box as he filled the glass Cush slid toward him across the bar. "I told McFarlane it would be a hell of a job gittin' it up here. But he claimed you ordered it fetched up no matter what it cost."

"That's right," Cush affirmed, as he weighed out the dust. "An' there's yer forty-five ounces."

The man tossed off his drink, pocketed the dust, and took his departure followed by his silent crew. As the door closed behind them Black John's glance focused upon the box. "What in the devil you got in there?" he asked. "It looks like a rough box. You ain't importin' no corpses are you, jest because One Armed John ain't found none in quite a while?"

CUSH DOWNED his drink and eyed the box somberly. "No," he replied, "there ain't no corpse in there. It's jest a caskit."

"A what!"

"A caskit. A coffin, most folks calls 'em. But the catalogue calls 'em a caskit."

"But—what the hell do you want of a coffin?"

"To git buried in. What else would one be good fer?"

The big man eyed the speaker narrowly, "What's ailin' you? You gone bughouse, er somethin'?"

"No, I ain't. Couldn't a man buy a caskit without he's bughouse?"

"But—who you aimin' to bury in it?"

"I ain't aimin' to bury no one in it. This here's my own personal caskit. The buryin' part will be up to you boys."

Real concern showed in Black John's eyes as he searched the other's face. "What's the matter, Cush? By God, if yer sick I'll take you down to the hospital, right now! Fergit this damn coffin business! Doc Sutherland'll have you fixed up in no time."

Cush's brow contracted in a frown of annoyance. "I ain't sick. But a man's got to die sometime, ain't he? Can't a man be forehanded without he's sick? Take it on a crick like Halfaday a caskit's somethin' a man couldn't git holt of if he needed one in a hurry. So I ordered me one. What I claim, a caskit's a handy thing to have."

A slow grin bared white teeth behind the black beard. "That's right," Black John admitted. "I rec'lect one time I got ketched without one. Way over back of the Endicotts, it was. I'd et my last dog, an' struck my last match. It shore looked like the end."

"What did you do?" Cush asked.

"Well, sir—when I run through my outfit an' found I didn't have no casket, I got to hell out of there. Ketch me dyin' in a place like that, without no casket handy!"

Cush scowled, sourly. "It's too bad you didn't have none. But jest the same, folks is habited to git buried in caskits, an' I aim to git buried in one, too."

"When do you figger this obsequy should take place?"

"What's obsequy?"

"Funeral, to you."

"When I die, you damn fool! When would a man git buried?"

The door opened, and with a great stamping of feet One Armed John, accompanied by Pot Gutted John, and Long Nosed John entered the room and ranged themselves beside Black John at the bar. Old Cush distributed glasses, and set out a bottle.

The one armed one downed his drink and eyed the box in the corner. "I seen Jake Moore from Selkirk an' a bunch of Siwashes packin' that box up the crick a while back. Jake claimed it was a batch of licker Cush ordered, so I slipped over to Pot

Gut's an' told him an' Long Nose where Cush had got in some bottle-in-bond licker instead of the damn bar'l stuff he's be'n feedin' us. An' we figgered it wasn't no day fer workin', nohow, on account of the wet snow. So we come on up." He paused and eyed Cush expectantly. "Should I fetch a hammer so we kin git into that bottle licker?"

"That ain't licker," Black John explained. "The fact is, boys, Cush has purchased a sepulcher."

"A which?" asked Pot Gutted John.

"A catafalque. A—"

"If John kin think up some o'nery name fer a thing he'll say it—jest so it's a long one," Cush cut in. "That there's a caskit."

"A caskit!" exclaimed One Armed John. "You mean a coffin?"

"Yeah—jest a common coffin," Black John grinned.

"It ain't no common coffin—by a damn sight!" Cush contradicted. "I could of got a wooden one in Dawson. This here's a bronze caskit."

"Bronze? You mean metal—like brass, er copper, er somethin'?" asked Long Nosed John.

"Shore," Cush replied, proudly. "What I claim, caskits is like anythin' else. If a man's gittin' one, he might's well git a good one, an' be done with it."

"Yeah," grinned Black John, "but a coffin's somethin' you ain't never goin' to be done with."

"I was readin' a piece in the paper along in the spring," continued Cush, ignoring the interruption, "where some fella in Buffalo, Noo York, had got him a bronze caskit rigged up with a spring lock, so when the lid was shet no one could open it agin."

"Who the hell would want to?" Pot Gutted John asked. "There ain't no room in a coffin except fer one fella."

"They didn't figger anyone would try to crawl in with the corpse, you damn fool! It was so no one could steal him."

"Steal who?"

"Why, the fella which was buried in there, of course."

"Why would anyone want to steal him?"

"Mebbe they buried a lot of his stuff with him, like Si-washes does," ventured One Armed John.

"Most likely he had a diamon' ring on, er a lot of gold fillin's in his teeth," suggested Long Nosed John.

"No," Cush explained, "the paper claimed how there's folks that makes a reg'lar business of robbin' graves an' sellin' the corpses to medical students fer to cut up."

"Cut up?"

"Oh, shore," Black John grinned. "Them students is great cut-ups, especially on Saturday nights."

"But that would be a hell of a prank," opined Pot Gutted John.

"It wasn't no prank, accordin' to the paper," Cush said. "It told how these here medical students is learnin' to be doctors, an' how they've got to git corpses to cut up so's they kin find out where their heart is, an' their liver, an' lungs, an' guts, an' all them inside parts, so if one of their customers needed one of them parts cut out, they could go ahead an' do it without wastin' no time slashin' around in the wrong place.

"I seen where this spring lock rig was a very good idee. So when I went down to Dawson I hunted up the undertaker, an' he got out his catalogue an' I ordered me one jest like the paper told about."

"But, Cripes, Cush!" One Armed John exclaimed. "There ain't no one on Halfaday learnin' to be no doctor! Who the hell would want to steal you?"

"You can't never tell," Cush replied. "The way Dawson's growin' they're liable to start some college there most any time. They've got a horspital there a'ready. An' if they was to run short of corpses—well, Halfaday ain't no hell of a ways from Dawson."

"I wouldn't give a damn if I was stole after I was dead," opined Long Nosed John.

"Oh, I don't know," Pot Gutted John replied. "I wouldn't like the idee of bein' dug up an' took apart jest to see how I was made. When a man's dead an' buried they'd ort to leave him lay."

"Yer dang right!" Cush agreed. "An, by God, they ain't a-goin' to git me!"

"S'pose we shuck off that box an' take a look at this tomb," Black John suggested. "Git an ax er a screwdriver, er somethin' an' we'll see what she looks like, Cush."

CUSH COMPLIED, and the rough box was removed leaving the dull bronze casket exposed to view.

"Cripes!" exclaimed One Armed John, his eyes wide with admiration. "Look at them silver handles runnin' the hull len'th of it! It's a damn shame to stick anythin' like that in a grave where there can't no one see it!"

"That's right," Black John agreed. "Instead of buryin' Cush we'll stick him up in a tree, like some of the Siwashes do. That big spruce at the top of the bank would be jest the place, so everyone comin' up the crick could see them silver handles."

Stooping, Pot Gutted John grasped one of them and nodded at Long Nosed John. "Git holt on the other side an' let's heft it."

The man complied and both heaved upward. "Good Lord!" cried Long Nosed John. "It must weigh half a ton. No wonder it tuk all them Siwashes to pack it!"

"It's good an' heavy," Cush said, eyeing it with admiration. "An' look at that row of angels around the top fer a trimmin'."

"What they suckin' on?" asked One Armed John.

"They're blowin'," Black John grinned. "Those are pipes. Didn't you never hear of the pipes of Pan?"

"Pipes—hell!" scoffed Pot Gutted John. "Angels don't smoke!"

"These pipes," explained the big man, "are musical instruments. These angels are s'posed to be escortin' Cush into Heaven with fanfare an' trumpetry."

STRANGE DOINGS ON HALFADAY CREEK

"I don't know nothin' about no fanfare an' trumpetry," Cush said. "Them angels is jest on there fer looks—like white rings on a harness."

"Heaven!" chuckled Pot Gutted John. "It'll shore be a big day fer Heaven when someone from Halfaday shows up there. Old Gabrial'll prob'ly blow his head off!"

"An' St. Peter'll begin checkin' up on the golden harps," Black John added, "an' worryin' about the gold paved streets." He turned to Cush. "But layin' all kiddin' aside, what does this here sarcophagus stand you, in ounces?"

"Well, it cost fourteen hundred' an' sixty-five dollars, in-cloodin' them angels, an' the silver handles, an' the inside trim-min's. The freight to Selkirk was eighty-four dollars, an' I paid Jake Moore forty-five ounces—that's seven hundred an' twenty dollars—to fetch it up here. That's twenty-two hundred an' sixty-nine dollars, all told," he added, after a penciled calculation. "An' it's worth every cent of it."

"I figger it's an extravagance," Black John said. "Cripes, if I ever git a yen to be buried in a coffin I'll buy me a wooden one in Dawson an' slip it in the river, an' set in it an' paddle it up here, an' save all that freight."

"A wooden one wouldn't last no time at all," argued Cush. "It would leak, an'—"

"Leak?"

"Shore—like if you was to bury a man where the ground's soggy."

"You don't need to worry about no water seepage—where you're goin'," grinned the big man. "But I s'pose these metal ones is more fireproof, at that."

"Wait till I h'ist the lid an' show you the inside," Cush said, ignoring the jibe.

Pot Gutted John shook his head. "Seems like a sight of money to have tied up in a coffin," he opined.

"I don't begrudge the money none," Cush replied. "It's worth that much to know I've got a caskit handy when I need one. It took dang near six months to git it shipped up here from Chicago. A man can't wait till he dies to order a caskit. He wouldn't keep till it got here." Grasping the cover, he raised it noiselessly on concealed hinges.

"It's got a winder in it!" One Armed John exclaimed. "What the hell do you want of a winder in yer coffin, Cush? You ain't goin' to look out at nothin'."

"That's so folks kin look in—not so I kin look out."

"But who the hell would want to look in it?"

"Before I was buried. Didn't you never go to a funeral back in the States? Every one walks past the caskit an' looks at the corpse."

"Hell, everyone on Halfaday knows what you look like without goin' to all that trouble!" Pot Gutted John exclaimed. "Look at that blue cloth all rumpled up fancy—like lace, er somethin'. The hull thing is lined with it."

"That there ain't blue—it's lavender," corrected Cush. "The catalogue said so. I could of had white, either one."

"Old lace an' lavender," grinned Black John. "A fittin' windup, I'd say, fer a career like yours."

"Jest the same, I'll bet you'd be damn glad to lay your career on it when you come to die, instead of bein' rolled up in a blanket an' tossed in a grave amongst all them hard rocks! I aim to lay comfortable."

"Damn if there ain't even a piller!" Long Nosed John exclaimed. "A piller, by God! Think of that—all his life a man lays with his head on a rolled-up coat—an' then havin' a piller after he's dead."

"They musta throw'd that in extry," Cush said. "I don't rec'lect no piller in the catalogue. It ain't a bad idee, though, at that." He turned abruptly as a scraping sound reached his ears to see Pot Gutted John, knife in hand, bending over an end of the casket. "Hey, damn you! Quit scratchin' that caskit!" he cried, indignantly.

"Bronze—hell! If you figger you got a bronze coffin yer out of luck! All the bronze is in the paint. It ain't nothin' but iron. An' I'll bet them handles ain't nothin' but iron if you'd scrape that silver paint off!"

"Bronze, er iron, er whatever it is, I don't want it all scratched up, er it'll look like hell agin I want to use it! Come on, you've saw all there is to see. I'll shet the lid an' then buy a drink."

"A piller," muttered Long Nosed John as he took his place at the bar. "What do you know about that! By God—even a piller!"

"I thought you claimed that onct the lid was shet it couldn't never be opened agin," said One Armed John, eyeing the casket across the room.

"There's a trick about that," Cush replied, as he set out bottle and glasses. "You kin open it an' shet it all you want to the way she stands now. But there's a dingus inside the lid in under them trimmin's. Onct you slip that over to the left an' then shet the lid, all hell can't open it. An' I'm the only one that knows where that dingus is at."

"Figger on crawlin' in an' lockin' the door behind you?" inquired Black John.

CUSH PAUSED with the bottle poised above his glass as his brow drew into a frown. "By Cripes—I never thought of that! I would be dead when you boys laid me in there. I'll show you how she works, John, the first time we're alone. So when the time comes you kin slip the dingus over an' seal me in. Hermetically sealed fer all time—that's what the catalogue said. But don't never tell no one else how to work it."

"You've got my promise, Cush," the big man said. "Yer secret will go with you to the grave."

Red John and Short John drifted in and many more drinks were had as the newcomers were shown the casket with all its various trimmings. Long Nosed John, who was notoriously a poor hand with his liquor, went to sleep in a chair as the others settled themselves for a session of stud.

After an hour of play someone ordered a round of drinks, and as Cush got up from the table to serve them his eye fell upon the casket, the top of which stood open. The next instant his roar of anger brought all the players to their feet, and they followed him across the room to stare down at Long Nosed John, who lay snoring serenely among the billowing trimmings, his head on the lavender pillow. Speechless with rage, Cush dived behind the bar and came up with a bung starter. Black John stayed his hand.

"Hold on, Cush," he soothed, "don't work him over with that. After all, he's jest ketchin' him a little sleep."

"But look at that! The damn cuss never even took off his boots! Look at that mud all over them trimmin's where his feet is!"

"You'll prob'ly be buried with yer boots on, so what's the difference?"

"Nussir! I don't give a damn about the rest of my clothes, but you boys has got to promise to take off my boots!"

"All right," grinned Black John, "put up yer bung starter, an' we'll promise. Shove out them drinks an' we'll be gittin' on with the game."

"Not an' leave him layin' there!"

"We'd ort to jest snap the lid shet an' bury him," remarked Pot Gutted John.

"Not by a damn sight!" Cush cried. "That's my caskit. An' besides he ain't dead."

"He would be, in time," commented Red John. "But come on, let's h'ist him out of there. It's my deal."

A coughing, sputtering sound came from the casket as One Armed John stepped back, scrub bucket in hand. Once again the voice of old Cush was raised in anger. "What the hell you doin' with that buckit?" he demanded, as the others again followed him to the coffin where Long Nosed John had struggled to a sitting position and was pawing soapy water from his eyes. Cush pointed to the bedraggled trimming and wet pillow as he glared at One Armed John. "What the hell's goin' on here?" he demanded.

One Armed John explained. "I tried to git the damn cuss outa yer coffin, Cush. An' when he wouldn't wake up I got the scrub buckit an' sloshed a damn good dost of water in his face. It fetched him to, all right."

"But look at the mess you made. Look at them trimmin's. It ain't bad enough he should climb in there with his muddy boots on, but you've got to smear up the other end with that damn dirty scrub water the klooch left in the buckit."

"He don't rate no clean water after the way he done," surmised the one armed one. "I plumb fergot about the splashin' on them trimmin's."

"My God! That caskit ain't be'n here half a day, an' it looks like a second hand one a'ready, what with Pot Gut whittlin' the paint off with his knife, an' Long Nose muddin' it up with his boots, an' you sloshin' scrub water in it!" Cush cried.

"Yeah, an' it'll look a damn sight worst," Pot Gutted John cut in, "if we don't git him outa there pronto. Long Nose don't hold his licker none too good."

Several pairs of hands laid hold of the befuddled man and he was lifted bodily from the casket and deposited on a chair. "A piller," he mumbled, half coherently, "by God, a nice soft piller to lay yer head on."

"Come on," urged Red John, after a round of drinks. "Let's git on with the game. Like I said, it's my deal."

"Not by a damn sight," Cush retorted. "Not till I git that caskit outa here! Cripes, if any more of the boys come driftin' in there won't be nothin' left of it by mornin'!"

"It ain't in sech bad shape," comforted Pot Gutted John. "That there mud'll bresh off when it gits dry. An' we kin turn the piller dirty side down an' rumple them fluffs so the scrub water stains won't show. What I claim, she's a damn good coffin yet."

"Yeah, but it won't be if a few more drunks wallers around in it! We'll take it to the storeroom."

"A better place would be One Eyed John's cabin," suggested Black John. "A lot of the boys goes in an' out of the storeroom.

"We kin stick it in One Eyed John's cabin an' lock the door. If we all git holt of it we kin pack it over there in five minutes."

"Guess yer right, at that," Cush agreed. "Come on, boys—give us a hand."

The heavy casket was removed from the barroom, carried the short distance, and safely deposited in One Eyed John's cabin after much maneuvering to get it through the relatively narrow doorway. Then the men resumed their game while Long Nosed John slumbered uneasily on his chair, mumbling incoherently from time to time about a "piller."

II

THE WIND WHIPPED into the north, that night, and for three nights and two days the little valley of Halfaday was a seething cauldron of whirling, writhing white snow particles that bit into exposed flesh like hot needle points, and reduced visibility to nothing at all. Men drifted into Cushing's Fort from nearby claims, and stud was the order of the day. On the third day the sun came out and the men returned to their work. Winter had come to the Yukon.

One morning, a week later, a dog team halted at the door and a man thrust his head into the barroom where Black John and Cush stood, one on either side of the bar, shaking dice for the drinks. "This here's Cushing's Fort, on Halfaday Crick, ain't it?" he demanded.

"That's right," Black John admitted. "Come on in. Cush is about to buy one."

"I got a pardner out here, an' we got to onharness the dogs," the man replied. "You got a place to put 'em?"

"You'll find shelters around back," Cush said. "An' be shore you toggle 'em."

"You don't have to tell me how to handle my own dogs," retorted the man. "An' you kin hold off on that drink till we git in there."

Black John grinned across the bar as the door slammed shut. "Our friend seems to be endowed with an evil face and a rough tongue. Ondoubtless a malefactor."

"He ain't no friend of mine, an' don't look like he ever would be," Cush growled. "What's 'malefactor'? Some kind of skuldug-gery?"

"One of the worst. An' there's two of 'em. I have a premoni-tion, Cush, that we may have to resort to drastic measures to disencumber ourselves of their presence."

"An' now you've got that said, what do you finger they done?"

"Have patience. They'll prob'ly boast of their misdeeds. I have be'n father confessor to many sech misguided souls."

"But if they done it before they got to Halfaday, an' don't do nothin' after they git here, there ain't nothin' we kin do about it."

"An observation that is ambiguous rather than succinct, but which seems to harbor a germ of truth."

"Dammit, John! Every time someone new shows up on the crick seems like you got to say a lot of big words about it."

"A newcomer, *per se*, tends to excite the imagination," observed the big man. "Who is he? What has he done? Why is he here? A hundred questions arise to arouse one's interest."

"Yeah—an' they'll say their name is John Smith. An' they'll claim they either didn't do nothin', er else they done twict as much as they ever done. An' we know they're on Halfaday 'cause there ain't no other place they dast to be! They're comin' in now," Cush added, as he set out a bottle and four glasses.

Two men entered the room, stamping the snow from their feet. Advancing to the bar they shook off their mittens and allowed two heavy packsacks to thud to the floor. The taller of the two spoke, blinking as his eyes accustomed themselves to the gloom of the room. "You'll be Cush," he said, in a gruff, truculent voice, and turned to the big man beside whom he had ranged himself. "An' you'll be Black John Smith, king of the outlaws."

"The roles is easily assumed," replied Black John suavely. "All but the 'king' part. That savors of rank flattery."

"What?"

"I mean you've correctly guessed our identities, except that I ain't king of nothin'—an' never was."

"They told me you could talk like a damn lawyer," grunted the man. "But it won't git you nothin'. We're plain men. We say what we've got to without ringin' in no fancy words."

"Drink up," suggested Cush, with a glance at the glasses on the bar. "The house is buyin' one."

THE TALL man picked up the glass before him, peered into it, poked a finger into the bottom, sniffed at the finger, then poured his drink. "I wasn't made in a minute," he said. "You couldn't run in no knock-out drops on me." The others filled their glasses and the man raised his own. "Here's lookin' at you," he said, and the glasses were emptied.

"We're men that looks after ourselves," the short man explained, as he returned his glass to the bar. "We don't never take no chances. There can't no one put nothin' over on us—not even the police."

"Yer damn right," the other agreed. "An' that's why we're here. We be'n aimin' to come up an' jine yer gang fer quite a while. But we helt off till we could pull a job that would show what we kin do. We ain't no pikers."

"Yer reasonin' seems sound," approved Black John. "Fact is, we're continually beseiged by small time malfeasors who never got beyond the henhouse an' clothesline stage of thievery. But we don't even consider 'em. We can't afford to have no weak links in our chain of crime. It's got so we don't even consider a horse thief any more onless he shows exceptional promise. But talk's cheap. Fer all me an' Cush knows you boys might be jest a couple of pickpockets. A man's word, onsupported by concrete evidence of his larcenous ability don't go very fer on Halfaday."

"You mean—kin we prove it? Prove we ain't no common sneak thieves?"

"Well—a man's looks might belie him. Trot out yer evidence."

"The evidence is right in them two packsacks there on the floor! Forty-eight hundred ounces of dust—a hundred an' fifty pound in each sack—better'n seventy-six thousan' dollars! Is that evidence enough? Er ain't it?"

"The amount, as sech, seems worth contemplatin'," Black John admitted. "But the manner of its acquisition remains in doubt. This dust, if honestly come by, would have no significance—would confer no prestige upon its owners, on Halfaday. What counts with us is—was it dug; er stole?"

"It was stole! Cripes, do we look like a couple of saps that would hang on the end of a shovel long enough to dig that much dust out of the gravel?"

"Well—not on the end of a shovel."

"What?"

"Go ahead an' elucidate. I jest said, no, you don't look that industrious. How was this wealth come by?"

"It come out of the strong room of the Yukon Dredge an' Navigation Company, on Bonanza! That's where it come from. An' we had to croak a couple of guards to git it. An' the police is runnin' around in circles, like the dog chasin' his tail around a stump. How does that suit you?"

"Suits me okay. A larceny of that magnitude, with a couple of murders throw'd in fer good measure, shore entitles you boys to special consideration, on Halfaday."

"I'll say it does!" agreed the taller of the two men. "Fact is, it sort of makes that there Army payroll job they tell about you pullin' off somewheres over in Alasky look like small time stuff."

Black John smiled deprecatingly. "Oh, that! Shucks, boys, I was younger, then. I lifted that payroll merely in a sperit of jest. No criminal thought entered my mind at the time. It was only a prank like any young fella would be apt to pull off. But—now yer here, what's on yer mind?"

"What's on our mind is like this—we don't figger, what with the gang you've got up here, yer gittin' all you'd ort to be gittin'. Accordin' to the talk there's fifty, sixty of you here on Halfaday. Yer right up agin the line where you kin duck acrost handy if it was needful. An' the police don't dast to bother you. What with that set-up you could reach out an' take any damn thing you wanted to. It would take an army to git you out of here. An' you know damn well the British army ain't comin' clean over here from England to mop up a gang of outlaws in the Yukon."

"Yer thesis seems onassailable, except fer the fact that it's based on false premises."

"What?"

"Jest a lot of big words," said Cush, somberly mopping at the bar.

"Reducin' my thought to its lowest terms, which seems to be the only terms applicable, I'll explain that while there's fifty, sixty of us here on Halfaday, there is no organized gang. We are, as you said, close to the line, which makes it handy at times. But yer dead wrong in thinkin' the police don't dare to come here. In fact, Corporal Downey visits us whenever he's a mind to. An' when he gits here, he's neither helped, nor hindered."

"All right—then you need us worst than you think!"

"It couldn't be worse—"

"What I mean," interrupted the man, "what you need is organization! An' I'm the man that kin organize you. First off, we've got to call a meetin' an' find out jest what every man's grift is—what every man is best at doin'. Like some is strongarm guys, an' some is burglers, an' some is petermen, an' some is prob'ly con men. Mebbe someone's worked on a steamboat so we could have him git a job on a boat that was carryin' a big shipment of dust outside, an' he could wreck her, er run her ashore some place where we could git away with her cargo. Then there's others that'll prob'ly have grifts that I can't think of. When we know all them things, an' git organized, we kin go ahead an' pull off any kind of a job. An' we kin keep on pullin' 'em—first one kind, an' then another. An' if the police horns in we'll shoot it out with 'em. Cripes, we could clean out all the police in the Yukon in one battle! We could take over the country. Then we could lay off the rough stuff an' let the big outfits an' the free miners git out their dust an' make 'em pay us, say twenty-five percent fer not botherin' 'em. An' when we git to that p'int we'll be settin' pretty."

Behind the bar Cush scowled as Black John smiled benignly upon the two men, and said, "Yer survey of the situation seems both comprehensive an' allurin'. It merits further discussion. So if Cush'll hand over three glasses an' a bottle we'll go over to a table an' do a little preliminary plannin' whilst he stays behind the bar to keep any chance customer from interruptin' our deliberations. An'," he added, "jest as a matter of good faith, you might fetch them packsacks over an' give me a peek at their contents. So fer as I know, they might contain three hundred pounds of rocks."

THE SCOWL on Cush's face deepened and he shook his head violently as Black John reached for the bottle and glasses when the two stooped to pick up the packsacks from the floor. But ignoring the disapproval, the big man led the way to a table out of earshot from the bar.

"First off," said the man who had outlined the plan, "we'll show you if these sacks has got rocks in 'em." Opening the packsacks the men disclosed numerous stout canvas sacks. Selecting several of these at random, Black John satisfied himself that they contained dust.

"I've always figgered I was doin' pretty well fer myself, in my feeble way," he said. "But you boys operates on a scale that's got me sort of bewildered."

"Oh, hell, you'll git used to the big time stuff! Trouble is you never worked with anyone with brains, before. Take me—I got brains. I ain't never be'n outsmarted; an' I never will be. I keep my eyes open, an' I use my head. What we need of you in this gang, ain't per brains—it's yer savvy of the men an' the country. I aim to be the general—figger out the jobs, an' how to pull 'em. An' you'll be like you might say, the captain, an' carry out my orders."

"That might work all right," Black John admitted.

"Shore it will!" The man talked on for half an hour, outlining a vast campaign of crime as Black John listened in apparent admiration. "So now," he concluded, "you git busy an' notify the men to come in here fer a meetin' tomorrow night."

"I'll send a couple of the boys up an' down the crick," Black John promised as he rose and drew on his parka. "I'll be back in an hour."

III

WHILE THE MEN of Halfaday banked their dust in Cush's safe, Black John also maintained a private cache of his own, unknown even to Cush. Leaving the saloon, he visited this cache, removed a number of heavy moosehide sacks, stopped at his own cabin to retrieve a bulky package from beneath his bunk, and proceeded to the cabin of One Eyed John. From there he continued, with the package under his arm, to the cabin of Red John, one of the more intelligent of the men of Halfaday.

"Want to make a hundred ounces fer an hour's work?" he asked.

"Why, shore! Who the hell wouldn't?"

"Okay." The big man removed the contents of the package and tossed them onto the bunk. "Tomorrow mornin' at exactly ten o'clock, you climb into them clothes an' harness yer dogs an' head fer Cush's acrost that stretch of open country we kin see with the telescope from the door of the Fort. Pretend to be foggin' hell out of yer dogs—but take yer time. Don't come to Cush's, though. When you hit the timber a couple of miles below the Fort, you kin slip back to yer cabin. That's all you've got to do. Tomorrow evenin' I'll slip you a hundred ounces."

"But," temporized Red John, eyeing the clothing doubtfully, "that there's a uniform of the Mounted."

"That's right," Black John agreed. "A year er so ago they got a consignment of these new winter uniforms down to Forty Mile.

"I happened to be sojournin' there at the time, an' in some roundabout manner, the details of which is inconsequential, I found myself in possession of this one. I figgered it might come in handy sometime. An' the present circumstances proves that I was right."

"But, Cripes, John—s'pose I'd git ketched wearin' it! S'pose Downey should come along. Impersonatin' an officer, he'd call it, an' I'd be in a hell of a jam."

"Downey won't be along. I'll guarantee to git you out of it, somehow. I'll think up some excuse. Hell, a hundred ounces is worth takin' some slight risk fer, ain't it?"

"Yeah. But I shore hope Downey don't show up. If he does, believe me, I'm goin' to hit fer the bresh even if I ain't half ways acrost that open stretch!"

Returning to the Fort, Black John stopped at One Armed John's cabin and gave him certain explicit instructions, promising him ten ounces if he should follow them to the letter, and threatening him with dire misfortune if he should not. In the saloon the two men stood before the bar as he entered.

"Did you send them fellas to call that meetin'?" demanded the tall man.

"Yeah. The boys had ort to be in here tomorrow night."

"Where we goin' to put up?"

"I figger One Eyed John's shack would be the handiest place," Black John said. "It's clost by, an' a good winter shack, what with a stove, an all."

"Hey—that caskit's in there!" Cush cried.

Black John nodded, and slipped him a wink. "Yeah, that's true. But these boys ain't superstitious. Superstition, which is nothin' more nor less than a fear er dread of the supernatural, is a prerogative of the ignorant. These boys is too smart to give heed to superstition, no matter how weird the supernatural happenin's seem to be."

"What about this here coffin?" asked the shorter of the two, a bit uneasily.

"Well," Black John explained, "it's got a hist'ry. One Eyed John was a character we was forced to hang, a while back."

"I've heard how you hang folks up here," the tall man said. "What did you hang him fer?"

"Some infringement of rectitude, no doubt. I disremember the exact irregularity he was guilty of. But in some manner he violated our iron-dad rule that any crime committed on Halfaday is punishable, by hangin'."

"That'll be changed when we git things goin'."

"Okay. But until we do, the rule remains in force. As I was goin' on to say, One Eyed John must of had a premonition of impendin' doom, because shortly before he died he ordered a coffin—" Behind the bar old Cush emitted a choking sound, and Black John frowned, and proceeded. "Well, shortly after the coffin arrived we had occasion to hang One Eye, which we done right here in this room. It was a rainy day, I rec'lect, an' we carried him to his cabin an' put him in his coffin without removin' his boots, after leavin' him swing fer a couple of hours to make shore he was dead. You kin still see the mud on the inside trimmin's which is also messed up some at the other end of the coffin, owin' to his head gittin' a little wet an' muddy where the boys dropped that end of him carryin' him over. We aimed to bury him next day if it would quit rainin' so we left him there in the coffin after closin' the lid. It cleared up durin' the night, an' when we went to git him, next mornin', by God, he was gone! Yes, sir, the lid was up an' he was gone! There wasn't a damn thing in the coffin but the mud off his boots, an' the marks where his head had dirtied the piller an' the trimmin's."

"Huh—he prob'ly wasn't dead an' clumb out an' beat it," opined the tall man.

Black John shook his head. "If he wasn't dead he was the best imitation of a dead man I ever seen. I rec'lect it was a hot day when we hung him—hot, an' muggy, an' rainin', an' I noticed when we cut him down he'd begun to turn a mite green."

"Someone made off with the body, then."

"Why would anyone? One Eye wasn't worth a damn alive— let alone dead. It ain't reasonable. Anyways, there ain't a man on Halfaday that would go near that coffin—not fer a million ounces, they wouldn't!"

After a few moments of silence the tall man spoke. "We ain't afraid of no empty coffin. We'll move in."

"Okay. Fetch yer stuff along an' I'll show you where it's at. You kin bank yer dust in Cush's safe. He'll weigh it in an' give you a receipt fer it."

"Oh, yeah?" There was an ill concealed sneer in the man's voice. "An' in case the dust would be gone when we wanted it, I s'pose we could keep on holdin' that receipt. I told you no one had ever outsmarted me, yet. The dust goes where we go."

Black John shrugged. "Suit yourself," he replied indifferently. "Most of the boys on the crick banks their dust in the safe, an' we've got the first ounce to be lost out of it yet. I jest figgered it was quite a heft fer you boys to be packin' around."

Picking up their packsacks, the two followed Black John through the fast gathering twilight to the cabin of One Eyed John. Producing a key from his pocket the big man unlocked the door, handed the huge padlock and key to the tall man, stepped into the room, and lighted the kerosene lamp.

Going straight to the casket placed along an end wall, he stooped, raised the lid, and proceeded to remove numerous heavy moosehide sacks. He grinned and winked at the two men, neither of whom noticed that his hand deftly contacted a small device concealed beneath the trimming. "Safest cache on Halfaday," he said. "Safer even, than Cush's safe. There ain't a man on the crick besides me that would raise that lid if his life depended on it. They won't even come near this cabin—think it's ha'nted, er somethin'." He paused and pointed to the stained and muddied trimming. "Look, there's where he messed up the coffin 'fore he disappeared."

The tall man returned the grin. "That's the same idee I had when you told me about it—usin' the coffin fer a cache. That's why I said we'd move in."

The shorter man glanced uneasily about the dimly lighted room after peering into the open casket. "But—s'pose there is somethin' to it? S'pose this here One Eye would come back an' want to git in his coffin, er somethin'?"

"Don't be a damn fool!" scoffed the other. "Did you ever see a ghost?"

"No, an' that ain't all, neither. I don't want to see none!"

"We'll take a chanct," the tall man insisted. "An' not only that, we'll sort of hint around that we seen this one eyed ghost prowlin' around, an' it'll make these Halfaday Crickers scairter'n ever."

"That's right," Black John agreed. "Well, I'll be goin', now. You boys might loaf over to the saloon after you've et yer supper. Some of the boys'll likely drift in, an' we kin have a game of stud."

"We'll prob'ly do that," the tall man said, and handed back the padlock and key. "You might's well take this along. I've got a lock of my own fer the door—a lock I know damn well has only got one key. When you know me better you'll see why I'm a hard man to outsmart."

"Guess that's right," Black John admitted, a look of frank admiration in his eyes. "You think of everything. A man would shore have to git up in the mornin' to outsmart you. So long. Be seein' you after supper."

Stopping at his own cabin to re-cache his sacks of dust, he proceeded to the saloon where Cush greeted him with a frown.

"By God, John, sometimes I think you ain't got no sense whatever! You foolin' around with a couple of skunks like them two!"

"Oh, I don't know, Cush. That tall one's a damn smart man."

"Huh—accordin' to his tell! What's so damn smart about murderin' a couple of guards an' stealin' some dust? Downey'll know damn well they hit fer Halfaday when he don't locate 'em along the river, an' he'll come up here an' git 'em—an' I hope he does."

"He better come before we git organized then," grinned the big man. "Didn't you hear that tall fella tell how we're goin' to organize a gang up here—a gang of specialists, an' take over the whole damn country, an' wipe out the police in one big battle? I'm tellin' you he's got somethin' there!"

"Yeah—he's got a pipe dream. Why, John, that's the cock-eyedist thing I ever heard tell of. An' you throwin' in with it!"

"But you don't know the whole set-up. He explained it to me over there at the table. Jest think, Cush, after we've took over the whole Yukon, lock, stock, an' barrel, we kin set back an' git rich off'n the royalty we'll collect—twenty-five percent, he said we'd charge fer every damn ounce of dust that's mined. Cripes, we'll have so much dust we won't know where to put it! I'm tellin' you it's the chanct of a liftime."

"Yeah—a lifetime in jail, if yer lucky enough to squeek out of a hangin'."

"You mean, you ain't comin' in on it?"

"No, I ain't comin' in on it. I won't have nothin' to do with it, nor no part of it! An' you won't, neither, if you've got any sense. An' what's more, I don't see no call fer you to let them damn cusses move into One Eyed John's shack, neither. By God, if anythin' else happens to that there caskit of mine it won't be fitten to bury a dog in, let alone me!"

"Wouldn't you contribute even a messed up coffin to a cause as comprehensive as our friend outlined?"

"Like I told you onct, he ain't no friend of mine! An' I wouldn't contribute no caskit, nor nothin' else to his cause. An' what's more, I didn't see no call fer you to make up that damn lie about the caskit belongin' to One Eyed John, an' us buryin' him in it, an' him disappearin' out of it."

"Oh, that was jest a bit of fiction, told merely by way of entertainment. The way I look at it, we'd ort to do what we kin to make the time pass pleasantly fer sech strangers as happens to be sojournin' amongst us."

"I wouldn't want fer the time to pass pleasant fer a couple of yeggs like them two is. The quicker they git off'n Halfaday, the better I'll like it. An' if anythin' else happens to that caskit, you bet they'll pay fer it."

"Well, seein' as they're friends of mine, an' seem' how it was me that induced 'em to move into One Eye's shack, I'll pay fer the coffin, myself. How much did you figger it stands you?"

"Twenty-two hundred an' sixty-nine dollars, countin' the freight."

"All right. Charge twenty-five hundred dollars agin me, an' credit yerself with it. That allows you some slight margin of profit. An' don't fergit, the coffin belongs to me."

"I'll order me a new one," Cush said, as he made the proper entries in his book. "An' by God, if anyone climbs into it with his dirty boots on, I'll split a bung starter over his head—drunk er sober!"

IV

THE TWO STRANGERS appeared early in the evening, several men drifted in from nearby claims, and a game of stud started that lasted until far into the night. As daylight grayed the east, late the following morning, Black John left his cabin, sauntered into the saloon, and had a couple of drinks with Cush.

"I didn't look fer you to show up 'fore noon, late as you got to bed," Cush said.

"It's goin' to be a busy day, what with that big meetin' tonight, an all. I've got to go over to One Eye's cabin an' confer with them two. There'll be a lot of details to iron out in a venture of this magnitude. I don't want we should make no mistakes."

Cush shook his head somberly. "A year ago you wouldn't of had no more truck with them damn cusses than you would with a couple of snakes. But go ahead. There ain't nothin' I kin say that'll stop you. You won't never listen to me. But yer slippin', John. That's all I got to say."

"You won't be sayin' that, this time tomorrow," grinned the big man, as he turned away and walked from the room.

THE DOOR of One Eyed John's cabin was jerked open by the tall man in answer to Black John's knock. "What the hell do you want—wakin' a man up this time of day?"

"Well, I figger we'd ort to sort of go over our plans before the meetin' tonight. I figger if we'd make a list of the boys here on the crick I could tell you what I know about 'em—what their qualifications is, as I see it. Course, there'll be other information they'll have to furnish themselves. But in an organization of this kind it seems like the more the leaders know about the men, the better it'll work out."

"Guess yer right, at that," admitted the other. "But it seems damn early to be gittin' at it. Come on in an' I'll light the fire an' git breakfast goin'. You kin be writin' out them names while we eat."

A half hour after the big man's departure from the saloon One Armed John burst into the barroom. "Where's Black John?" he demanded.

"Over to One Eyed John's shack visitin' with a couple of fellas. What do you want of him?"

"There's a police comin' up the crick! He looks like Downey."

"Good!" uttered Cush, fervently. "Now mebbe John'll listen to reason, 'fore it's too late."

One Armed John disappeared, and a few minutes later he pounded on the door of the cabin where the two strangers were eating breakfast while Black John busied himself with pencil and paper. Invited to enter, he thrust his head into the room. "There's a police comin' up the' crick. He looks like Downey!" he announced, with parrot-like precision.

"How do you know?" Black John demanded.

"I seen him. He's below here, lookin' in all the cabins. I come like hell to tell you."

"We better git over to Cush's," Black John exclaimed.

"What," cried the tall man, with a glance at the casket, "an' leave all this dust here! Not by a damn sight!" he rasped, a hard gleam in his eye. "Downey's only one policeman—an' there's four of us here. We'll blast him down."

"You fergit," Black John reminded, "that I told you the police are neither helped nor hindered, on Halfaday."

"An' I told you things would be changed when we got organized."

"We ain't organized yet. The rule stands."

"Who says so?" demanded the man, reaching swiftly for one of the two rifles that stood in a corner close beside him.

"I do."

The man's hand dropped, and his eyes widened at sight of the blue-black six-gun that suddenly appeared in Black John's hand. "What's this? What the hell?"

"The captain's took over, instead of the general."

"But, man—if the Mounted ketch us here we'll git hung!"

"Ondoubtless. An' that's why, if I was you boys, I wouldn't let him ketch me here."

"You mean we should pull out? Hit over acrost the line?"

"That would seem the obvious solution of yer difficulty."

"By God, I smell a trick. I don't believe there's a policeman on the crick."

"We kin soon find out," Black John said. "If there is one on the lower crick he's got to cross three, four miles of open country about five miles below the Fort—an' we keep a telescope handy fer jest sech emergencies. We'll go take a look. An' jest in case one of you boys might take a shot at Downey, One Armed John'll take charge of them rifles."

The four proceeded to the Fort where Black John pointed to a moving black object far down the creek. "Someone's comin'," he said, and reaching into a section of hollow log, withdrew a brass telescope, wiped the lens with his handkerchief, and held it to his eye. Then, without a word, he handed the instrument to the tall man.

"By God, it is the police!" the man cried, after a moment of scrutiny. "An' he's about Downey's size. An' comin' like hell!" He whirled on Black John. "There's somethin' damn queer about this!"

"I don't see nothin' queer in Downey's takin' out after a couple of thievin' murderers. It would be queer if he didn't."

"What I mean—you're mixed up in this, somehow. Yer tryin' to put one over!"

"Cripes—how could I put one over on someone who's never be'n outsmarted, an' never will be? It's ridic'lous. You know I ain't got no brains. You said so yerself. An' how the hell could I have got in touch with the police sence you got here—even if I'd wanted to?"

"But if we can't knock Downey off, what kin we do?" cried the short man, a look of terror in his eyes.

"If it was me I'd load up a sledful of grub an' hit over into Alaska as fast as my dogs could leg it. Downey won't be here fer an hour an' a half yet, even if he makes good time. You've got time if you hurry."

"But the dust!" the tall man cried. "There's three hundred pounds of dust."

Black John shrugged. "Well—it's yours. Take it along with you. We shore as hell don't want Downey to find it on Halfaday. He might think some of us boys here on the crick was mixed up in that job."

"But we can't make no time with all that weight on the sled."

"It's only about a mile to the line," Black John said. "An' onct you cross it you kin take yer time."

"We could go acrost an' wait till Downey went back to Dawson, an' then come back an' git organized."

Black John shook his head. "Nope. Onct you git acrost the line you boys better keep on goin'. That there play you made a few minutes ago fer yer rifle sort of give me a premonition that you ain't a man to be trusted. An' besides, thinkin' it over, yer dream of a vast northern empire here is a mite too comprehensive fer my limited intelligence to grasp."

"We can't stand around an' talk all day!" exclaimed the short man. "We know if Downey comes, we'll git hung. Let's git goin'!"

"Harness the dogs an' throw a load of grub on the sled," ordered the tall man. "I'll go to the shack an' git out the dust an' roll our beds." He turned upon Black John. "You damn fool!" he cried, beside himself with rage. "Yer passin' up the chanct of a lifetime. An' yer too damn dumb to see it."

"That might be," admitted the big man mildly. "But you can't blame me. Dumbness is a misfortune—not a fault. I guess I'll have to jest struggle along like I've be'n doin' before you boys showed up. Better trot along now, an' git yer stuff together. I'll help yer pardner load the sled."

FIVE MINUTES later, as Black John and the short man were carrying supplies from the storeroom, the tall man reappeared, his eyes blazing. "How the hell do you open that damn coffin?" he demanded.

Black John shrugged. "You shet it. You'd ort to be able to open it."

"But I can't open it! I've pulled, an' pried, an' pounded it with an ax, an' the lid won't budge. It's stuck tight as hell—an' all our dust is in there."

"Tight!" exclaimed Black John, looking at the man in surprise. "Cripes—you didn't shet it tight, did you?"

"Course I shet it tight! You don't think I'd leave it open—an' better'n seventy-six thousan' in dust in it, do you?"

Black John slowly shook his head. "*Tch, tch, tch,* my mistake, I'm afraid. I plumb fergot to tell you about slippin' a chip under the lid so it couldn't shet tight. Onct that lid is down tight, nothin' in the world, short of a cold chisel could open it. It's hermetically sealed—prevents grave robbin', you know. That there's a damn good casket—chilled steel an eighth of an inch thick. It would take a week to chisel a hole in it. Takes six men to lift it, empty."

"But—you claimed you shet the lid with that one eyed corpse inside! How did he git out?"

"That's what the boys is wonderin'. That's what makes 'em scairt."

"But our dust! How the hell we goin' to git our dust?"

Black John shrugged. "That's your problem; not mine. You put it there—I didn't. Smart as you are, an' dumb as I am, you can't expect me to do yer thinkin' fer you."

"But, heck, man—all that dust in that coffin, an' we can't git a damn ounce of it. Look at the fix we're in."

"Yeah. But look at the fix we'll be in when Downey comes along an' finds it there! You boys are the lucky ones. You'll be where he can't git holt of you."

The blazing eyes of the tall man fixed Black John with a glare of hate. "Damn you—you put one over on us. Give us our rifles. We've got to go now. But we'll be back!"

"You can't be trusted with rifles. You might shoot Downey an' then come back an' start to work on us. As fer comin' back, I wouldn't try it, if I was you. Both Cush an' I kin testify that yer both guilty of connivin' an' conspirin', which is both hangable offenses on Halfaday, comin' as they do under our skullduggery law. It wouldn't take a miners' meetin' no more'n ten minutes to hang you higher'n hell."

"If we stay we git hung," cried the short man, "an' if we come back we git hung! All that dust an' we can't git an ounce of it! We're worst off than we was when we started."

Black John shook his head as he eyed the enraged men benignly. "I wouldn't hardly say that. At least you boys has learnt what some men never do learn—that *crime don't pay*. An' you better git goin'," he added, glancing down the creek. "I don't see Downey on that flat no longer. He might show up here any minute."

Old Cush stepped to the doorway as the two men disappeared up the gulch that led to Alaska. "What did they do to yer caskit, John?" he asked. "I heard him say somethin' about poundin' it with an ax. I'm shore glad I got shet of it. I told you not to have no truck with them damn skunks!"

"That's right," the big man agreed, a grin twitching the corners of his lips. "Yer lucky. I got stuck with that damn coffin—an' forty-eight hundred ounces of dust locked up it it. Give me a couple of cold chisels an' a hammer, Cush. It won't be long before Downey *does* come huntin' them birds, an' I'd hate fer him to find that dust—he might git the idee that I was mixed up in a venture that was somehow onderhanded."

BONUS MATERIAL

THOSE BEAR PAWS

IT ISN'T OFTEN that Jim Hendryx writes us a letter about his yarns ; they come as is. So we were particularly interested in the following about the Bear Paws tale in this issue. We have been completely intrigued with the idea of the sourdough who lost his toes, ever since we read the story when it first came in, so every bit of Hendryx's letter about it was eagerly perused in the office. We pass it on with interest to our readers—who number so many Hendryx fans.

"I must tell you that Francis Rotch, former captain of the *Midnight Sun,* a gas boat that ran the Yukon, the Porcupine, and the Tananna, wrote me a year or so ago and told me a yarn about Old Solomon Albert, a queer old cuss (now dead) who lived up on White River, near Canyon City, a trading post, which is near the line at the mouth of the creek I have used as Halfaday. It is a fact that he used the front paws of a bear for moccasins after losing his toes—and that he was suspected of a murder because of the tracks in the mud. From these facts I built the yarn. I wrote to my friend, Bettles—the 'Old Bettles' of my yarns—asking him if it were true as Rotch had said that it was he and Tagish Jim who had cut off Old Albert's toes with a butcher knife. His reply was that they had cut them off all right, but had used a razor, not a butcher knife. He asked me specially to notify Rotch of this fact, but as this all happened some thirty years ago, I thought he might be excused for not remembering all the details!

"The renewal of my acquaintance with this same Gordon Bettles is interesting, in itself. During the early days of the gold rush I was a chechako, but went to the Yukon from Montana where I was punching cattle, so I mixed with the sourdoughs, Bettles, Swiftwater Bill, Jimmy the Rough, McMahon, etc., rather than with the chechako element. Dawson was a lively camp, and we were all forthright two-fisted drinkers and card players. Such being the case, years later, when I got into the writing game, I used many names of actual characters, supposing most of them to be dead. At the clip they were going, it's a damn wonder they aren't, because all of them were older than I am.

"A couple of years ago Dr. Southerland, of Fairbanks, Alaska, wrote me a letter of appreciation of the Black John yarns, and I answered his letter, asking him if he was the Dr. Southerland who used to do female impersonations in Dawson in the old days. I remembered him well, but never happened to meet him at the time, though saw him frequently. He was practicing medicine, and gave these impersonations at the amateur shows. He admitted the fact, and as he and his wife were coming outside for a visit, he swung up to my home and stayed a couple of days with me; we sure did chew the fat! He told me that Old Bettles was alive and had married a teacher! Also that Swiftwater Bill Gates was alive and living in Peru where he has some kind of a mining concession from the Government. This was very surprising to me, as I had supposed them dead. Then last fall Dr. John N. E. Brown, of Toronto, President of the National Sourdoughs Association, also one of the early physicians of Dawson, and at one time territorial commissioner, wrote a very nice appreciation of my book, *The Outlaws of Halfaday Creek*—which as you know is a collection of the Black John stories from *Short Stories*—for the Alaska *Weekly*. Bettles read it, and wrote me from Chanego, Alaska, and we got to corresponding again.

"You will note that my acquaintance with him dates from 1890—eight years before the rush and six years before Carmack discovered gold on Bonanza! I was in my early twenties, very early twenties, in 1901-2 when I was on the Yukon—and Bettles was then what seemed to me an old man! He must have been in the forties—and that was thirty-six years ago. It looks like the tougher they live the longer they live!

"I'll tell you a good one. There was a bunch of the boys one time in the saloon at Forty Mile and Bettles began shooting at the bottles on the back bar—trying to knock the corks out without breaking the bottles. He is, or was, a dead shot with a rifle, and was having more or less success with the corks when he noticed that a number of his bullets were knocking out chunks of the chinking between the logs of the wall, there being no mirror behind the back bar. He eyed the holes and turned to the proprietor with the utmost gravity. 'You better patch those holes before spring,' he said, 'or when the river rises yer damn saloon's goin' to sink.'

"JIM HENDRYX."

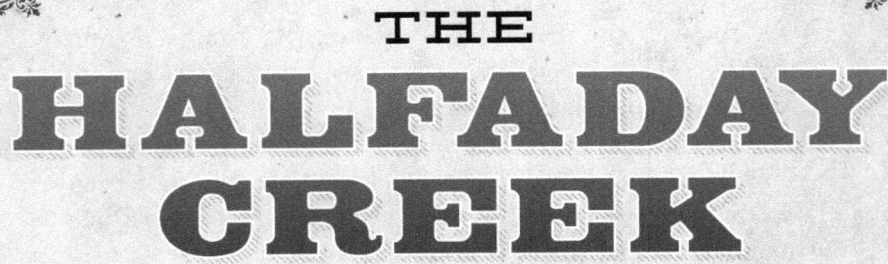

THE
HALFADAY
CREEK
LIBRARY

JAMES B. HENDRYX

James B. Hendryx's classic series returns to print! The author of more than 50 novels and anthologies, he's best known for his characters set around the outlaw community of Halfaday Creek in the Yukon. Set during the Gold Rush of the late 1890s, Hendryx penned over a hundred stories featuring these characters over the span of 25 years for a variety of pulp magazines.

Now, Altus Press has committed to return these to print. Using the original pulp magazines as the source material, along with the illustrations from their original pulp magazine appearances, and augmented with rare material.

Leelanau Historical Society

Celebrating 150 Years of Leelanau History

Leelanau County was officially established in 1863 when the State of Michigan was a young 26 years old. People were attracted to the natural resources from the beginning—first as a way to earn a living and build a home, and later to enjoy recreation away from the cities. Early settlers arrived on the islands beginning in 1839, while Native Americans populated the Leelanau peninsula until pioneers began exploring the area in 1847. For the next 45 years, the villages known today—and some that are abandoned—were settled. North and South Manitou Islands and the Fox Islands officially joined the county in 1895.

The Leelanau Historical Society was launched in 1957 by a group of residents dedicated to collecting and preserving Leelanau's history. Leland, first established in 1853 and later the county seat, seemed the natural location for the Society. When the old county jail became available in 1959, the museum found its first home. Through generous donations and grants, a new museum was built in 1985 and later expanded.

Today, the collections and archives contain more than 11,000 items. Visitors to the museum learn about Leelanau life and maritime history from exhibits, educational programs and publications. The Society continues to collect, document and preserve items relating to Leelanau history.

203 East Cedar Street, Leland, MI 49654

Tel. (231) 256-7475

info@LeelanauHistory.org

http://www.leelanauhistory.org/

www.ingramcontent.com/pod-product-compliance
Lightning Source LLC
Chambersburg PA
CBHW051639050726
47502CB00011B/1301